R. M. Ahmose

Tales Off The Rails

authorHOUSE®

AuthorHouse™
1663 Liberty Drive
Bloomington, IN 47403
www.authorhouse.com
Phone: 1-800-839-8640

First published by AuthorHouse 3/2/2011

ISBN: 978-1-4567-3757-3 (sc)
ISBN: 978-1-4567-3758-0 (dj)
ISBN: 978-1-4567-3759-7 (e)

Library of Congress Control Number: 2011901583

Printed in the United States of America

Table of Contents

The Quiet Town Mystery

Officer Dan Kopochek had only driven from the Saeton Hill section of town just minutes earlier. He intended, next, to make the same slow, cruising rounds through adjacent city areas within his purview. In so doing, it was customary to stop, paying visit to various establishments, on the lookout for suspicious behavior from loiterers and wanderers. It was a pattern Kopochek and other officers followed, particularly with the arrival of night.

There were a good number of sections to cover in the city of Grafton. It was especially so for the district to which Kopochek and some other officers were assigned—upper eastside. In spite of this, Kopochek reasoned, there should be time left in his watch to return to Saeton, if he so desired. And he did *so desire*, perhaps a little too much. Consequently, he found himself turning onto a street leading back to Saeton Hill.

The patrol car dash read 10:07 p.m. Kopochek's work shift this month was "the ol' five to one," as dubbed by the Grafton police force. Therefore, nearly three hours remained this night, within which to fit in a return to Saeton Hill. Somehow, though, he wouldn't, or couldn't, postpone the revisit. But, then, Kopochek knew what was *really* driving him. It was the prospect of another chance to harass Philip Peutret, even if it was with no more than his iciest policeman's stare.

Philip Peutret, though, was nothing if not clever. Always, he avoided encounters with the police, even in the most casual of circumstances. It wasn't his style to be outwardly defiant. In the twenty minutes, tonight, that his "uniformed" enemy patrolled around Saeton, Peutret kept out of sight. He caught a fleeting glimpse of the patrol car, but the view had been one way.

While Peutret was known by friend, foe and the fearful, alike, as a

1

low-profile personality, he had, nevertheless, gained an ugly reputation in Saeton. Above all else, he was a reputed local gang-leader—a powerful and vicious one. As such, he was behind much of the city's crime. Second, as his rap sheet revealed, he moonlighted as a sort of part-time flesh-peddler. He was known to keep his few "girls" in line with vicious beatings, for which he showed no conscience. These factors, taken together, made officers like Kopochek want to see Peutrek taken down.

Gazing into the darkness of Billow Street, Kopochek drifted into reflection on an earlier event of the day. It was the latest disagreement he'd had with his wife over his career choice. He hated those occasional spats with Julie. Always, they seemed to flash in his mind during his patrols—not, he concluded, the right times to revisit unpleasant memories.

Slowing nearly to a stop at an alley-street entrance, the officer's focus was abruptly averted. He saw what appeared to be a man striking a woman with an object. As he turned sharply into the alley, Kopochek's headlights revealed that it wasn't just *any* man—it was Peutret. The woman, stooping, clasped her head in her hands, as dim light from an above lamp revealed red seeping through her fingers.

Watching Peutrek turn and run, the officer considered himself, now, to be in pursuit of a criminal. But he knew that, out of protocol and general decency, he should stop briefly. The objective was to assess the woman's condition—a gesture which was as cursory as it was irritating, for the officer. In fact, Kopochek recognized the young woman as an illicit "employee" of Peutret. She wore a cynical expression, as Kopochek pulled up next to her with his inquiry:

"Are you all right? Look, I'm calling for an ambulance. You need to be near here, when they arrive."

With that six-second delay, Kopochek was off, screeching his tires in pursuit. Down the alley-street, Crow Terrace, he sped behind the dark and vanishing blur that was Peutret, in the distance.

If not his timing, at least Peutret had chosen his assault *location* well. He knew Crow Terrace and nearby streets inside and out, in daylight or darkness. Through a gap in the line of adjoining, dilapidated gray-brick houses he darted. In a second he was out of view for anyone on Crow. His mission: get to a three-story, abandoned building a block and a half away on a parallel street. Once inside, he could "lay low" or make his way to the roof, if necessary.

Kopochek had vaguely seen his quarry vanish into the black space between the alley houses. At present, he was on the radio reporting his pursuit and requesting medical help for the assault victim. In seconds, he devised the plan to bypass the locus of Peutret's disappearance and continue to the alley's end. There, he would, with vehicle light's flashing, turn north onto the southbound one-way, Bogg Street. With a little luck, he thought, he might just catch a glimpse of Peutret sprinting in one direction or another, or applying a cover.

Turning, now, onto a parallel street to Crow Terrace, Kopochek saw no sign of the man he sought. Within the minute, he started losing hope of having the confrontation he craved with Peutret. On Dawning Street, Kopochek cruised slowly, eyeing one and another group of men standing about. Just beyond the middle of the block, the officer saw something that got his attention. Hastily, individuals of seedy appearance tumbled, in succession, from the doorway of a rundown three story building.

Via the legendary "policeman's hunch," Kopochek made a guess. He thought the activity he witnessed at the entrance of 444 Dawning may have something to do with Peutrek. He knew the correct procedure: Call and wait for a backup before pursuing a suspect inside an unfamiliar establishment. This was especially to be the case, when neither the life nor safety of an innocent hung in the balance.

Kopochek made the call as required. Afterward, he did something that was patently not standard police procedure. Divesting himself of the radio apparatus, he laid it on the car seat. He thought the sounds it emitted might hinder an upcoming pursuit. Often, when he undertook sudden chase of a suspect, Kopochek was given to risk-taking, sometimes at high-stakes. In the present pursuit, it seemed that the *gambler* inside him won out, again.

Kopochek leapt from the patrol car and, with weapon drawn, bounded the outside steps of the edifice. In his free hand he carried a flashlight. Once inside, he found that the gloomy darkness was mitigated only by the filtering-in of illumination from outside streetlamps.

Within the great vacant structure, corridors and portals abounded. Wandering about, the officer saw ample evidence that some of the city's most unsavory individuals staked out, or camped out, or got high and passed out, in every visible area. So dismal were the surroundings that Kopochek began to wonder if he should await arrival of his backup—outside. On the other hand, that might provide just enough time for Peutret to escape. Already, the officer could hear rumbling sounds coming from floors above him.

Just do it! That was Kopochek's mental command to himself as he made the decision to find the source. Somehow, he thought he could *feel* Peutrek's presence above him.

"It's the police!" shouted Kopochek, once he'd arrived at the top of a flight of stairs. "Whoever's here—make yourself known! Come out in clear view of the flashlight!"

He was now moving through an area of the second floor peering along the hallway. Down at the far end, the officer more *heard* than *saw* the blur of a figure "taking" to a back staircase. Kopochek automatically gave chase.

"Stop running!" he called out loudly. "It's the police! Stop running! Lie down on the steps!" By the time he got to the alternate set of stairs, however, the figure he'd spotted was soundly on the third floor selecting the best room of escape. With weapon drawn, the officer ascended the stairway. Moving cautiously through the third floor, Kopochek paused at the one *open* door.

Three conditions set the stage for the set of events to follow. First, Peutret didn't close the door behind him when he ran into the room leading to the fire escape. If he had, there would have been no reason for Kopochek to choose the correct one so immediately. Second, the fire escape window, which always opened easily, was secured by window lock. The third condition was the presence of Nelson Weasler, who stood within the dark room, between wall and door, when Peutret entered.

Suddenly, now, Kopochek appeared in the doorway with weapon and flashlight trained on Peutret, who stood at the window, unlocking it.

"It's over, Phil," the officer called out. "Down on the floor, with your arms and legs spread! You know the drill. Do it now, Phil! …Now!"

Weasler stood on the other side of the half-open door. Unwilling to risk his own discovery, he pushed hard at the portal, knowing the officer's left shoulder touched the wood surface. Kopochek was knocked to the floor, in the semi-darkness, and struggled to keep possession of his weapon. He could only watch the shadow that was Weasler, quickly exiting the room.

Peutret's window was now unlocked. As he could see, Officer

Kopochek, kneeling, still had not regained a proper grip his service revolver. There were no witnesses present. It seemed an ideal occasion in which to kill a cop who had become a real "pest" in his life. Peutret brandished the same pistol he had used to strike the woman in the alleyway of Crow Terrace. As he aimed he spoke:

"This one's for you, 'Koppy.' You've been askin' for it a long time." Peutret casually pulled the trigger. The gun hammer slammed down on the bullet's back surface, but did not fire off the lead.

Kopochek was now in crouched position and fired his own round. The .357 slug caught Peutrek dead center at his heart, obliterating it. So violent was the force of the blast that his upper body crashed through the window glass, while his legs dangled, lifeless, inside.

In his rush to deliver justice, Kopochek had left his portable radio in the car. Now, however, he could hear the sounds of human and radio voice-communication downstairs, in the building. He hurried to shout, down to his backup, the report of his being all right. The same, he informed, as the officers stormed up the stairs, could not be said of Philip Peutret.

Everyone in the Grafton police force, including those investigating the incident, agreed on at least two matters. The city was better off with Peutret lying perfectly at rest, in the morgue. In addition, the shooting was unanimously viewed as a justifiable homicide. But that's where the consensus ended. The point that greatly concerned Officer Kopochek's supervisors was his decision to enter the building in pursuit without his radio and backup. In so doing he violated protocol. He had put his own life at undo risk and possibly the lives of innocent people illegally inhabiting the edifice.

The controversy just would not blow over. Once news reporters began revealing details of the case, troubling questions arose. One asked whether the earlier *assault* that was witnessed warranted a police pursuit, with that level of intensity. Another concerned the *alleged* initial crime itself—for example, had there *really* been an *assault*? The female of interest in the case, Andria Craug, denied having been struck by Philip Peutrek. She claimed to have sustained her injury, in a fall.

Some of the cynical wondered why Officer Kopochek hadn't stayed with the alleged victim, until an ambulance arrived. At that time, he could have taken her statement and initiated a search for Peutrek, later, if appropriate. In a relatively short period, the Kopochek shooting was generating way too much attention and negative buzz for the Grafton police department. The officer at the center of the controversy was actually being labeled by some "a rogue cop." It was a term with which the force wanted no association.

Neither did it sit particularly well with Kopochek's wife. Already unhappy with her husband's line of work, Julie Kopochek found her discontent now intensified. Consequently, she began joining the chorus of voices strongly urging Dan Kopochek to accept a "reasonable" offer. It was for him to transfer to another, more outlying and serene, department within the state. Julie found promise in reports that Dan's supervisors knew just the little out-of-the-way town, presently seeking a good, dedicated officer.

Pondering the prospect of the family's move to Mount Pleasant, Julie's first thought was of career change—Dan's, that is. If Mount Pleasant was nearly as *laid back* as her informal research indicated, Dan should have no trouble taking college classes while working. She was thrilled at the very idea. Certain that her husband had "brains" untapped by police work, Julie appointed herself his new occupation-change facilitator.

Always, it gave Julie a rather warm and fuzzy feeling to contemplate the work of influencing Dan's direction. For Julie, her world consisted of "the girls" and Dan. Nothing pleased her more than putting her powers of persuasion to work, nudging and impelling them all toward the *right* course.

Dan Kopochek didn't appreciate, at all, how Grafton P.D. folded under pressure exerted from outside the force. To him, they had, as the saying goes, "hung him out to dry." Deep inside, he knew they had, in the end, cut him a good deal, though. But the whole matter just had the feel of a betrayal, at least on the surface. *Sure,* he thought, *they say I can 'apply' to return, after some time has passed. Well…how much time? And what was behind use of the word 'apply'?*

In the end he decided not to fight but to go quietly. At least, he continued in his reflections, he could recognize one benefit in the outcome. Julie was now more chipper than he'd seen her, in months. Indeed, the girls seemed happier, too, of late—even his one-year-old, he mused, *as if she's old enough to know anything about anything.*

In the ensuing weeks, the Kopocheks—Dan, Julie, Danielle, Samantha, and Faye—settled into their new environment. They were lucky enough to transfer the mortgage paid in Grafton to a house in Mount Pleasant, in a pleasingly short time. But to the family's added delight the new home was bigger, more rural and sat on more land. The next item on the agenda was to become acquainted with those most important to know in town. In the process, the Kopocheks planned heartily to familiarize themselves with the *culture* of Mount Pleasant.

One thing jumped glaringly out at Dan and Julie after they'd been in Mount Pleasant two weeks. It was how seriously "Pleasantians" (Dan's appellation) took their local politics. Arriving home, at 6:00 one evening, in the patrol car assigned to him, Dan found Julie riveted by a TV news report.

"Hi, sweetie! ...Look at this! All these...people...standing around the Town Hall...protesting results of a little *school board election!* Oh my God! Look at them! They're all up in arms...mad as heck...mostly middle aged and old folks!"

"If you think it looks bizarre on TV," Dan commented dryly, "you ought to see 'em up close. It doesn't show on that replay you're watching, but I was there monitoring them about half hour ago. I've gone from chasing down armed, hardened felons to watching over a whiny, *over-the-hill gang.*"

Julie watched the broadcast from the living room sofa. Simultaneously, she wiped little Faye's face, hands and bib, following a lively *baby food* feeding. Happy sounds emanating from upstairs were an indication that the couple's five and seven year olds were in their room, playing.

"Oh, my God...this is precious! This town has no more to get excited about than a *school board election*—and a *minor* one at that."

Standing near Julie, Dan asked: "What *seat* was it for? Let me guess: the *Grand Poobah of Textbook Designation?*"

"No, it's something equally 'imposing,' like the *High School Truancy Czar*—." At just that moment baby Faye signaled her desire for attention by her father.

"Oh, I didn't mean to ignore my little angel...you come right on here, sweetie pea. How's my pumpkin pie, huh? How's my punkin'?"

"I told you, Dan. I told you. Mount Pleasant is the perfect place for us right now—easy-going, laid back."

"Yeah, if it was any more laid back, it might snooze off into a twenty year sleep, like Rip Van What's-His-Face."

"*Tee-hee*. But, you know, that's actually a good thing. Sleepy, snoozing, quiet—it's what *the good life* is made of, when you're raising three darling girls and married to big, strong man with brains and ambition."

"Well, as you know, Jules, I prefer to be big, strong, and on the prowl for dangerous bad guys. The only *bad guy* I've seen in this town is old Mr. Balzton, who owns the central movie theaters. You should have seen him kicking the Town Hall door, from outside, after they'd closed it and terminated the meeting. That was before the camera people arrived. I thought I might have to put the cuffs on that old rascal."

Dan headed for the stairs with the baby in tow. Without turning, he called back to his wife:

"What's for dinner, Jules? Better still, I'll derive the details from Faye-Faye's inscrutable vocalizations. *I'll bet you know what's for dinner, don't you, little chubby legs? Miss Faye-Faye knows all and tells no one. Isn't that right, my little munchkin?*"

"Dan," called Julie, "you must remember not to call our baby 'chubby legs.' We don't do 'complexes' in our family."

"Yes, dear. ...Can I call her 'Tater Toes'? ...No? What about 'Puff-n' -Stuff'? ...No?"

Julie, still watching images on the TV screen, could hear her husband's voice fading, as he ascended the stairs. In smiling disbelief, she shook her head, taking in details provided by the evening-news reporter.

The contest for the school board seat in question had been won by a Mr. Pike Stencil. By a mere seven votes, he had, in the final moments of tallying, "squeaked" pass a theretofore *even* count of ballots. For those who had protested inside, and outside, of Town Hall, discontent centered on nine votes that were intended to be, but were not, cast.

Tidying up about the living room, Julie never broke her focus on the news report. *Nine votes*, the news caster emphasized. The erstwhile unruly mob outside of Town Hall claimed actually to know just who the nine were, who had missed the opportunity to have their votes recorded. They knew and would have no problem naming names, upon inquiry. In fact, they didn't even wait to be asked.

Among those cited was Mr. Waxlo, slipping ever so gradually into an Alzheimer's state, at a local assisted living facility. He had forgotten to request shuttling to the poll. Mrs. Lumpel and Mr. Tumers were each recovering from surgery at a Mount Pleasant hospital. Answering an emergency call from a relative, the day before the election, Mr. and Mrs. Nookery were absent on election day. They, in fact, stayed out of town nearly a week. The remaining four Mount Pleasanters, the Waverlys and the Deckers, were vacationing on a luxury liner. Due to unforeseen circumstances, the trip extended a day beyond the election.

From what Julie could gather, the race's closeness, to the very end, had surprised everyone who followed the tally. The incumbent, Jill Graves, had been favored to win by a large margin. Based on assumptions of a Graves landslide, many of those favoring her simply had not come out to vote. For sure, there was much regret over the error in judgment made by the no-shows. But that wasn't the focus of the dissenters' argument.

"All the *hell-raising*," said the newscaster, irreverently, "is over votes not cast due to what might be viewed as *acts of God*. Now, study over that awhile." The lightly derisive tone shifted:

"But, all jokes aside, we can appreciate the protesters' position. Nine known supporters of the incumbent were unable to cast ballots, quite due to forces beyond control."

The newscaster referenced signs the protesters carried, displaying: WE WANT GRAVES! "So, viewers," she quipped, "these folks want you to know, in no uncertain terms: They are solidly *into* Graves. Here's an idea. When *this* protest is over, let's a bunch of us borrow those nice plaques to protest for more cemeteries. What do you think?"

Laughing, Julie mused, *Well, the town's got a sense of humor.*

As Officer Dan Kopochek discovered, Mount Pleasant was a good sized town with an appreciable population. It just seemed to *get about* with a certain ease. He took note of what he referred to as the "retired or retiring Pleasantians," of whom there seemed a sizable number. Setting aside the cantankerous display of that "old gang" at Town Center, Dan had to admit that these *up-in-agers* appeared serene. He learned gradually of their caring and helpful ways, with regard to those around them of lesser ability and means.

Daily, Dan made updates to Julie on his views of the town's demographic "design." He shared his intrigue of the *social class* situation in Mount Pleasant. According to his observation, the three classes lived interspersed. For sure, there were differences in the quality of the residences. Upon close inspection, there was notable variation in the manner and elegance of their dress. Anyone paying attention would even detect significant nuances in parlance shaped by early "usage" influences. Yet, somehow the citizens had achieved a sort of unity that showed very little segregation by locality.

So, the newly arrived patrol officer marveled at what he took to be a societal wonder. At the dinner table with Julie, it was one of his favorite topics. It wasn't long before he thought he should like to explore the phenomenon farther. If Mount Pleasant was incorporating a system, of some sort, that could be a model for other cities, it might be worth discovering.

Accompanied by her three girls, Julie Kopochek did some light shopping at the area super-mart. Sitting and riding in the smoothly rolling cart beside a few purchased items, baby Faye seemed non-envious of her pedestrian siblings. The child, secured in a seat at the basket's upper level, faced her mom and took joy in the moments of attention allotted her.

In her casual perusal of store goods, a conversation she overheard got Julie's attention. The participants were two ladies looking over a selection of children's wear. With an ease reflective of familiarity, Sandy Shork spoke to Melissa Finkel:

"I can't believe those old fuss-buckets are raising such a stink over the damned thing. Talk about having too much time on your hands—."

"Sandy, that group is as peculiar as a green goat. Normal folks just don't get that worked up over a school-board election."

"So, now they're demanding a whole new one. God, you should have heard Mr. Battle. *It's not a democratic election unless every intended vote is counted! We demand justice!* Whiny, whiny, fussy." In the next second, Sandy made note of the woman standing nearby, browsing.

"Hey, look, there's—." Sandy paused, to recall Julie's name. "Hi. Aren't you the new policeman's wife?"

"Guilty as charged," the younger woman quipped. "Hi. I'm Julie… Julie Kopochek. And these restless little munchkins are our daughters. This is Samantha…here's Danielle and this is our little cupcake, Faye. Say 'hi' girls."

"Oh what beautiful little girls!" Following that compliment, Sandy and Melissa introduced themselves. After some seconds of talk, Sandy offered:

"Look, let me give you my phone number, and anytime you'd like to pay me and Claus, my husband, a visit, just call. We'll arrange for our 'grand' girls to come by to meet your little angels."

"Oh, that is so…neighborly of you!" Julie was genuinely moved.

"Yes, and here is *my* number" Melissa added. "My house is just a little ways down from Sandy's. Stu and I would love to have your family over, anytime it's convenient."

"Well, thank you so much."

"Julie, this is a great place to live and raise your kids. Every now and again…things happen, but that's everywhere. I understand that you and your husband came here from Grafton. …Well, compared to what I hear goes on there, Mount Pleasant is *green pastures.*"

Melissa glanced cynically at her friend when she replied. "Sure. Pastures visited by an occasional cow and 'pies.'"

"Well, I suppose if you live in green pastures, a 'cow' every now and again ain't too bad." Julie's comment drew chuckles from the ladies.

It was the perfect Sunday afternoon in Mount Pleasant for the Fraternal Order of Police to have its quarterly outing, in Rosary Park. The entire Mount Pleasant force seemed in attendance. To Dan and Julie Kopochek, it had the feel of a church outing. Sitting at the round family-dining table they'd chosen, the Kopocheks marveled at the orderly layout.

Browsing about the picnic area, a ranking officer of the force, Captain Letigo, oversaw the festivity. His spontaneous visits didn't cause resentment of any kind to the various groups playing host to his brief presence. In his random wanderings, he stopped at a bench where some officers made brief convention beyond earshot of their wives. The captain, helping himself to an iced tea, joined the ongoing dialogue.

"Who're we talking about here, men, our newest addition to the force?"

"Yes sir, Captain, none other." It was Officer Wiggins answering. "Dan was just over, a few minutes ago. Real likeable fella', that. He's kind of a *serious* type though. That's what we were talking about. He's one of those that, at least when *we* see him, is never really *loosed up*. You know what I mean?"

"Oh, yeah. I've seen it. But, you know, he comes from over there in Grafton. That's a *hard* place—a hotbed of all kinds of crime. You name it; they do it over there in Grafton. So, I guess you had to be *hard* to make it as a cop in that hell-on-earth, for seven years."

Officer Saylyn spoke next: "I like him. I think he kind'a gives the force a more...rugged look. Any of you ever see how townsfolk react when he pulls up in the squad car?"

"I've seen it," answered Officer Dovey. "In the whole twelve years I been keeping the peace, I ain't never got that much respect. Like Al said, it's a *good* thing.

"Hell, I've actually been thinking about trying to imitate Kopochek. Approach people, not with a mean face, but like I'm looking straight through, to their souls. Unnerve the hell out of them good, God-fearing folks."

"They'd likely call another police officer on you, Ned," warned the captain, jokingly. "Can't you just hear 'em: *'That there Officer Dovey's actin' strange. You all better have him looked at!'*"

Several yards from where the conversation buzzed between the captain and officers, the Kopocheks occupied their table. There, Dan spoke with mock seriousness:

"Looks like Faye-Faye's prepping for a career as a pitcher. Hey angel-face...don't you know that tossing projectiles from a highchair is unlawful? Julie, this one's headed down misdemeanor highway, without a brake-peddle."

"Nahh—no criminal inclinations there. She's just high-spirited and maybe a bit of a risk-taker, like someone *else* in our family."

"Well, those days of *pushing the odds* are all behind me now. The old *tornado of fate* has dropped us off in *Oz*—and *Emerald City* at that. I feel like one of those Oz *flying monkeys* with his wings clipped."

"Experiencing pent up energy and drive? Well, I have the perfect solution to that: evening classes at the local college. I've already looked at their list of study areas. It's pretty impressive."

Dan was picking up and sanitizing toys Faye earlier tossed in the grass, as he replied: "Oh really? Did you see anything that might fit my temperament, as much as policing a crime-ridden city?"

"As a matter of fact, I did. I saw programs for *construction engineer, civil engineer, architectural design*—courses that go right along with interests you used to talk about."

"Julie, that was a long time and three children ago. I've got a full time job and three sweethearts to help raise. So, unless you're in the market for some serious spousal neglect, how about just help a cop ride out this Mount Pleasant daydream."

"I'm sure you know I'm more than ready to make the sacrifice for our future. Dan, I just don't like you risking your life as a policeman. Of course, here, it seems I don't have much argument, with conditions being as mild as they are. Does Mount Pleasant have a crime rate at all? So, far I haven't been able to tell."

Dan reflected on his brief perusal of department files from time to time. "Welllll," he dragged out thoughtfully, "they've actually got a few *UHs* in the archives. And, of course, like any other town, there are the usual *missing persons* cases."

"Heck, Dan, there goes my *New Eden* theory. So, Mount Pleasant has blemishes. Missing persons, unsolved homicides—that's hard to imagine here, based on the impression so far."

"Well, honeybee, it's not exactly discovery of secret mass graves within city limits. Still, it got my attention—and *in*tention to look a little farther."

Julie noticed a group of officers' wives gathered around a refreshments table in the distance. Within seconds, some of the ladies making eye contact waved. Reciprocating, Julie turned to Dan:

"Officer Sweetie Pie, I have your next assignment. Continue guardianship of our cherub. I think I shall like to collect Faye's sisters then join some of the other wives over there, in chitchat."

"It's way too pleasant a day to mar by being disagreeable. I will monitor our toy-tosser with due diligence."

"And, Dan, give some thought to the college courses we talked about. Once you're back in school, I know you'll feel that old academic *fire* again."

The MPPD clocks read 7:41, a morning within the following week. With cool deliberation, Officer Kopochek moved about the records room, engaged in private research. There was no rush to punch his time-card, as the morning shift didn't officially start until 8:00. Taking advantage of permission he'd obtained earlier, he studied paper reports, as well as those displayed in other mediums.

Mount Pleasant had a crime rate, alright, Dan mused, albeit a tiny one. In addition, Dan believed he saw reason to suspect—of all things—*gang* activity. It was the crime-victims' ages that drew Dan to that conclusion. Yet, not a single one of the police briefings he received made mention of a problem with gangs in Mount Pleasant.

Punch-in time was still nine minutes away, but Kopochek decided to get his patrol started early. Quietly, he returned to the cabinet the last of the files he had spread across a table.

At that moment, a call from his radio blared out the urgent command for available units to make haste to an address on Fowler Bend, west. It was a domestic situation that had escalated to brandishing of a firearm. Sliding his card into the clock, Dan just barely caught a glimpse of other officers rushing to the emergency

Everyone speeding to the domestic disturbance site, except Dan, had a sense of what he was likely to face. It seemed that old "Mr. Jessie" Crawstuf felt compelled, yet again, to show his three grown sons his less civil side. The old man didn't take well to his authority being challenged. When he discovered his sons' latest intentions, it fairly set him off. To save the family business, the sons wanted to have him legally declared unfit to continue management of *Feathered Friend Birdseed*.

Now, the Crawstuf "boys" stood defiantly on the edge of their father's property, verbally firing *at him* their ultimatum. He should concede power of company management over to them, willingly, or face legal repercussions.

After an abrupt stop behind the three vehicles parked near Mr. Jessie's property entrance, Officer Peas alit from his patrol car. Standing at the driver's side, he began a mixture of pleading and chastisement directed toward the senior Crawstuf. The latter continued to point his rifle at his three sons, who alternated between shouting a few words and ducking.

"Mr. Jessie," scolded Officer Peas, "have you lost your mind pointing a weapon at people—your sons, at that?! Is that thing loaded?!"

"You're damned right it's loaded. Look, I'm on my property. These three damned *jackals* I raised *want* to get shot. They know I don't put up with this kind of crap from anybody!"

"Mr. Jessie, we've told you before: You can't aim a loaded weapon at people just because you're mad!"

"Do your job, Sam," Mr. Crawstuf demanded. "Arrest the *real* criminals here! You should be hauling these three…*traitors* in!"

"Mr. Jessie, now you got to put that rifle down. You're gonna' get yourself in a world…."

"You come from behind that car, Sam, and I'm gonna' start shootin' *jackals*—and I mean it!"

The sound of the two other squad cars coming fast could be heard a hundred yards in the distance. The one driven by Kopochek stopped not on the side of the road like the others, but *in* the road. Spinning and glowing in the daylight, his red and blue police emergency lights signaled crisis. From his vehicle, Kopochek made his way in a cautious hurry to where the Crawstuf sons half stooped on the side of the elder brother's pick-up. When he had determined that no one, to this time, had been injured—not even a shot fired—he stood to cast appraising eyes at the elder Crawstuf.

"Sir," Kopochek began, "you must realize that pointing a rifle at a police officer is one of the worse decisions you can make."

"I'm aiming to part the hair of the first one of these *hyenas* I raised that I can get a bead on. I got no beef with you. How about you get out of here and let me handle my matter. I'm on my own property. I know my rights." As he spoke Mr. Jessie kept his rifle pointed at the bobbing heads of his offspring.

Once again, the gambler in Kopochek surfaced. With athletic ease, he hoisted himself up and into the flat bed of Jessie Jr.'s pick-up. The added "height" gave him, in uniform, an added imposing appearance. As he spoke to Mr. Jessie, his tone was both matter-of-fact and authoritative.

"*Now*, you're aiming that rifle directly at an officer of the Mount Pleasant law, sir. I don't know if you're aware of what's called proper police procedure, but I am obligated, now, to draw my weapon and shoot. I've given you a warning that I'm a police officer."

"I'm on my own property!" Mr. Crawstuf demanded. "You can't come around here threatening me!" Mr. Jessie, in his rage, watched Officer

Kopochek climb over the pick-up's side facing him, and jump to the ground. The two were now just a few yards distance from one another.

"You notice I haven't drawn my service revolver," Kopochek commented. "And this means I'm not following proper procedure. But the reason is this: I'm a new officer in Mount Pleasant, and I just haven't had time to make a proper meeting with everybody here, as yet. I'm sure, though, that you are one of its finest citizens."

Just as if their encounter were under cordial conditions, Kopochek walked right up to where Mr. Jessie stood. As Crawstuf had reminded the officers, that position was just inside the entrance to his front lawn.

"So, let's just *not* allow this terrible misunderstanding to go any farther," Kopochek advised. His expression showed complete confidence, his stare was piercing. Calmly, he stepped across the gateway threshold onto privately owned land.

"You're going to hand your rifle over to me and I'm going to turn it over to Officer Peas and Officer Dewey," Kopochek directed. "And after that, I'm leaving, to take up my normal patrol duties in Mount Pleasant."

Taking hold of the rifle, Kopochek was careful to point its barrel upward. His dialogue continued in an unbroken string:

"If it's all the same to you, I'd just as soon let my fellow officers handle the matter from here. I hope I can say, convincingly, that it was good meeting you. And I do hope to drop by sometime in the future, to make acquaintance under much *easier* circumstances."

At the turn of events, Mr. Jessie was enraged and outraged. The one consolation "allotted" him, though, was a firm belief that he knew, at least, how to handle Dewey and Peas. They had each worked for him when they were boys, underscoring years of acquaintance. Once that crazy new officer was gone, he surmised, he stood a good chance of making his case, even without his rifle.

By about midday, Kopochek made the assessment that all seemed well in Mount Pleasant from a policeman's view. Not so much as a case of school truancy was apparent. The aging townsfolk within the various communities were out and about, tending to their various affairs. These seniors, Kopochek noted, appeared to lack the fearful uncertainty and caution characteristic of their Grafton counterparts. Indeed, they seemed, at times, not only confident, but cocky—even aggressive—in an elderly way. Thinking on it, Dan supposed the latter to be a good thing. Better to have ornery old people, letting off verbal steam every now and again, than overly assertive youth, elbowing their way through town.

At just around the end of the traditional lunch hour, Dan pulled into a section known as Sap Tree. The community abounded in arboreal giants which, as the name suggests, oozed fluid at rips in tree bark. Piney Street, along which Kopochek steered, was lined also with modest homes for which the trees provided a natural shade. Dan estimated that many of the dwellings were quite old but wearing refurbishments that hid their true ages. Down the road several blocks, he could see outlines of homes that were small mansions in comparison.

What a town, he thought, as he had many times before. The well-heeled and the humble living practically side by side.

As he had earlier expressed to the senior Jessie Crawstuf, it was his intention to get to know the citizenry in a nonofficial capacity. To that end, Kopochek looked for an opportunity to initiate dialogue with someone at leisure within the neighborhood. The occasion presented itself when a small group of porch-sitters eyed the officer and gave a friendly wave. Trained in observation, Dan took note of the "234" address, as he slowed to a stop. In the tone of a dedicated town's peacekeeper, he issued a greeting:

"Hello. How are you-all doing?"

"Oh, we're fine." It was Mrs. Florn who replied. The forty-year-old woman was enjoying the spring day with two friends and her disabled father-in-law.

"Great weather we're having today. If I wasn't working, I'd be at home relaxing on my front porch, just like you." The four showed pleased smiles at receiving such cordial commentary from Mount Pleasant's newest patrol officer.

From his position some distance away, Dan could make out that each member of the group attended a glass of beverage of some kind. It was his policeman's attentiveness going "into gear." The assessment was automatic, for Dan was, in fact, not at all in a prying mood—not then. Suddenly, as if aware of the officer's mental note-taking, the other woman, Ms. Spark, made her offering:

"Would you like a cold cup of lemonade, officer? We just made it—big, ripe lemons, a real thirst quencher."

Typically in these situations, Kopochek, gave a staid *No, thank you.* In Grafton, he would no more accept—much less ingest—food or drink from a resident than swim with pariahs. Here, however, he was exploring possibilities for doing, sort of, community-based policing. Most importantly, this was Mount Pleasant, not Grafton. Here was a town, he assessed, that could find no more to get worked up over than small-time, local elections or one's trio of mischievous and prematurely balding sons.

He'd only paused a couple of seconds. Then Kopochek made his calculated delivery: "Just a half cup would be fine. I haven't had fresh, homemade lemonade in…well, too long."

With that announcement, Dan motioned the cruiser into an available place right in front of the house, at the curb. From the porch, he was watched carefully, as he exited the car and approached. As he got closer, each of the four made similar assessments: They saw a tall man, sure-gaited, with an almost menacing appearance. This was in spite of Dan's attempt at a smile—a clamped-teeth, squint-eyed, controlled, but sincere smile.

The woman, Ms. Spark, who had offered the lemonade, made the one-way introductions of her group to the officer. Afterward, Dan gave his name, pointing to the tag on his uniform as confirmation.

From where he stood on the porch, Dan could see all the way through the house to the open back door. While chatting with the remaining three of his hosts, he simultaneously watched Ms. Spark journey to the kitchen. He saw that she opened a refrigerator, lifted a pitcher from inside, and pulled a paper cup from the top of a stack on a table.

Quickly, as if suspecting she was being watched, Spark made her way back to the porch. There, she handed the police officer the cup and poured to half its capacity.

"I don't mind telling you," Kopochek informed, "I never was treated this kindly in Grafton. I was just telling Mr. Gouss, Mrs. Florn and Mr. Pathwinder that I transferred from Grafton to here." At the end of the statement, Kopochek took a long sip of the savory, cold drink.

"Now, this is what I call *real homemade* lemonade," he offered. … Oh, no, no, no. This is quite enough. I just wanted a small taste, to jog my memory. It's just the incentive I need to persuade the wife to put lemonade back on our menu at home."

"Truth be known, I'd say just about everybody in Mount Pleasant knows you were policin' in Grafton, before comin' here." It was Mr. Pathwinder's statement. "Mount Pleasant ain't a tiny town, but it's pretty close-knit. Word, of one sort or another, gets around over time."

"I suppose," Kopochek replied, "that can be good sometimes. Well, I just wanted to start getting familiar with folks of your community. I thought, rightfully, I could start with you. I'm hoping to do likewise with all the areas I patrol. As is often said in law enforcement: There's nothing better than police and community working together. It just gives everyone involved a better feeling of safety and satisfaction."

Before he could get out his last expression of gratitude for the treat, Mrs. Florn allowed a deep sentiment to spill forth. "I hope you can help them other police find out what happened to my Lonnie."

"Lonnie?" inquired Kopochek.

"Yes, my son. He disappeared two years ago. Them other police... they say they can't come up with anything...so he must have run away. But I know my son ain't run away nowhere. He ain't had no place to *run to*. All his family—and friends—is right here in Mount Pleasant."

Gouss spoke next: "Don't get yourself all back in that kind of way again, Mayzie. You gotta' just let it go, after a point. The police, they—." He ended abruptly, shaking his head.

"I know they ain't really tried to find my son," demanded Mrs. Florn. "Lord knows they coulda' done more. Lord knows they *coulda' done more!*" She tried to cover the tears falling down her face.

"Some things," averred Mr. Pathwinder in a near chant, "you have to leave to the Lord. That's just how it is: You got to leave it to the Lord."

"I can see how upset you are over it, Mrs. Florn. If you don't mind, I'd like to get your son's full name, his age and date of disappearance. Maybe I can look the case up in the records and maybe... find out something."

Kopochek sought the fine balance between commiseration and non-commitment. Saying something that appeared to override earlier, official, determinations was strictly taboo. After taking a few statements, Dan graciously departed.

When Dan disappeared down Piney in the police cruiser, the four associates spoke their impressions of him. Gouss led the colloquy:

"He ain't like them other ones. You can see that. I don't know that I'd trust him, though. He looks *hard*...like he ain't really got no feelin's. Even when he smiles, his eyes look like a jungle cat."

"He sure don't seem scared or phony, like our police that's been here, for-*ever*. So, who knows? He might look into it. If he does, he might get interested in some of the other ones, too." Sonja looked thoughtful as she spoke to her companions. She was the ex girlfriend of Mayzie's youngest brother. Although he was long since married—to someone else—Sonja kept a good friendship with her "ex's" older sister.

Melan Gouss, at age forty-five, was a good friend to practically everyone in the neighborhood. He was enjoying a scheduled day off from his job as a grocery store employee. He addressed the wheelchair-bound Mr. Pathwinder:

"What you think of him, Gumpy? You usually can size a person up pretty good. You think he's any better than the other ones?"

"Tell you the truth—I can't tell, as yet, what to make of him. He ain't like our regular police. That's for sure. But he got a...I guess what I'd call a *mystery* with him. It could be a bad mystery or a good mystery. As yet, I can't tell—too early. If he's good, he may get some things looked into—cause he ain't scared. But if he's bad, he may be that ol' wolf wearin' part of a lamb's skin."

Patting her friend lightly on the back in consolation, Sonja formed a cynical expression. "I wonder what's behind his coming to Mount Pleasant," she uttered, thinking out loud. "He don't seem to fit Mount Pleasant. I wonder...why *here*."

Dan and Julie were just about finished packing the minivan with items for an overnight stay in Grafton. According to plan, the eighty mile drive should get them to the home of Julie's parents by noon. From that point the Leipzigs would have all day and night to enjoy their granddaughters. Bright and early the following day, the family would depart, en route to the Kopochek home in which Dan was raised.

Those early morning hours of preparation had seemed to fly by, given all that was required for a good trip. Dan had hoped to be on the road at ten and it was already 10:28. Finally, the three girls were all strapped in place in the minivan's back seat. Having double-checked the house windows and doors, Dan secured the front, as he exited, heading for the vehicle driver's seat.

"Alright, you ladies back there," Dan urged, "any sudden bathroom *gotta-goes* before I put it in gear? ...Okay, we're off."

"Faye-Faye might, but she's falling to sleep," announced Samantha.

Julie was turned backward helping the older girls hold their juice cups properly. "Hopefully," she commented, "she won't ask for potty until we get to Grandma's and Grandpa's."

"Well, all of you just remember—." In speaking, Dan affected sternness. "Faye-Faye's the only one of us who can make potty where she sits. So, no accidents. ...Julie—?"

"Officer, I'll have you know I'll make potty when and where I choose." As usual, their parents' playful talk, when understood, brought giggles from the girls.

Half an hour into the expected hour-forty-minute drive, "Dan-na," "Sima" and Faye were fast asleep. It was at just about this time that it occurred to Julie to re-animate the topic of college. In her thinking, it was crucial for Dan to take immediate advantage of the calm work and living conditions that Mount Pleasant offered. Who knew when things might change? For as long as the tranquility lasted, it seemed to her a good idea to make the best use of it. In that frame of mind she initiated the discussion.

"Did I tell you, Dan, that the *Mount Pleasant Technical College* has a summer session?"

"I believe you may have mentioned it once or eight times."

"*Funny*. Well, don't you think this is just the perfect time to resume your studies?" Julie tried to make her tone sound light. "I mean, things are so mild in Mount Pleasant. You'd have very little distraction.

"And at home, I'd make sure the girls were quiet while you're in the books. And, of course, I'd do everything at home. All of the chores and errands and upkeep you help me with now—I'll work day and night to keep it all together by myself. And...."

"Jules—I get it. I know how much you want me to take the beginning steps of career change. I've been giving the return-to-college thing some thought. But only because I know you won't rest until I commit to a decision. Still and all, I like police work, Julie. I just *like* it—it's in my blood."

"So, you've actually thought about it and you're considering it!" Julie's hopefulness showed in her voice.

"You might say so," Dan replied cavalierly. "I've been down to *MPTC* on my breaks to check out their programs. But the summer session is only three weeks away. I'd have to get transcripts from my other schools… enroll…get set up with a counselor…find the first semester's tuition. That's a lot in three weeks."

"What if I told you we already have the transcripts? I mailed the requests in your name last week They arrived at the school yesterday. And the tuition…we've got 'rainy day' money in the bank. We'll pretend it's raining."

"Gees. You're a real steam-roller, when you're after something. I don't know how I can stand against such an irresistible force."

"Yes, yes, that's what I like—surrender! So, it's all settled. All you have to do is choose a program."

"Man. Too much of a pushover—that's my problem. I should have taken notes from those old protesters in front of Town Hall that day."

"Oh, did you hear?" Julie asked. "They got their way. The election is being done over. Can you believe that?"

"That's wild." Dan thought on the matter awhile, shaking his head. "How does the saying go?" he asked rhetorically. "Great minds rehash great issue; small minds stir up the dead ashes of a school board election."

"Why do I think you just made that up?" As she spoke Julie was still elated over Dan's implied agreement to renew his years-past academic goals.

Parked side by side in an area of the Oakford mini mall lot, the two police cruisers faced opposite directions. That alignment allowed the drivers to converse while keeping an eye on goings-on in the broad expanse. In the prior week, on this same day, some roaming teens staged a pocketbook snatching outside of *Food Time* market. The two elderly people who were victim and co-victim of the crime were not hurt. But they were angry, and demanded that the local constabulary apprehend the robbers sooner than later.

To Kopochek, a crime was a crime. Be it an armed bank robbery or the unlawful relieving a senior of her valuables, such an act was intolerable. And however low the town's crime rate was, he considered it the job of the police department to *try* to get it zero. He continued his talk with Officer Tredlight.

"I understand the investigator has a few leads on that purse snatching. Not real smart to do that in broad daylight with people moving about nearby."

"These kids don't think. They see what they take as an opportunity and go for it. Could have been on a dare or to prove something...who knows?"

"What about gang activity," inquired Kopochek. "A lot of times, these kinds of crimes are committed as an initiation. And it starts expanding from there. In Grafton, they bring in an organization called *Gang-Stoppers*, launching them in prone neighborhoods, to try and nip it, early."

"*Gang-Stoppers*...catchy name. Sounds like a good idea, too. But I don't know if I can get *on board* with the theory of budding street-gangs. I've lived here all my life, Dan. And I can tell you, the only time I recall the word 'gang' popping up in Mount Pleasant was in reference to a gang of wild turkeys. Wild as hell they were, for sure. But...."

"I know—they never committed a crime. That's pretty funny, Mort." Kopochek smiled and nodded at his colleague. Such instances of small-town humor had grown on him. "I'll say this," Dan continued, "you'd be surprised to know, these days, how fast and unexpectedly that *gang* phenomenon can crop up."

"Well, bud, I can tell you, we sure don't need that developing in Mount Pleasant. This town is slowly but surely finding its way on the map. You notice the new construction that's going on downtown?

"...Oh, yes, it's impressive," continued Officer Tredlight. "You probably don't know what Mount Pleasant looked like twenty-five years ago, when I was coming up. Oh, it's changed *big time*. A lot of folks don't like it, though, as you can imagine. But progress is progress. This town had to join the 21st century, for it own good. Those days when every other *Mike* worked on a farm are gone. And Dan, I say good riddance."

Kopockek nodded as he scanned the parking lot. "Yeah, I think I know what you mean. Change is pretty much inevitable."

"Absolutely. But it's not just change we're seeing in Mount Pleasant. It's progress, like I said before. Almost everyday, you see new faces coming and going about town. Fresh blood, Dan…it's fresh blood being infused into this old town—and it's good. …Well, hell, take…like you, for instance. Far as I know, everybody agrees that you are a great addition to the force—."

"I appreciate that. I certainly want to fit in."

"Well, you do more than fit in, bud. You give the force a new…*look*, sort of. I think the guys even act a little more like cops half the time." As he thought on his statement, Tredlight laughed a little.

"You know, Mort, I've been looking through old police reports, you know, to get familiar with some of the criminal history, and…."

"There. You see—that's what I'm talking about," interjected Tredlight. "The rest of us have been leaving it up to our tiny band of investigators to rehash through those old records. But since you've been doing it, a number of us have been talking about gettin' our butts over there and studying with you."

"Yeah, sure, that will be great. But, like I was about to say, it looks like you-all got a collection of unsolved homicides and disappearances."

"We got 'em, alright. I guess I could remember most of 'em that happened here from time to time, if I looked over 'em. I don't think they're all that uncommon, though, Dan. I'd say every town's got its *unsolved*."

"True. I guess they just stand out for me given Mount Pleasant's serenity. People here are so law-abiding."

"Well, on the bright side," added Tredlight, "you've been policing with us for, what, five months now? And we ain't had a homicide or a missing person in that time. So, by-damn, whatever's in the past, we got reason to celebrate the present. And, bud, when I get off in a couple of hours, I plan to do just that—with a cold beer and a comfortable seat in the back yard, in the shade."

"Sounds like damn good-times, too," said Kopochek wryly, but with humor.

Julie Kopochek, in her amiable style, met a woman whose family made the perfect child-sitters, on occasion. Actually, only about twice a month was required, evenings when she and Dan went out on a date, of sorts. This evening the couple had retrieved their precious triplet from the O'Shamus's care. Now, they were getting settled back in at home.

Following the obligatory night bath, the sleepy girls were readied for bed. Upstairs and downstairs, the televisions were tuned to the same late night news station. In this way, one was only a few steps away from attending, more closely, something of interest in the broadcast. That *something* came as Dan descended the stairs after having tucked the older girls in.

The report revealed that the bodies of two males were found along a stretch of railroad tracks. While the cause of deaths had yet to be formally determined, both apparently resulted from gunshots. Identities were being withheld, but by all appearances the shootings were less than twenty-four hours old.

The Kopocheks talked, some, about the report but very little. Discovery of the bodies had just been made, so Dan was in no position to speak knowledgeably on the case. Fact is, even if he knew more, he would have been inclined toward reticence, as Julie was well aware. For her, it was unwelcome news, for more reasons than those related to the tragedy itself. She had a vested interest in the town's serenity.

Dan may not have said a lot about the railroad track discovery, over several hours at home. But he sure thought a lot about it. At the station the next day, he found the place abuzz with discourse on the case. Together, the town's homicide investigator and its head coroner determined something that gave everyone a start. It was that the actual shootings had occurred in a different place than where the bodies were found.

As a police officer, Dan knew to leave the investigatory part of law enforcement to those who specialize in it. His role was to patrol, watch for criminal or untoward activity, answer calls to check out problem events. He was part of a team that stopped bad behavior in the city, as it was detected. Regarding investigations, he only assisted, as required, in the process.

Fortunately, Detective Beauford Boner had no problem with Dan's interest in the *cold* case files. Showing the same non-territorial bent as did the rest of the force, Boner took Dan's research as a means of getting to know the town better. No more, no less.

Even within the relaxed atmosphere, Dan was too keen of mind to appear to be abusive of the leeway given. He asked no more about "hot" and "cold" cases than that which seemed reasonable for a mildly probing new officer. He not only avoided over-inquisitiveness, he was also careful not to come off as critical. His real impressions he kept private; his real interests he pursued unannounced.

Summer began, in earnest, two weeks before the official start, temperature-wise. The preceding showers and blooms gave the city an Eden-like aura in places, even in the intense heat. As he patrolled the streets and byways, Dan had a particular interest, now, in the Mount Pleasant youth. It concerned the ways in which they might comport themselves during the break from school. Would the summer sun, he wondered, work a similar "magic" for driving recalcitrant impulses here, as it did in Grafton?

It was the Friday before the start of his own classes at *MPTC* that Dan had his interest indulged, regarding youth behavior in the summer break. The event involved Mount Pleasant's *Red Herring Social Club*, a popular venue for various kinds of social gatherings. Today featured a mid-afternoon, all-you-can-eat seafood extravaganza. Locals, young and older, were admitted for a modest fee, while seniors were charged a mere dollar to enjoy the festivities. So, popular and desirable was the event that the line to enter typically reached a half-block.

Arrangements could have been made for more efficient admittance. But taking small steps toward the entrance door for several minutes had become a tradition. It allowed the smartly dressed patrons to be on display for passers- and drivers-by. Overhead, colorful awnings leaned elegantly to protect the line-walkers from the sun. At ground level was a red carpet that gave them the feeling of being *royal* Red Herring guests.

As Officer Kopochek could see, from where his cruiser sat in the distance, folks of all ages stood in line. The $1-entry "set" typically arrived in taxis or were driven to the locale by relatives. For Kopochek it was amusing to watch but, after a time, also tiring. He was seconds away from the decision to move on, when he took note of Mrs. Swayer's slow but determined exit from her taxi. He saw her scan the line of people with an odd mixture of apprehension and distain.

Some quality in the old lady's demeanor made Kopochek hesitate before putting the cruiser in gear, to drive off. In fact, the woman's *apparent* attitude brought memories of the old people's indignation at Town Center months earlier. Dan knew body-language, and hers practically shouted her unwillingness to shuffle down to line's end.

Like an opportunistic bird of prey, Mrs. Swayer chose a gap within the colorful human chain making its slow procession. The space toward which the elderly woman moved was bordered at one end by a similarly-aged member of the line. At the other was a teenaged girl attending her great-grandfather. Boldly she ensconced herself between the woman and girl, simultaneously making affectedly friendly conversation with the former.

The gambit placed sixteen-year-old Mandy Skool an extra person farther away from the entrance door. She thought she should make known her dissatisfaction with the turn of events:

"Excuse me, Miss. You can't…. I'm in line." Mandy waited for a response. But, Mrs. Swayer, stepping slowly and leisurely, with the line in front, pretended to be oblivious of the information.

"Excuse me, Miss," Mandy reiterated more directly, "this is a *line*. You cut into the line. You have to go to the…to the *back*."

Having had enough, Mrs. Swayer spoke: "I'd like to know who you think you're talking to, missy. You mind your manners and address me properly. I have a name that you'll do well to learn and learn fast. And it's not 'Miss.'"

"And mine is not *missy*. You cut in front of me, in line. You can't do that."

With smoldering indignation, Mrs. Swayer turned forward again, toward Mrs. Guerthe. As the two continued their previous small talk, the line crept slowly onward.

"Great Grandpop, can you believe that?!" grumbled the teenager. "I don't know who she thinks she is. And I don't *care* who she is. She's no better than anybody else!"

With that outburst, Mrs. Swayer turned her aged frame around to address Mandy. "What is your name, you young snip?!" she demanded. "You tell me what your name is, so I can have your principal deal with you proper!"

"Principal?" inquired Mandy. "You think this is a line—to the school cafeteria?"

Present, also, were other youth, of or about Mandy's age. At the teen's last comment, they began to snicker and then laugh out loud. It was clear their derisive chuckles were aimed at the elderly woman and not Mandy.

"What are you laughing at, you little acorn-heads?! Do you know who I am? I'm Mrs. Swayer! How dare you laugh at me?! Why, I'll.... I want your names! I want *all of your names!*" Mrs. Swayer pointed a mean and trembling index finger at those to whom she spoke.

Damn, thought Kopochek humorously to himself within his patrol car. The expletive followed his notice of motions by some of the older people in line. They began to appear restless, antsy, as it were. Though subtle, it was clear their sidling motions took them partly out of line. In addition, from far front to far back, they postured such as to face Mandy and the laughing youthful cohort.

The phenomenon had not the least appearance that a physical confrontation was in the making. In Kopochek's estimation, a curious display of intensely unhappy sentiment was all that it was. Nevertheless, it seemed an eerie symbol. Formerly tranquil faces became suddenly dour, the old people apparently united in bold and evident misgiving.

Somehow, at this point the line became still. Then, suddenly, an elderly man at the door stepped out to summon Mrs. Swayer. Calling gently, Mr. Cragmoor waved the flustered aging dowager forward, beckoning her to take his place in the line.

With pride and haughtiness Mrs. Swayer made the little trek to the establishment's entrance. From her tiny, and ancient, two-finger snap-open/shut coin purse, she retrieved a silver dollar. She sported a victor's countenance as she tendered admission, moving regally to her favorite area of the ballroom. Outside, the line of people resumed its slow movement. Advancing inch-by-inch toward admission, the human cord lost the brief period of tension experienced earlier.

From Dan's view, it was like having watched the passing overhead of a dark cloud. Not one that forecast a threat of rain and wind, but one which blocked all sunlight for an apprehensive quarter-minute. Carrying out his earlier intention to move on, Dan put the patrol car in gear. As he did, he muttered to himself, "Well, that was...interesting. I learned *something* here. Be damned, though, if I know exactly what."

In civilian, or "home," attire, Dan Kopochek stood in his living room, affecting a playfully sour mood. From makeshift seats on the carpet,

Danielle, Samantha and Faye looked up at him with pretty, beaming faces.

"I don't want to go to school," Dan whined. The older girls laughed behind hands covering their mouths.

"Oh, it's not going to be so bad Officer Kopochek," Julie assuaged in pretense. "I just know it's going to be a lot of fun. You're sure to make new friends and everything."

"I don't want to make new friends, and I don't want to go to school. You can't make me go."

"Now, now, Officer, we don't want to set a bad example for our children, do we?"

"Oh! I didn't realize they were all sitting there. Of course, I'm looking forward to my evening classes at the college. Any of you young ladies want to come to school with me?" Dan and Julie looked with amusement at all the exaggerated head shaking and expressions of, "Noooo."

"There'll be ice cream and cookies and cake," Dan fibbed.

"Meeee! I want to go! I want to go!" the older girls chorused.

"Daddy's just having fun with you. He can't take you to his evening classes. Now, if you sweethearts are good while Daddy's in school tonight, maybe we can have a little ice cream before bed. Okay?

"...Now, Dan—oh, look at the time. You've only got fifteen minutes to get to the college and find your first class. You don't want to be late on the first day."

"Plenty of time—it's just a seven or eight minute drive. You three *Dora-Explorers* be good and mind your mother. Come here and give me my big going-off-to-college kiss. Yes, you too, Miss wobbly-legs--."

"Dan, don't call Faye-Faye that. Later, it could give her a complex." Julie was only a tad serious.

"Oh, okay, but actually I was, you know, addressing you. ...Hey, hey, hey! No fighting in front of the children."

As usual, at their parents' banter, the older girls were reeling with snickers and mirth. "Alright, princesses all," Dan continued, opening the front door, "I'm on my way. I should be walking back in, at just about nine—maybe earlier if they cut us a break on the first day. Be good."

In the drive to *Mount Pleasant Technical College*, Dan thought about the schedule he'd decided on. Three 50-minute classes, two days a week—probably a bit much to start off, he thought. But, if he was going to do it at all, he may as well jump in, chest-deep, and just swim like hell to the finish line.

Just as he had planned, he noted the time of 5:54 while pulling into the campus parking space. *Back in school,* he thought, making way to the building of his classes. *Who would have thought it? Why do I let Julie talk me into these things?*

In spite of his fussy inner attitude, Dan was quite aware of his pattern with regard to school. Once his professors had given the assignments, he'd be off and running, determined to achieve maximum absorption. But right at this time, he would much prefer the comfort of being at home with his family. When he found room 331, there were seven other newly arrived students sitting about.

Cordially, everyone glanced up at the newcomer entering, giving his and her greeting. Among all the faces, it was that of the woman sitting in the front that most got Dan's attention. The countenance appeared to him more suited for modeling class than *civil engineering.*

When the professor arrived, the scheduled class of twelve was showing ten students present. As the course title indicated, over time, Dr. Nishfala's instruction would focus on topics largely concerned with municipal infrastructures. Included was a study of city mapping procedures and of the associated symbols and terminology employed in the field.

Next, came the student introductions. Dan's response was succinct. After giving his name, he said only that he worked for the city of Mount Pleasant. In his experience, people's awareness of a cop in the midst, made them act...well, unnatural. If pressed farther he planned to say he was "in" traffic and road sign maintenance.

With minutes remaining, before the formal start of his patrol, Dan chatted lightly with other officers at the station. In the exchange he made mention of the little scene alongside the *Red Herring Social Club* the prior week. It was Captain Letigo that passed to Kopochek a revelation:

"Kops, my boy, you were bound to find out sooner or later. I heard about your suspicions that the rudiments of gang activity may be in evidence here in Mount Pleasant. Well, by Smokey, you were *almost* right—in a slanted, off-center, *oblique-as-hell* sort of way.

"We got a gang here, alright—a gang of old fogies that meet and talk local politics and a whole slew of other stuff, from what I understand. Who's got how much money still in their families, who's going broke, who's risking investments, who's offspring are besmirching the honor of their surname—all kinds of private, idle talk like that.

"Proud? Holy hell, the older ones are the worse. But they stick together. Now, it ain't but about twenty-some among the ring-leaders. They got influence—that is, with the other old-timers, and near old-timers, in town."

"Are we talking a major *political* force here, Captain?" Dan inquired.

"I wouldn't say…*major*, Kops." The captain trailed the comment off, in way that showed deep reflection. "I might say…*marginally* significant, regarding the politics of the city, overall. Even at that, it would have to involve some issue on which Mount Pleasant was split, like fifty-fifty. And that don't happen much.

"But *small-time* political, and other, offices that don't get a whole lot of attention, or that don't get the masses too excited—there, they can be a *body* to be reckoned with."

The captain continued in a sudden turn of thought. "One good thing I can say for the old geezers: They never cause *the force* any problems, like with complaints and whatnot. They sure don't give us worries as law*breakers*. Most of them are too old to even 'bend' the law, much less break it. But you know, it makes 'em feel good to be in touch with one another, sort of…unified. I think that's great.

"Too often old people of a town just lose touch and fade away. Not here, though. Old timers walk the streets like the good Lord draped *Do Not Disturb* signs around them ancient frames."

Dan issued a bland chuckle, as he spoke. "That's really funny—and all the more so, because it describes the picture I have of them in my mind. But like you say: What the hell? Good for them, if they got a little club-like association to belong to."

"That's right, Koppy—right as rain."

The shooting deaths of 18-year-old Monterey Morgan and 19-year-old Wilson Casey remained under investigation. By the start of August, the case was barely two months old. The detective in charge and his assistants still did not know who dropped the bodies along the tracks.

Nor had they determined where the homicides had originally occurred. To the credit of the investigative team, they did have nearby tire marks believed to be associated with the crime.

Also, the advent of August saw Dan immersed in college studies. As he saw, Julie had made good on her promise to provide the space he needed. At work, he was building an intense interest in what he considered an *inner* layer of Mount Pleasant's outer "skin." Keeping separate his academic pursuits and his interest in Mount Pleasant's hidden inner workings was a balancing act. For him, neglecting either one was unacceptable.

As the college summer session drew to a close, Julie saw even less of Dan at home than had become the norm, since its start. She didn't like it. For her, it was a difficult adjustment to make. Of course, on the other hand, she knew that making the sacrifice was her role to play in their new "program." Dan was taking the first steps toward a new career. She was overjoyed at that part of it. But all the time he spent at the college, at libraries, and at home secluded within the makeshift study—it was difficult for her.

Every now and again, within his patrols, Dan took license to come home and have lunch with Julie and the girls. At other times, he told her where he planned to grab a sandwich, to eat at a counter or within the cruiser. That was only if no emergency occurred, altering the course. From these revelations Julie conceived the idea to fit, into her routine of travel-related errands, a *browse-by* one of Dan's favorite lunch spots.

This particular day, Julie timed her arrival to an auto repair shop, for 11:45. The service requested was guaranteed to take half an hour or less. She and the little ones would then have at least fifteen minutes to get to the café where Dan anticipated having lunch this day. 12:30 was his usual time for break.

While Julie awaited the repair, Dan patrolled near the Mount Pleasant community of Sap Tree, a mile away. It was in his mind to drive, yet again, through the block where he was given the lemonade treat those months prior. Since then, in his patrols, he had seen one or more members of that earlier group sitting on the porch of the 234 address. A few times he had exchanged cordial waves. But he had not mustered the enthusiasm to apply a new volley of questions, concerning Mrs. Florn's missing son.

Somehow, this day, he felt different. It was just an inexplicable "sense" he had, that today could prove auspicious for gleaning more information. Who knew what tidbits gathered here and there, down the road, might aid in the discovery of something significant? Approaching Piney Street on Fern, Dan noted the shapely form of a woman crossing the street. In seconds, he was able to make out that it was Sonja Spark.

Pulling close to the curb where the woman walked, Dan lowered his window and spoke. After the greetings, he mentioned that he'd hoped to see Mrs. Florn enjoying the late morning on her porch. He had a few more questions to ask, informally and unofficially, about her missing son.

"Would you know whether or not she's at home," Dan inquired.

"I doubt she's back yet," answered Sonja, "but you can go by and see. She had somebody take her across town—I'd say…almost an hour ago. I would have taken her myself, but my car wouldn't start back up this morning, after driving it earlier."

"That's too bad. I hope it's not in a bad place."

"No…it's still in front of my house a block down the street."

Feeling an enterprising mood, Dan quickly assessed possibilities. Mount Pleasant was so orderly, for the most part, that any *protect-and-serve*-related break from his mundane patrol seemed welcome. Essentially, he wanted to ask Mrs. Florn about her son's personality and general comportment. The problem with taking a parent's account, he knew, was the bias factor. But maybe a non family *friend* might render a more accurate report.

"Would you like for me to take a look at it," Dan asked evenly. "Or do you have other plans in the works that you're following?"

Julie and the girls had been cruising down a street running parallel to Piney. There were many streets she could have turned onto to get to the one she desired. But she chose Fern. In so doing she wound up at a stop sign not far behind Dan's patrol car.

The cruiser Julie eyed could have been any of twelve patrolling Mount Pleasant at that hour, but somehow she knew it was Dan. She watched as the pretty thirty-two year old walked around the front of the cruiser and got into the front passenger seat. As there was no traffic behind her,

Julie waited at the stop sign until the cruiser pulled off. In seconds she saw it go to the next block and stop.

It was always a gamble of sorts—that is, timing just right her arrival at a location where her husband earlier expressed intention to buy lunch. It proved at best to be a 60-40 proposition with the odds slightly in her favor. She now concluded that today had fallen in the *40 percent-of-the-time* category.

Normally, Julie would simply have driven home to test the "odds" another day. But something about the woman who ambled so lithely around the patrol car gave Julie pause. She appeared about "five-five" of height, one hundred twenty-five, or so, pounds, twenty-eight to thirty-ish, like Julie herself. But there seemed to be something, well, *exotic* about her—her complexion, her eyes, the apparent texture of her hair.

Julie circled around discreetly surveying the scene of her interest. From a distance, she saw that the woman, now, sat in the driver's seat of a vehicle that Dan inspected.

"I believe it's your fuel pump," Dan commented, looking under the hood of Sonja's aging car. Leaning out the driver's window, Sonja listened to the officer's recommendation.

"You said you were pumping the gas pedal, trying to give it gas? … Well, I think you've flooded the *intake*. Your battery sounds good. …I'll tell you what: This time when you turn the ignition, keep your foot pressed on the gas pedal. Don't let up until you hear ignition."

Following the directions given, Sonja kept the ignition switch whirring until, in a few seconds she heard, and felt, the roar of the engine.

"Oh, my God…it started up!"

"Yeah, we lucked out," Dan offered. "Now, of course, it's up to you—. But *I'd* go straight somewhere and have it looked at. If it's the fuel pump, it might cost you a couple of hundred depending on where you go."

From Sonja's happy expression, emerged a stunningly attractive smile, as she watched Dan close her car hood. "Thank you so much," she called out fervently. Her eyes met his as he walked around to the driver window. In the officer's posture of making official inquiries of a stopped motorist, Dan made his pitch:

"Miss Spark, did you know Mrs. Florn's son, Lonnie?"

"Um-hm. Everybody around here knew Lonnie."

"This is unofficial, but…you mind saying what kind of young man he was? You probably recall that Mrs. Florn gave me some general info. But I'm wondering, now, if there were ever any problems that you know of. You know—neighborhood stuff or otherwise."

"Well, he dropped out of school, the way some of the young guys around here do. I don't know of him having been a trouble maker or anything, though.

"Work…? Well, I know of a few jobs he was able to find. But it seems he always got fired for one thing or another. That's what I remember but I don't know what it was all about.

"…No, I don't know of any enemies he might have had. But then, I can't really say for sure."

"Thank you, Miss Spark. That's good enough. If there's anything more that's significant, maybe I can get it from Mrs. Florn, when I see her again.

"Thanks, again, for sharing your impressions. And, Miss Spark… good luck with your car."

During the entire exchange, Julie was parked in the minivan in a place that disallowed her husband's view of her. She assuaged her concern by viewing the matter from an altogether plausible standpoint. The entire meaning of what she witnessed could be summed up as acts of official duty, on Dan's part.

Just two weeks. That's all the time Dan had for winding down between the summer and fall sessions at the college. Julie was grateful for even such a brief period to have, again, normal access to her husband. It had been for her a tough nine and a half weeks. As she had predicted, Dan became preoccupied with his studies, once he had gotten back started. And she couldn't have been prouder of him. Still, it was a two-edged sword, cutting a path toward the desired goal but also lopping off large segments of their time together.

Eight days into his break a call came to Officer Kopochek over his patrol car radio. Fellow officer, Samuel Peas, had walked in on an armed robbery in progress. Although not voiced, the immediate suspicion of the dispatcher, as well as informed police, was that the criminals were from out of town. It was the way the store employees making the call described the robbers, their manner, and methods.

As Dan was informed, Peas had, upon entering the store, surprised two masked hold-up men. Thereupon, he drew his weapon and was duly fired upon. Even with a grazed shoulder, Peas' return-fire kept the bad guys kneeling behind the store counter.

From information given by store employees, the ensuing gun battle was a stalemate. Peas had found shelter behind a rack of some sort, on one side of the establishment. At present, he was obstructing the robbers' escape from the niche in which they were holed up. That place just happened to be a break in the counter near the cash register. But as employees, hiding in the back of the store informed, the crooks appeared to be growing more desperate and determined. The concern was that they may find a way to split up and sneak up on Peas from an unexpected vantage.

Kopochek was the first back-up to arrive on the scene. From the front lot, where he stopped his cruiser, he could actually see Peas through the store window, crouching. Peas' weapon pointed toward the store's cash register, sitting atop a counter running perpendicular to the store's front. In seconds, Kopochek knew exactly what he'd do next.

It didn't take a session of *pros and cons* thinking, or weighing of possible consequences. Dan put the cruiser *in gear* and sped straight for the store's front glass window. Once he'd crashed through and was inside, he quickly crawled out his driver's door. Having created a car "shield" and a wide opening in the store for escape, Dan urged Peas to move cautiously to the street. The store employees, he assured the wounded officer, were safe.

While Peas was making a quick and careful return to outside, Dan, fired his weapon in the general direction of the cash register. He seemed totally undeterred by the return fire.

In seconds he was running through a short isle to the back of the store. There he stood watch, crouching, until he heard other police units arriving. At this point his objective was to prevent the robbers from occupying a place in that back area. He also wanted to make sure the employees, wherever they had found refuge, would remain safe.

Realizing they were "surrounded," the robbers surrendered. They didn't know how many officers had run to the back of the store, in order to ambush them from that direction. One thing was sure: the *front* was covered well enough. Adding to the bleakness of their situation, the two men had been a tad disoriented by the patrol car crash through the window. That event had gone totally *counter* to the dearth of resistance they expected to encounter, from a "job" in Mount Pleasant. *You can't even trust the quiet towns anymore,* they lamented.

Officer Dan Kopochek had received respectful glances and a healthy amount of public deference before the attempted store robbery incident. Now, folks were inclined somewhat toward awe. Pedestrians jaywalking in a slow-traffic thoroughfare, typically disregarded the presence of patrolling officers, continuing in casual pace. However, when Dan appeared, cruising carefully, they livened their steps—even the older people.

In visits to various businesses to check conditions, Dan now received wide-eyed smiles from patrons and proprietors, alike. Then, within seconds, some apprehensive customers tended to move hastily to their missions. The combination of aura, uniform and reputation gave him the image of the hard, uncompromising lawman. It showed in the manner and private speech of Mount Pleasant folk. They were glad he was on their side.

In his second semester at the college, the *civil engineering* cohort was encouraged to collaborate in pairs, or groups of three. There was a lot of work to cover and a benefit to be accrued from dividing and sharing the workload.

It just so happened that Dan and fellow student, Jennifer Plaetonik, had made scholastic conference in preceding classes. It served as the basis, now, for a more formal study partnership. From his notice of her on the first day of class the last semester, Dan was pleased at her manner: He found Plaetonik to be firmly "grounded," in spite of her good looks.

Neither spoke of his or her occupation, in the beginning. Dan preferred to keep a *low profile* concerning his police work. As an office secretary of moderate status and pay, Jennifer wasn't exactly *on fire* to share the boring details of her employment. She did, however, make known that she was married to a Mount Pleasant investment broker.

Although the CE majors studied in groups of two and three, they, in fact, set a pattern of free communication among them. Accordingly, they exchanged phone numbers and called one another, as need arose.

Listening to the muffled sounds of her husband's evening phone talks sometimes increased Julie's feelings of being shut out. Exacerbating the "sense" was the fact that he spent most weekday evenings sequestered in the home's makeshift study. Often, it seemed that he talked more in conference with classmates, than with her. Nevertheless, she comforted herself in the knowledge that it was all for the good of their family.

The single one of Dan's "associations" that agitated Julie most concerned the woman she saw him giving aid to, in the in Sap Tree district. She had never known Dan to taxi pedestrians in his cruiser. If only, she lamented, the woman hadn't seemed to possess such allure, such charming effervescence.

It would have increased Julie's concern had she known that Dan made the Sap Tree neighborhood such a frequent area of his patrol. As he had in a number of communities within his overall assignment, he visited the little shops there. His intent: to make connections that might prove valuable at some future time.

Yielding to curiosity, Dan developed the habit of looking for the presence, or absence, of Ms. Spark's car, while in Sap Tree. Ms. Spark, he reflected on occasion, had an interesting way and manner about her. To him, she seemed a woman with rare self-possession, someone who could be trusted always to be candid and upfront.

When not engaged in typical police matters, officers of Mount Pleasant often parked their cruisers beside one another, within big and small lots, and talked. In the case earlier described, Dan and Morton Tredlight made chat. Now, the communicants were Officers Kopochek and Ezey, Tom Ezey. One of the younger cops of MPPD, Ezey was a few years Dan's junior. He spoke in the kind of easy drawl of the typical Mount Pleasant citizenry.

"Jeeesus, I'm glad school is back in session. Them boys of mine and Lora's were about to run her bats. I'd slip in, at home, on a break, and she's chasin' 'em around the house like they was two thieves discovered at a house warmin'."

"Whoa. That conjures one hell of a picture," Dan replied smiling.

"I just hope they ain't as high spirited *in school* as they are with Lora. So far, though, no complaints. I guess those teachers are used to rambunctiousness. Hell, I think it could be simply that Lora is too damned soft. Some women shout a lot; but it seems *just not in 'em*, to pick up a belt."

"Got to be careful about that belt, these days—you know that." Dan's expression was mildly advisory.

"Oops. I forgot I'm *the police*, for a second. But, Dan, my ma, God bless her, used to whip the pants off me, when I was little. I bet your folks did, too. You can always tell those of us that got a good ass-wackin' when we deserved it. We're the ones who minded our manners in school. We're the ones upholdin' the law instead of smashin' it."

The mention of school brought a question to Dan's mind:

"The Mount Pleasant Public Schools System—did they ever get that election thing solved way back months ago? As we live on the county line, my girls go to Mutton Elementary, just down the road from our house."

"Ohhh, they're in Mutton County Schools, huh? Great *system* from what I hear. Um, the school board elections? Oh, yeah, they held the one for the disputed seat a second time. Ol' Pike lost by over a hundred votes the second time around. So, Mrs. Graves is still the Mount Pleasant truancy *dictator*."

"You got kids cuttin' school, you don't want it to be gettin' her attention, if they're in the local system. She's hell *on school-bus wheels*—letters to parents, harassin' phone calls, court. She's good."

"Does the city have many truancy issues," Dan inquired.

"It has its share. You'll come across a few school-skippers, here and there—especially after the Christmas break. By then the older kids know whether they're keeping up or not. I guess they decide it's not worth it, to hang in there, for the other two-thirds of the school year. It's just like it was when we were kids. That stuff never changes."

"Yeah—unfortunately. But back to the runoff—I understand that doing a *reelection* is expensive—even small ones. I guess the city government considered it worth it, huh?"

"You guess wrong, Dan-my-man. There's no way that thing would have been done over, for the reasons the complainers stated, if the city had to pay for it."

"Well, how...who--?"

"The QH-QCs—that's what some of us call 'em. They're a group of *oldies* that are always about a quarter-hundred in number. And they're also all within a quarter century of being a hundred years old. QH-QCs—catchy ain't it?"

"For sure—*quarter of a hundred* and within a *quarter of a century*. But...what do they...?"

"Oh, they paid for the reelection. Moneeeey! Holy jaspers, they got money! And from what I understand they're tight as hell with it, too. Now, they'll part with some to move forward with crazy, eccentric stuff only *they* have interest in. You ever notice the statue of the collie dog in Wilkey Park? They funded it. One of them had owned the dog decades past.

"Everything," Ezey continued, "from the awnings on the Red Herring front wall, to *prime* seats at the ballpark, for those 70-plus in age—it's their doing. God bless 'em they're a feisty set of old fossils. And they influence the other oldies in town to walk around like they're part of the 'Qs.'

"You've seen 'em, Dan! They, all of 'em, can be funny as hell, too. I get a kick out of watchin' 'em walkin' around like old, Wild West gunslingers—ha! It cracks me up just thinking about 'em!"

Ezey's mirth was contagious and elicited amused snorts from Dan.

It was a little more than midway into Dan's second semester, the college's fall one. During most of the day hours, while he worked, Julie had only little Faye to care for. Danielle, now eight, was in third grade while Samantha, nearly six, romped about in "first." Thus, weekdays during the school year were times of much more relaxed pace for Julie.

At 12:17 this day, Dan was in the Sap Tree district making his rounds. Cruising ever closer to Mrs. Florn's residence, he took note that Ms. Spark's car was parked in front. Perhaps, he thought, she had stopped to pay a visit on her way home from somewhere. As it was a cool, late-October day, Dan held out little hope of finding any of the "original" four sitting out, on the front porch.

Following an impulse, Dan stopped the patrol car a little behind Ms. Spark's Toyota. He had a few minor reports to write. This seemed as good a place as any to get that small obligation over and done with. And who knew, he thought, maybe Ms. Spark might see him, and come out to chat. Whether or not it was his false perception, she somehow seemed, to him, a possible "well" of pertinent information. Maybe, upon request, she'd deign to dip once more into the fount and toss some sprinkles his way.

He had been sitting there for about three minutes when, from the corner of his eye, he noticed a figure waving at him. It was Ms. Spark, alright. She stood on the porch holding open the front door with one hand. Dan took a standing position at the open door of his cruiser, as he spoke:

"Hi, there. I saw your car here and I kinda' hoped you might come out. Is Mrs. Florn at home?"

"You just missed her. She has some things to take care of. I'm watching a couple of kids she babysits, until she gets back. It shouldn't be more than half an hour."

"Oh, well, I don't want to obstruct your keeping an eye on the little ones. I just had another little group of nosy questions to ask. No big deal, though—I'm sure I'll see you another time and can run it by you then."

"Never put stuff off, Officer. That's what I always say. If it's just a few questions, come on up and you can tell me what it is, inside."

Giving the proposition barely more thought than he'd given the idea of crashing through the store window that day, Dan conceded. Crossing the threshold into the living room, Dan could see the two toddlers sitting in their playpen. Ms. Spark walked the distance to resume her seat near them, in a gesture that maintained their calm.

"These two little 'Hershey's Kisses' are Earlwyn and Venetia. And, Early and Ven, this is Officer Kopochek. He's a nice man. When you get bigger, Officer Kopochek is gonna' help teach you how to cross the street. And if you're real good he might even buy you an ice cream cone, too."

Dan smiled and waved. "Hi, there. What a precious couple of little muffins."

Sonja Spark wore a knee-length cotton dress with a leaf-like design over a white fabric background. In her sitting posture, rounded, light-coppery knees were exposed. Her dark hair was thick with waves and an oily sheen. Pulled back, it formed an intricate single plait that fell well below her neck. Displaying a look of indistinct racial backgrounds, she appeared elevated from any reasonable stereotype.

Glancing, alternately, downward at the children and upward at Dan, Sonja awaited his question.

"Would you happen to know anything about a group of twenty or so older people of this town, who, I hear, are *aligned* as a…I don't know… band of local, political…*movers and shakers?*"

"Are you talking about the 'Qs'...the 'Quarters'?"

"Yes! It's the same name, almost, that I've heard from others." Sonja's quick and *on-target* answer confirmed, for Dan, his appraisal of her.

"The Qs...so everyone in Mount Pleasant knows about them?"

"More or less, I'd say. They're kind of a legend. You don't, like, *see* them together walking down the street or anything. We just know of certain ones that you might run into, on occasion, or hear about on the news. They're known to have money...major money. And I hear they *think* they run Mount Pleasant. But they're not *all that*, not like maybe they used to be.

"Most people around here know they're fading out. A fading bunch of *have beens* and *used to bes* is what people around here take them as. Now, that, Officer, is just one part of the story."

"What's the...other part?"

"I've heard that they have these *secret* meetings, that they invite *other* old people to, ones outside their group."

Dan's expression requested Sonja's further enlightenment.

"I work the middle shift at Cedar Hospital. It's the one that's adjoined to the assisted living home? Some of the old people talk to me. But, like I said, they're old. Many of them are forgetful. Some are confused or just plain *non compos mentis*, if you know what I mean. So, you have to take what they say with a 'grain.' But, on occasion they've talked about meetings—real sketchy stuff without detail.

"So, that's basically all I have, Officer. I hope it was of some help to you."

Reading accurately Sonja's expression, Dan knew his time was up. He duly thanked her for her time and willingness to share information. In a sudden remembrance, he asked about the disabled Mr. Pathwinder.

"Oh, he's all right. He doesn't get out much as you can imagine. But when he takes a notion, he'll wheel on over—sometimes stay with Mayzie for days. ...Oh, and no Qs involvement there, as I know of."

As he backed away toward the front door, Dan smiled and waved again at the toddlers. It hadn't escaped him how curious and seemingly in awe they appeared, concerning his presence there.

He now stepped back into the brisk fall early afternoon. As he did, he missed by seconds something that surely would have gotten his attention, had he exited moments earlier. It was the sight of Julie, pausing a moment in the minivan, ogling the two cars in tandem outside of the 234 address.

For the remainder of Dan's fall semester, Julie was haunted by suspicions about his visits to Sap Tree. The fact that she had questions about his fidelity *at all* was painful enough, to her. The idea that Dan may have interest in the woman with the Toyota was tormenting. Never once did he even mention the Sap Tree district. If he had, she could have found it easier to believe he was there on official police business. He talked about other areas of his patrol in Mount Pleasant and interests he had in individuals and events. Why not the same for Sap Tree?

Many were the times she started to interrupt their talk with a question like: *You ever run into anything of note in Sap Tree?* But then, she'd have to make it segue seamlessly from whatever was said just prior. Fact was, she and Dan knew each other all too well, regarding their manner of conversing. A nuance of deviation from the norm would pique curiosity, perhaps bring probing questions.

What makes you ask that, she could hear him saying, in her mind, if she released such an inquiry. Of course, if she wanted to be upfront about it, she could simply reveal that she'd seen him in the area twice. Then the ball would be in his court. Somehow it wasn't *in her,* at just this time, to take that route, either.

Dan found Jennifer Plaetonik to be a conscientious study partner. With admirable diligence, she carried out the parts of projects assigned her. Dan, scholastically "revved up," was, as the saying goes, *no slouch* himself. He, too, gave their assignments his complete attention and effort. So closely he and Jennifer worked on school assignments that Dan felt it wise not to reveal the extent of it to Julie.

There seemed to him no need to put upon his wife the extra burden of knowing he was welded, coursework-wise, to another woman. He guessed that the image of them in often dimly lit rooms, scouring through giant pages of city infrastructure designs, might be a little unsettling. Her knowing, too, the sense of interdependence they shared—for *course* survival—might also give her unease. It just seemed to him something better left un-broadcasted.

When the fall semester was over, and the winter holidays arrived, Dan dutifully resumed his *exclusive* alliance with Julie. He was aware, however, that the exclusivity could only last a few weeks. There was every reason to expect that the academic partnership with Jennifer would pick up, anew.

Two semesters down and two to go—that's where Dan and classmates were, at the arrival of January's second week. The year was off to a cold start, the town and surrounding counties held in winter's frosty embrace. Gone were the bright, colorful, picture-postcard scenes and landscapes of summer and fall. In their place were ice-crystal grays and glistening whites, from the occasional overspread of ice and/or snow. The holidays had lavished upon the Kopochek family warm and cozy times together adorned with spectacular wintry scenes. But all things earthly blissful come to an end, and in this case the terminator was the return of scholastic obligations.

In spite of the rigid focus on schoolwork, Dan would find himself lured toward an *extracurricular* interest. At some level, mentally, he harbored a fervid interest in uncovering more about the "Qs." He kept this fascination largely a private matter, though. And it would remain so, unless and until he found someone, a native "Pleasantian," in whom he could confide. Some "gut" instinct suggested to him that the town had tantalizing secrets. The Qs, he thought, may or may not be part of them.

For Dan, it was all about whom, outside his family, he could trust, for revealing his growing curiosity. Over months of working so closely with Jennifer Plaetonik, he detected no hidden agendas, no pretences, no red-flag personality flaws. Here, at last, seemed the possible link for connecting him with important aspects of his imagined mystery.

For three days of the workweek, Dan and most of his study cohort had no scheduled classes at the college. It was just a fact of life that research outside the home on these evenings was often required. Although rare, once in awhile on these days, Julie could not count on Dan as a participant in dinner at home. As a courtesy, he would call and report to her his intention to grab a bite at some nearby restaurant.

The clock on the *Suitable Café* wall read 6:17. Already, night had fallen upon all outdoors. Inside were the dimly-lit tables and booths spaciously arranged throughout the establishment. On one side of a semi-secluded table sat Dan Kopochek. Facing him at the opposite side, Jennifer, at twenty-nine, cast a dazzling image.

Only rarely before had the two spoken of their private lives at any length. Dan knew of her marriage with two kids and her secretary's job in a city *projects* office. In turn, Jennifer was aware of Dan's pride in his family. She still believed, from Dan's report to the class, that his employment was in street-sign maintenance. While they awaited their orders, Dan resumed light conversation, glancing about the surroundings:

"This place is nice. I think Julie would really like it. From outside, I would never have guessed it was so elegant. The staff, too, seems top notch."

"It's just like they say," Jennifer responded. "You can't always judge a book—. I'm just as pleasantly surprised as you are."

"You think Lander will like it?"

"He would, if I could get him over here. He doesn't like going out... you know, like cafés and clubs and other entertainment venues. Now— staying home with our boys, while I pursue my school stuff—? He's a total sweetheart about that."

"Yeah, I think some guys, after marriage, just get thoroughly domesticated—lose the ol' drive to do the *evening out* thing."

"And, especially after a bad experience with it. I was making some headway getting Lander to take me out, then that pea-brained Brent Belcher had to ruin it." Jennifer glanced up at the waiter who professionally and unobtrusively brought their iced teas. In seconds he was gone.

"Belcher—that's one of the guys in your office, isn't it? I've heard you mention him, and not very flatteringly either, as I recall."

"I'm sure the fact that I hate him likely comes through, in any incidental mention I make of that rodent."

"He's some kind of assistant supervisor or something?"

"Yes, that and total *scum-of-the-earth.*"

Dan's expression showed his amusement at the harsh words. He made a joke: "Unconditional positive regard—I like it."

Shaking her head and looking into the distance, Jennifer was seeing what she regarded *Belcher's detestable image* in her mind. She muttered, "You just don't know—."

"So, you and Lander are out and you run into Belcher?"

"We didn't exactly run into him. He's a part-time...*peacekeeper* at

Pauly's Pavilion. I know you've heard of it. It's *thee* most popular nightspot in Mount Pleasant."

Dan did, in fact, know of the place. But it was in an area outside his normally assigned patrol. "You're right. Julie's mentioned it a few times."

"I don't think I told you Lander's eleven years older than I am. I love his maturity. He doesn't fly off the handle and go nuts about things.

"Like our disagreements and stuff? He just says his *piece* and he's done. No grudges or smoldering quiets or long periods of bad temper. After he let's me know how he feels about something he bounces back to being more concerned about my happiness. In that way, he's priceless to me."

"Sounds like a great guy," agreed Dan.

"And he doesn't like public displays, either."

"You mean he's against which: *making* them or *seeing* them?"

"Both, actually. He's just not the kind to make a public scene—or to enjoy seeing one. My husband is laid back, cool headed, doesn't like trouble."

"Nothing to see fault in, there—still sounds like a good guy." No sooner had Dan gotten the last word out than he noticed the arrival of the sandwiches. As before, in seconds the waiter was gone, blending with the dim surroundings.

"That's what made Brent Belcher's little performance that night all the more demeaning."

"Okay, let me guess. You and Lander treat yourselves to a night out at *Pauly's*. This Belcher guy is *bouncing* that particular night. And there was a confrontation of some sort?"

"On purpose, Dan—he did it on purpose, to get at me. Belcher is the office *pig* in our section. He's big and loud and obnoxious, petty, mean and vindictive. Oh, I *hate* him!"

In the soft candlelight, Dan could see Jennifer's eyes becoming moist. Her face showed distress that followed from a bad memory. After a brief pause, Dan bade her to continue.

"Sooo…what happened? Are you able to talk about it farther?"

"That…*reptile* came over to where Lander and I had finally gotten a table near the dance floor. Then, he just starts harassing us. First, he tried to say the table was reserved. A couple of *VIPs* were expected to arrive too late to buy good tickets. *'They must be accommodated accordingly.'*

"Can you believe that?! Those were the words he used. Lander and I told him the ticket guy gave us those seats and we weren't moving. After that, he starts making veiled threats—crazy stuff.

"He warned us," she continued, "not to spill any drinks on the dance floor or he'd be forced to throw us both out of the club. Next, he goes on about the 'other' club rules. *'Get drunk in here and start acting foolish—'* he said, looking mostly at Lander. *'And you'll find out the hard way what two hundred twenty pounds of weight-lifting fury looks like.'* ...It was something close to that, he said to us."

"Yuk! I hope you contacted the manager."

"It was so crowded in there by that time. Lander didn't want to leave me at the table alone and he didn't think I should try to find the manager alone. If we had both gotten up, other than for dancing, Belcher would probably have taken our 'occupied' plaque off the table. We would have lost our place, especially if management was unsympathetic.

"But, really, it was more Belcher's attitude than anything else. Do you see what I mean?" Jennifer asked. "He just wanted to humiliate *me*—to goad and provoke Lander into something, in front of me. It was getting so noisy inside that the only way Lander could have put him in his place was by standing up and getting into a shouting match. And that's probably just what that *Neanderthal* wanted—an excuse to fight."

Through Dan's silence, Jennifer continued. "It was horrible. But it wasn't long and drawn out. After he'd done his *dirt*, Belcher moved on. Every so often, though, he came back around giving Lander and me his 'evil eye.' As you might imagine, after a little while, Lander had had enough—and so had I. We just left. ...I never told Lander that the club 'peacekeeper' was a worker in my office. It would have been more than he could take.

"Already, Lander knew of 'the office idiot,' as some of us call him at work. If he had known Belcher was the same guy at *Pauly's,* I'm sure he would have wanted me to find another office job. And that would be fine except that Lander's investment brokerage work is paying less and less these days. I just can't afford to quit a job at a time when unemployment is so high."

"I'm feeling where you're coming from," Dan assured.

Jennifer exhaled a long sigh. "You know, that actually felt good to get it off my chest. There's nothing like having a sympathetic ear to 'bend.' I hope I haven't overburdened you with my issue."

"No—not at all. I have to confess: I have a little issue of my own that I need to air."

"Oh, really? You don't seem to have a worry in the world outside of our schoolwork."

"It's more like a *mystery* that I need help in solving. But it's a thing where the person I share it with has to fit two major qualifications. First, is that of being a native of Mount Pleasant. That let's my wife out. Second, it must be someone I trust a great deal. At this point, you're at the top of the list of candidates."

"Well...how intriguing! A man with a mystery to solve—whatever could it be?"

"I don't mean to be *mean*, but I'd really like to save it for later, when we're not pressed with research obligations. Looks like we're at the end of the time we allotted for a break. No sense in jeopardizing either of our career goals by cutting into our research time. Don't you agree?"

"You make a convincing point there, sir. But, I'll say this: You sure know how to present a cliffhanger."

"It's the least I could do considering you insist on paying your own tab."

"I appreciate your listening to my *third-worst-event-of-my-life* story."

"It means a lot to me that you felt free to share it. In the meantime, I'll be preparing for when, and if, you pull the curtain on the *second-worst*."

"I recommend spinach, extra vitamins, and plenty exercise."

Over ensuing weeks, Dan finally got around to mentioning the 'Qs'. Sure enough, Jennifer had heard of them. But like, seemingly, everyone else in Mount Pleasant, she never gave them much probing consideration. To her knowledge, the Qs were just a group of moneyed old elitists and exclusivists. They were aging throwbacks from a bygone era, dependent upon close intra-affiliations for feelings of relevance.

Also, like everyone else, she could identify them at sight, usually by chance—downtown, at outings, at this or that function. Even the *names* of some came readily to mind for her: Mrs. Brisket, Mrs. Fallon, Mr. Keye, Mrs. Gizolene, Mrs. Houte, Mr. Caransino, the Hogmatee sisters,

Mrs. Swayer, Mr. and Mrs. Rolling. Each of the surnames was given frequent and favorable mention in the news—TV, radio, newspaper.

Dan concluded that it wouldn't be difficult to gather a complete list of names, for the "quarter-hundred." But rather than taking the time and energy to compile such a roster, he felt that gaining *audience* with one or more of them might be more fruitful. Of course, it would have to be accomplished in a way that provoked no special attention or wonder. The more he thought on it, however, the less likely it seemed that he could meet that standard. For the moment, the prospects for a quick payoff did not seem good.

Upon satisfying, one by one, all obligations of his classes, Dan's spring semester wound to a close. Now, an important decision the Kopocheks would have to make became ever clearer, especially for Julie. The question was: Would Dan enroll in a second *summer* session, to complete the final quarter of the four-quarter program? If so, he would continue the grueling pace of study, virtually nonstop, in a period that actually extended *beyond* a year. At issue was whether or not the family was up for the sacrifice?

On a Friday before semester's end, Dan found himself obsessing over an idea that had come to him a week prior. It began as a fanciful flight of imagination. Over time and with sustained deliberation, it evolved into a coherent plan. He recalled the nightclub episode Jennifer related to him, involving that assistant office supervisor. He remembered her report that it had occurred on a Friday.

Day and evening hours plodded inexorably on to 9:45. Giving in to a tendency to act quickly on a novel idea, Dan fabricated a pretext for use with Julie. In it he told her he'd just remembered a book he meant to borrow from a library that closed at 11:00 p.m. The tome, he said, was one with important information related to his planned weekend studies.

When Dan arrived, alone, at *Pauly's Pavilion*, the wall clock read 10:34. He considered it a benefit that few people, outside his fellow officers, recognized him without the policeman's uniform. Once inside, the *first* objective was to see if the club "peacekeeper" fit Jennifer's description of Belcher. The *second* was to make sure Belcher, upon seeing him, was oblivious as to Dan's occupation. Out of uniform, there was nothing to link him to the police force.

Before leaving home, Dan had inconspicuously smuggled out a sport jacket to don at *Pauly's*. While he was far from *high fashion* upon entering the establishment, his dress was at least acceptable.

Making direct eye contact with the man—six-two and beefy—standing near the inside entrance, Dan felt certain it was Belcher. By state law, Dan knew, security people were required to wear a visible nameplate. It was just a matter, then, of making his way over to the human hulk and carrying out the examination.

Belcher was not used to patrons approaching him so deliberately and with such apparently glaring intent. Yet, he could see that the plainly attired guy who'd just purchased his entrance ticket was doing just that. In response, the club peacekeeper intensified his scowl. There seemed no doubt to Belcher that this brazen individual was sizing him up.

The clenched-teeth expression, the cold intense eyes—these features Dan took note of, as he secretly confirmed the bouncer's identification. It was Belcher alright, Dan determined. Dan's face now showed a hint of mischief.

But, then, Belcher knew how to make his own *first impression*, with cheeky newcomers:

"What the fuck do want?" he inquired, displaying full aggravation at being stared at.

Dan knew well the game he was going to play, for the short time he intended to be at the club. Always, he estimated, a certain type of "loser" visited clubs and bars, looking for a cheap thrill. These were want-to-be tough guys who possessed a genius, of sorts, for testing the limits. It was through that method that they gained a kind of *dark* respect from those frequenting these places. In seeing how far they can go, with displays of crassness, they gain a reputation for being shady and unpredictable.

Dan believed that those with insight know it's all an *act*. Behind the show of audacity is usually an unmitigated coward. According to Dan's experience, club bouncers know them on sight. He had seen, also, that peacekeepers were not accustomed to becoming targets of these paper tigers.

To Belcher, there seemed every indication that he had become such a target—at least until Dan spoke.

"Huh? Oh, nothing—. I just thought I was supposed to see you about getting my seat."

"Do I look like a fucking escort to you?" Belcher blurted.

"No, sir. I just…let's see…'area A.' I believe I can find it on my own. Sorry if there was a misunderstanding. So…hey, nice meeting you, man."

Dan quickly walked off. As he did, his former baleful expression returned. He had observed the pretend-to-*fight* and subsequent *flight* tactic of "bar jackals" so often, he could imitate it effortlessly.

Having found a table, Dan placed his "hold" notice atop it and then began to wander about sections of this ground-level of the nightclub. The mission was to find just the right spots for his next *aggravation* assault. From these he resumed intermittent stern stares at Belcher.

Mostly when Belcher caught Dan's ogling, Dan would look away quickly. At other times he would maintain the vigil until Belcher began to approach angrily. Then Dan would make a hasty retreat to his table. After the second of the latter events, Belcher had had enough. He followed Dan back to his allotted seat.

With hardly any exceptions, *Pauly's* patrons were of an orderly ilk. From time to time, one may require a warning glare from the peacekeeper. It seemed to Belcher this night, though, that someone might be looking for real trouble. With that thought in mind, he stood, toweringly, at Dan's table.

"I um, I heard that people can browse around and mingle—." Dan sounded apologetic.

"You didn't buy a ticket for the *Browse-and-Mingle* section. That's for groups who know each other and look out for each other when they leave their seats. You can get up to dance, order drinks, use the restroom. But, damn-it, I don't think you know enough people here to justify trying to be a browser."

"Oh…well, that's true. But, I was also looking for some friends who are meeting me here. Is that all right?" Dan tried to sound pleasant.

"New customers are always welcome at *Pauly's*. Now, you seem like a nice fella'—maybe a little misguided. We appreciate your business, but there's some things we need to get straight right now.

"There's *rules of the club*—and then there's *me*. Club rules are pretty commonsense: Don't act like a fucking jerk while you're here. Now, *my main* rule: Don't fucking *test* me. I'll mangle you just as sure as there's shit in sewage."

51

Dan stretched his eyes, in a pretence of imagining being mangled.

"Now," resumed Belcher, "let's not get our balls *all on fire*, here. You keep the rules, while you're here, and you and your friends are gonna' have one hell of a good time." Belcher saw a waitress nearby.

"Sandy...Sandy! Please, if you will. ...Now, here's Sandy, Mr.—." He gestured for Dan's name.

"Pimple," Dan invented hastily, "Francis Pimple." It was the most non-threatening name he could think up, at a moments notice. Belcher smiled broadly.

"Alllrrrighty then. Well, Pimple, why don't you be a good *Pauly's guy*, order yourself a nice drink, and act like 'folks'."

"Uh. Hi, Sandy. I'll take a gin and tonic, please. Thank you very much. ...Uh, is it okay to kind of walk near the door every now and then to watch for my friends?"

"I'll beat the hell outa' anyone who tries to stop you, Francis. Just keep the house rules that I mentioned, okay?"

"Absolutely."

"Good deal. I always say, Fran-my-man: A night without bloodshed is a good night at *Pauly's*. ...What the hell are you laughing at, Sandy? Sheesh. Where do we get these waitresses," Belcher inquired rhetorically.

Dan waited until Belcher was tending to matters that put him out of seeing range of his intended exit route. With his drink paid for and a tip left, Dan quietly left the club. He felt that he had gained the information and insights he sought.

It was exactly a week later. That, sort of, *reconnaissance mission* had taken place the Friday, past. The present one was to be full of finals at Mount Pleasant Technical College and of turning in term papers.

Periodically, during that seven day stretch, Julie was on the verge of tears. The scent of gin and tonic Dan sipped at *Pauly's* remained with him that night. It had in fact defeated all his efforts at concealment—gum, mouthwash, etcetera. Yet, Julie never inquired about the uncharacteristic drink she knew Dan took, before or after the supposed library visit.

With Dan in the final stage of his third semester of study, she wasn't about to risk averting his focus with potentially unsettling inquiries. Inside, though, she was becoming an emotional wreck. Evidence seemed to be mounting that the Sap Tree woman of Dan's evident interest was stepping up her "rivalry." Now, she wondered if Dan was actually creating pretexts to meet with her for whatever time he could manage. Maybe they'd even had a drink together.

But, how could it be so, she asked herself, over and over. At home, he showed no signs of guilt—just preoccupation with schoolwork. How could a man she knew so well, or thought she did, demonstrate such perfect deception? It didn't add up. *If there was another explanation,* she asked herself, *what in God's name could it be?*

Finally, it was the last day for wrapping up the semester—yet another Friday. Doing his routine patrol through Mount Pleasant, Dan felt upbeat. Semester-wise, he had good reason to feel so. His cohort's last final exam had been completed in-class the evening before. They now had only to turn in a paper, for one of tonight's classes. And that was *it* for the semester.

Happily, Dan reflected on the fact that very early that morning, he secured the thirty-pager in a binder, ready for submission. Now, as it neared his usual 12:30 lunch half hour, he had time to chauffer the document to the college. The professor had a "turn-in" slot affixed to her office door, for early drop-off of papers. Instead, Dan opted to call Jennifer Plaetonik on her cell, at her job. It was time, he thought, to make her a proposition.

Over the past weeks, Julie, with relief, had not seen Dan's patrol car parked again in Sap Tree. Most importantly, there had been no sign of it anywhere near the one belonging, apparently, to her supposed rival. But that was just one ray of light penetrating her dark mood. If Dan was meeting her *someplace else* and even having drinks with her—that was just simply intolerable.

In Julie's mind, it was time for a bold move. She had noticed that the Toyota of her interest was typically parked at, or near, the same place she first saw it. In addition, it was usually still there as late as 2:15 p.m., the latest time of Julie's periodic "surveillance." Having recorded the address as 331 Fern, Julie assumed it was "the other woman's" home. It was time, she thought, to pay a visit there and not put it off another day.

Dan reached Jennifer by cell just as he often did to discuss course-related matters. When she heard his proposal—the overview, before details—her eyes widened in astonishment. His voice was staid:

"I'm sorry I can't give you a lot of time to think about it. Do you want to fix this thing, once and for all, or do you want to let the opportunity close—forever?"

He had come to feel he knew Jennifer really well. Like his own wife, he thought she showed an unusual selflessness in her general negotiations with people. Also like Julie, he thought she showed signs of being either attracted to or in deference to perceived *strength*. Accordingly he planned on the use of forceful persuasion, carefully modulated, to compel her acquiescence. He wanted her to agree to something that would likely have great benefit for them both.

Dan's location, vis-à-vis that of Julie, was over a mile away. While he engaged persuasive efforts with Jennifer, Julie was parking behind the Toyota on Fern Street.

As fate would have it, Sonja Spark had no before-work obligations on this Friday afternoon. She was relaxing, watching the "soaps" in the time she had, before preparing for the second-shift. The ring of the doorbell interrupted her fervent attending the TV screen.

Julie looked for signs of faint recognition or apprehension in the eyes of the woman answering the door. One thing was for sure: It was the same woman who had elicited Dan's uncharacteristic indulgence that day months prior.

"This is very unlike me, but I had to come by." Julie was visibly not-at-all *at-ease*, although mild of tone. "Do you know who I am? ...Do you have a guess, as to who I am?"

Just as she had upon answering the door, the woman, Julie noted, showed only signs of curiosity.

"...Uh, no—*should* I know you?"

"I'm the...policeman's wife?" Julie's tone formed a question, as she tried to compel from the woman a revealing response.

"Oookaaaay. Aaand...." Both Sonja's hand gesture and tone were designed to coax out of her visitor the *point* of the encounter.

"You have no idea who I am." Julie had believed herself capable, in this case, of Sherlock Holmes-like detection. She would discern, figuratively, the tiniest "red dot" of guilt against a rose-colored camouflage of innocence. And yet there was *no dot*. That is to say, there simply was no evidence of *secretive knowing* by this woman. If there was, she knew she would have detected it.

"I'm afraid I don't. ...You say, you're married to a cop—?"

Julie thought she'd take it one step higher: "Officer *Kopochek?* Officer *Dan* Kopochek? Are you saying the name has no meaning…?

As she had spoken in uncertain pauses, the woman before her, Sonja, interrupted. She was clearly happy to have found something with which she was familiar.

"*Kopochek—the policeman!* Yes! He's the one you're talking about? He's your husband? Sonja was smiling and nodding her head, as if to inquire: *Well, am I right. Am I right? Did I get it?*

"He's my husband," Julie confirmed. But the tinge of embarrassment she felt caused her to make the announcement with a noticeable dearth of pride. That, in turn, gave Sonja alarm. Her expression quickly changed to one of concern.

"Is he all right? Oh, no, don't tell me got shot or something—."

"Oh, no…he's fine. I just…well. I guess I need to explain. I actually was wondering if you and he were…friends. You see, I saw the two of you talking one day, right…there…out in front…and I began to wonder if…. Oh, this is embarrassing…I'd really like to just turn around and leave now."

After a few seconds, Sonja got it. She donned a look of genuine sympathy for her "guest." She spoke slowly, hesitantly:

"Oohh. You thought…. Oohh, no. I'm sorry…. Wow. I can imagine how you must feel, though. But nooo." Sonja shook her head as if she were talking to a child who had fallen and scraped her knee.

Julie was backing down the porch steps, while speaking. "I appreciate your being so understanding. It's just that…. There's actually more to it than…but I can see that everything was merely circumstantial, or something like that. I'll have to let Dan know I made this error."

Sonja still wore a deeply commiserating expression, as she spoke:

"Yeah, I…yeah. Are you sure you don't want to come in and talk about it? It might help…a little."

"Thank you, so much. I really do appreciate your understanding. But, no—I'd better be getting on. I told my sitter I wouldn't be long. Please have a nice day. I hope you can forget my mistake"

Sonja called out to Julie as the latter was pulling off in the minivan.

"Yes, have a talk with him. I'm sure he can explain whatever the problem is. He seems like a really decent guy."

When Dan pulled into the driveway, in his old, to-and-from-work clunker, he was full of anticipation to see his "ladies." School matters were virtually off his mind. He felt like the cross-country trucker who, by necessity, left his family for days or weeks at a time. Even though he hadn't actually been "away," Dan knew he had been "missing," sort of. It was so, even when he wasn't in class or doing field research, but was at home studying. The way he shut himself away within the converted study, he might as well, he knew, have been in Canada.

When he opened the front door, the four distaff members of his family were sitting in the living room. The three girls seemed to wait for his cue as to whether his mood would be light and playful or heavy and sedate. As for Julie, she knew that all the academic oppression was over, for now. Thus she anticipated the jocular, happy officer who entered the front door. In dark glasses he pretended to be without sight.

"Where is my family?!" he dramatized, falling to his knees. "My wife, my three girls—has anyone seen them?! I need my family!"

"Here we are, Daddy!" Danielle and Samantha, fully inclined to play along, rushed over to give their father hugs and kisses. Little Faye was standing braced against the sofa on which Julie sat. Infected by the excitement of her sisters, she made her way to the spectacle's epicenter.

"I seem to recall a third one of my angels," Dan emoted, in a gesture of looking around with blind eyes. "Faye-Faye-the-Fat! Yes! Yes! That's her name. Where, oh where, is the chubby one?" The two older sisters could not contain their laughter at Dan's new appellation for the toddler.

"Dan, you know that's not nice," chided Julie. "We will not call my baby any *Faye-Faye-the-Fat*, even if she doesn't understand it yet."

"My wife! Oh wondrous, thunderous heavens! How I have missed that scolding, annihilating tone. Come to me, woman! Make me your grateful slave!"

"Wish granted—only don't call my baby 'fat'. You know our rule about name calling."

"I curse the demons that make me backslide! I shall fight them, feed them cold French fries, if need be—and win!"

"Alright, *Sightless Igor*—stand and give 'the Queen' a hug and kiss before I have you broken on the wheel."

"You mean, broken on the wheel...*again!*"

During the family merrymaking, Julie and Dan, each, knew they kept a secret from the other. How it would be taken, once revealed, was of major concern for them both. Nine years they had been married. Each was a wall of fortitude for the other. Even now, a near decade later, when Dan looked at Julie he saw in her *his life*, in metaphor. From her perspective, in Dan Julie saw the central gear that turned all parts of the family "mechanism." To her he was indispensable. Although the revelations to come were expected to be hard to deliver, they each felt certain their union would not be compromised. They hoped against hope it wouldn't be even moderately altered.

In addition to holding a secret, Dan's burden was compounded by his intention to lie, quite deliberately, to Julie this very evening. Later, and as a result of a certain deed he planned, she was in for an "awakening." The total effect it would have on their lives—he was not sure. But, whatever the cost, his determination was already set. First, though, Dan needed to create yet another blatant deception.

The planned prevarication was actually inspired by events occurring days before. Earlier in the week, he made Julie aware of a plan the *civil engineer* students had discussed loosely. Rather than submit the last paper and be done, they spoke of convening, in class, a final time for the semester. In fact, though, the plan never reached consensus. Other concerns and long delayed home obligations of the students diminished their willingness to tarry, for rejoicing the semester's end. It was a thing desired but just not all-around practical.

According to Dan's report to Julie that evening, the students' intent to assemble was *still alive*. The gathering was to start at the end of their eight p.m. class, that is, about 9:00. After turning in the term papers, the group, including the professor, would head to *Pauly's Pavilion*. There, in the *restaurant* section, they would discuss aspects of their learning experiences. As most everyone, including Julie, knew or had heard, *Pauly's* nightclub didn't open until ten. Dan indicated that they should be exiting the café, by then.

To Julie, the affair represented the semester's final, dying, grasp of her husband, before its expiration and irretrievable slippage into the past. *Sure, why not*, she conceded in her private musings. It was, after all, Dan's last day at the college, for awhile. An *added* benefit came clear to her, too. The gathering of classmates conveniently postponed Julie's revealing to Dan her Sap Tree incident, at 331 Fern. Certainly, it didn't make sense to tell him of it *before* the assembly of students, for celebrating academic triumph.

So, he was having one last night with "the college," for the semester. Maybe in the course of festivity, mused Julie farther, he'd take a light drink at the restaurant. It seemed clear to her now: That must have been what happened the night he went to get a book from the library. Then she recalled he never mentioned stopping anywhere, before or after. Yet, he was gone longer than what seemed usual for borrowing a book.

But then, on the other hand, she could not recall a single instance that Dan acted guilty or distracted when they were alone. *How,* she wondered, *could someone you know better than anyone else in the world be involved in something so profoundly despicable and you never detect emotional signs of it?* Therefore, she reasoned, it must not be true.

Finally she decided: *Waaay too many thoughts—one thing at a time! If Dan comes home buzzed by a little drink, it'll just make it that much easier to tell my story. In fact,* she continued in reflection, *maybe I'll have just a tiny one myself when the girls are asleep and while I wait to hear Dan's car pull into the driveway.*

When Dan arrived at the technical college at 8:51 there actually were two other students submitting papers before the 9:00 deadline. One was Ralph Tredwater. He was always full of self-effacing humor:

"Hot off the presses, folks—this *baby* just rolled, *sizzling*, out of the printer. Not only should you not *touch* this smoker, don't inhale too close to it. You'll be risking a wet-ink *chemical high.*"

"The paper can't be that fresh," spoke Glen Altern, playing along."

"*Can* be and *is,*" corrected Tredwater. "Behold the king of procrastinators!"

"Well," Dan added, "it's like the professor said: Any paper submitted before nine tonight is as good as if it was handed in a week ago." He gave Ralph a friendly pat on the shoulder.

"That's what she said, alright, and leave to me, to put it to the test. Well, it's good seeing you-all this one last time before the end. Now, I gotta' run and buy the ol' lady an appeasement gift for living with a zombie over the past three months."

Pauly's patrons who dined at its adjoining restaurant often left their tables, at just about the 10:00 hour. From there, they had but to trek a ways over and up some stairs, to purchase club tickets. This evening, as prearranged, Jennifer Plaetonic was among them. Although it was not essential to the course planned for the evening, she had been able to persuade a girlfriend to make this outing with her. Indeed, it had the appearance of a bribe, as Jennifer promised to bear the entire expense for a ritzy *Pavilion* night out.

The two women sat in their assigned seats, while discretely, Jennifer watched for Dan's intended 10:10 arrival. Lisa Deering had no reason to pay particular attention to any of the people entering the club—including Dan. But Jennifer saw him the moment he made his ticket purchase. As she noted, he wore a necktie under his sport jacket, a difference in his attire on that first visit. Now, he appeared as one dressed for a formal night out.

Jennifer and Lisa talked in private tones to one another across the table. As they did, the latter was forming hypotheses about what may have precipitated her friend's invitation. It saddened her to speculate that Jennifer and Lander might be having marital problems. She knew Jennifer to be a woman dedicated to her marriage and not likely to go out clubbing without her husband. Suddenly, amid their talks, she noticed Jennifer eyeing intently a patron who appeared to be waiting to get the club *peacekeeper's* attention.

It wasn't long in coming, and it was clear that the peacekeeper was in no mood for banal and idle exchanges. At some point, Jennifer tapped her friend's arm, imploring her to maintain a vigil of what seemed a brewing confrontation.

"Okay, look, let's get something straight." It was advice from *Pauly's* peacekeeper. "I'm not *Officer Friendly* who wipes your nose for you when you have the sniffles. Don't ask me for any directions, for any help, or to solve any problems that you're not competent enough to figure out on your own.

"Now, *Mr. Helpless*, I'm going to point you in a direction, then, you just get the hell away from me, as quickly as possible." With that last command, the bouncer clasped Dan's shoulders, attempting to give a turning push.

Dan's voice was audible, clear, and stern, as he freed himself from Belcher's grip:

"Yeah, yeah, sure, sure...somebody died and made you king. Just, whatever you do, don't be dumb enough to put your hands on me, again."

It turned out that Belcher, in fact, proved himself to be "dumb enough." Or maybe *misinformed enough* is the more accurate description. He allowed himself to be goaded into a physical confrontation with someone, knowing nothing of his adversary's combat training. Within some seconds Belcher was incapacitated.

At the nearby hospital it would be determined that Belcher suffered a splintered fibula and fractured rib and jaw. As would be discovered later, these injuries, even when healed, would render Belcher unsuitable for future club "bouncing."

The evening-shift police arrived with the paramedics. It was with a mixture of astonishment and numb disbelief that they discovered Officer Kopochek's role in the disturbance. Sure enough, he was taken in, for questioning, while other officers gathered reports from witnesses at *Pauly's.*

"Self defense"—Dan repeated it quite matter-of-factly, whenever he was asked to make a statement. It was his "plea" whether asked on, or off, the record.

Self defense—it was what observers at the club said it looked like to them. Essentially, the MPPD had no problem with that. They just hoped it couldn't and wouldn't be viewed as a case of self...*over-defense*, by one of their own. Being on good terms with the DA's office was something the captain, in particular, wanted to maintain. While the officers found the *self defense* excuse "digestible," one thing they all knew for sure: No *other* member of the Mount Pleasant force had been trained to do anything like that. Not in, and under, the time and circumstances reported.

BURLY BOUNCER VERSUS CANTANKEROUS COP! The news headline sprawled across local newspaper fronts. Television news reporters seemed unable to get enough of featuring the story. And it was the talk of the town. Dan did his best to try to take it all in stride. Actually, he had gotten used to Mount Pleasant's regard of him as, sort of, *the good cop from hell.*

Released on his own recognizance that night, Dan drove home. The cell phone conversation with Julie lasted from the stationhouse, through half an hour on the road, to his walk to the front door.

So, Dan had lied, Julie discovered. There had been no meeting of classmates at *Pauly's Pavilion*. Instead, he had just gone there to fight. It was a bizarre scenario, for sure. But, it was one that came with consolation for her. Julie's battle with distrust in Dan put them, sort of, on equal terms. His issue involved lying to her; hers lie in imagining his infidelity—so, *even-Steven*.

Dan, it turned out, displayed not the least disappointment or even annoyance at learning of Julie's, well, indiscretion. Indeed, he almost seemed amused. For her part, Julie had multiple reasons to feel relieved. Dan, all too often, in her view, the risk taker, had emerged from an ugly situation, again unscathed. In addition, she felt she had no further reason to be concerned about the woman on Fern Street. She was content to let the whole matter rest—almost. There was still one thing on which she needed to have total clarification. It concerned just why *this Jennifer Plaetonik* was worth Dan's entering into a nightclub brawl.

Dan had no problem explaining that:

"Now, she owes me," he uttered lightly. "I would never put it to *her* like that. But, she *must* feel, now, that she *owes me big*. Think about it Julie. She's the only Mount Pleasant native I know who is suitable to find out things for me. You know what I mean…things about this town that I find mysterious.

"How many times," Dan resumed, "have you and I both said Mount Pleasant is like some odd town in a…*movie?* Something's 'underground.' There's no way I could work and live here without knowing what it is.

"It all boils down to trust, Julie. You know how I am with people. Plaetonik is the only person in this town I'd trust enough to ask for help."

So, there it was. Aside from school, her husband had yet *another* burning interest, outside their household. She thought he had put his "Mount Pleasant mystery" aside, ready for permanent discard. But all the time it was sitting on a back burner, simmering quietly. And *hang it all*, she conceded, there was no disputing the honesty in his voice and demeanor.

Not only that, but with his explanation, everything fell into place. She knew that once Dan locked onto something, he became almost fanatically engrossed. With a sort of paradoxical *sad* happiness, she had to admit it was the same quality that made him a dedicated, *and loyal*, husband and father.

So, most of Julie's concerns were laid to rest. Now, however, she wanted to know the answer he gave the police force, when the inevitable question had been issued: *What in the world was he doing at Pauly's, alone, in the first place?* Dan had answered simply that he sought to determine, beforehand, if it was a suitable place of entertainment for his wife and him.

"And what have you determined?" the officers had rejoined, facetiously.

"Well, it is *now*," was Dan's reply.

As far as Julie was concerned, at this point—the die was cast. Dan would have to be convinced to "march on" through the summer session, foregoing break. It must, she thought, be *police work* that was compelling him to keep pushing the limits. Always, he seemed ready to find and confront "evil underpinnings" that exert negative forces in communities.

At this point, Julie felt even more desperate, than usual, for an alternate course. Eleven weeks more of the academic grind and Dan's program of study would be completed. A two-year curriculum condensed into four quarter-semesters—she knew it was brutal. But, when it was over, their options regarding how to proceed would be significantly increased.

When Julie finally presented the proposal, Dan, as she knew he would, took the mission. The bliss of a summer free from academic trial would have to be put off just one more time. In lighthearted spirit, she advised Dan that she was forever in his debt, given that he was the world's best husband.

Dan's assumption that Jennifer would be grateful for his *Pauly's* "intervention" was borne out. Due to his industry, the scourge of Jennifer's office was on leave for a few weeks. He was also vacationing from his side work as a peacekeeper at *Pauly's*—but, there, it was *for good*.

In addition, Jennifer dared imagine that which seemed starkly *not* "in the cards" earlier. It was that, once he returned to his *day* job, Belcher's obnoxiousness may be a tad less on display. After all, *his* had been, by all appearances, a most humbling experience. With a sort of awe, she reflected that it was all due to Dan's handiwork. Prior to those newspaper reports that described Dan's endeavor with such levity, she'd had no idea he was a policeman.

Acting on Dan's stated objective, Jennifer went to work immediately, gathering information relative to his mystery. Her subtle inquiries were made, here and there, without ever mentioning Dan's name. Lander, her husband, was a good source of people-information, as well she knew. Incidentally, Jennifer noticed that Lander's gracious manner had increased a degree or so, lately. It coincided with reports, from both Jennifer and media, describing the recent big incident at *Pauly's*.

The small break between quarter-semesters allowed the Kopochek family extra time to spend together. Then, all too soon, Dan was back, starting the summer semester. As before, school and schoolwork filled the evening hours, just as police work filled workday mornings and afternoons.

As the time approached 4:00 p.m. on this day, Dan parked his cruiser, curbside, on a six-lane street. It was only moderately busy, as everything in Mount Pleasant seemed almost to move in slow motion. He watched the citizens going leisurely about their businesses, and as he did he indulged himself reflections on Julie.

Full of surprises, that one, he mused. In a million years he'd never have guessed she'd go visiting a strange residence to inquire about his fidelity. He shook his head at the thought. But, then, gradually his mind shifted to noticing a pattern among the pedestrians.

Some of those older citizens, ambling in small groups, appeared, like Dan, to be monitoring activity in the surrounding area. They walked and watched, stopped and watched, sat and watched. In Dan's estimation, it was done with such subtly, that he wondered whether he should attribute to it any significance. In any case, there were no signs of disorder within the scope of his surveillance. Dan thusly took his people-watching and intermittent thoughts of Julie farther down the road.

Given the extent to which Julie had been looking forward to a summer free of studies, it mystified Dan that she'd apparently changed her focus. This was his thought as he drove a half mile down the street and parked once again. He had actually considered stonewalling, insisting that they keep their summer plans. What was the rush to finish the program? He had labored academically, like a man *possessed*, for three straight semesters. It seemed unlike Julie not to want him to take a break.

That's a woman for you, he griped mildly. *You just never know exactly where they're coming from.* With that last musing, he took note of a scene outside his cruiser seeming to mimic that which he'd witnessed at the earlier location. It was the elderly people, again—seemingly engaged in subtle and orchestrated survey of the environment. Interrupting his reverie, a call came in over the radio.

There was a report of gunfire at a home on Landstone Way. It was a mile or so out, and Dan rushed to the address with lights flashing intermittently. When he arrived, he saw a man in overalls standing in his spacious yard. Dan assessed the gentleman's age at around seventy or so. He seemed to be just about to mount a riding mower. To the right, a large, redbrick home stood, with curtain visibly drawn at a side window. A face could be seen peering out at the scene of Dan's arrival.

"What's going on here, sir? We got a report of a weapon fired at this address." As Dan scrutinized the man farther, he could see a gun handle showing prominently in a side pocket of his overalls. In the investigation, he would learn that the old fellow was a Mr. Ben Fiker

"Damned buncha' teenagers—three of 'em. Oh, I saw 'em watchin' me gettin' my lawn ready for mowin'. They even asked if I wanted some help. I told 'em, *'No thank you. I can manage just fine.'* I wanted to say *'Get the hell out of here. You look like you're up to no good!'* I could see that those little acorn-heads were intent on nosy-ing around.

"Now, see, I learned long ago," the man added, "it's a good idea to lock your house doors even when you come out to do yard work. But some'em just told me to go back around to the front of the house. Well, officer, sure enough, they was tryin' the front door and the windows! When they saw me, they looked like they might want to try to rush me. That's when I pull out ol' *Bessie,* here, and fired a shot in the air. You should have seen those jackrabbits hightailin' away from here.

"I see you lookin' at *Bessie* stickin' out of my pocket. I got me a permit. Let's walk on over to the house, and I can get it for you."

"I'd appreciate that. You mind handing me the weapon so I can add a good description in my report? …Thank you. And you say you fired a single round in the air? …So, as far as you know, no one was hurt."

"Only if you'd call gettin' the hell scared outa' you *hurt*—. As you can see, *Bessie's* a right mean-looking piece of firearm."

"No argument there," Dan conceded. "Can you identify the teenagers? …It'll help if you can give a description of them."

"Hell, they was just three *acorn-heads*. All the young people around here look alike to me. I don't know if I'd know 'em, if I saw 'em again or not."

On the classroom wall the clock read 8:43. The instructor for this third of Dan's classes this evening gave signs that a slightly early termination was in order. When all except the instructor had filed out of the room, Dan and Jennifer Plaetonik stood alone in the vacant hall. He took note of her smile as they began the walk toward the elevator to the ground floor.

"You look like someone's who's had a happy day, Miss Jen."

"It's the look of someone who's finally struck pay dirt, Officer Dan."

"Don't tell me you've solved the problem of ventilating an underwater tunnel, already—the assignment Dr. Pratt gave us."

"I wish. Actually, I have something for *you*. You did something that has had a very good impact on my and Lander's relationship. As you know, I've been making inquiries—looking for a lead, of the kind you desire, concerning those Qs."

"Okay, I'm the proverbial kid in a candy store. What've you got?"

"It's something that, in a way, was in your own back yard all the time. As you know, I told Lander that *I* was the one interested in learning more about the Qs. He asked around, like he said he would. Well, through one connection and another, he came up with the name F. L. DeMendt— sound familiar?"

"F. L. DeMendt…I can't say that it does."

"He's reportedly one among a line of Qs *organizers*. It's like the Qs go back a pretty good ways and they've always had individuals who served as, I guess, a *galvanizing* force. That's the term Lander quoted from a source among layers of people *in the know*. Are you sure you don't know the name, 'DeMendt'? From what I hear, he performs some function at the Mount Pleasant police department. But, then, it's part-time, and kind of voluntary, and in the evenings."

All the rest of the evening and into the night, Dan's mind fixated on the name and description given him of F. L. DeMendt. It sure looked like Jennifer had delivered, alright. According to what she had been told, his "stats" were these—age: at or near seventy; height: about five-ten; general stature: lean, fit. Lander's "sources" even mentioned the hobby of which DeMendt was such an avid practitioner. It was birdhouse building. After some thought, Dan believed he *had* encountered DeMendt once or twice, in the police-records room. An old guy, apparently retired—he seemed, in Dan's recall, to be engaged in transferring various documents to microfiche.

If DeMendt really was a key figure in the Qs mystery, Dan thought, *talk about your 'embedded images'!* There it was all the time right under his nose. In Dan's excited assessment, everything was in place. Conditions were entirely suitable for engineering a very "innocent" encounter.

Even the *history* was right. That is to say, Dan had past experience with the MPPD records room that was well noticed. Briefly taking up the searches again would not seem out of the ordinary. Although the old guy he remembered seemed a solitary, uncommunicative type, that was no problem. Many were the times Dan had applied interpersonal skills to loosen up a *non talker*. For this case, he felt more than up to the challenge.

It was nearly two weeks later that F. Laek DeMendt requested assembly of his special protégés, the latest in a long series. The so-called *Qs* were, at present, only twenty-two in number. Provisions had to be made for voting in three that would give their number the traditional "quarter of a hundred." In Mount Pleasant there was no shortage of folks within a *quarter-century* of centenarian status, from which to choose.

While proper age was traditionally the first criterion for membership, *thorough* indoctrination into the Qs' philosophy was of utmost importance. Of lesser significance were factors of lineage and family wealth. The vicissitudes of life and financial investments had, over years, taken a toll on many a prominent family of yore.

Significantly, DeMendt was not himself a member. First, he was six years shy of the age requirement. Second, he did not descend from a family of early affluence and prestige in Mount Pleasant, as all Qs must. In addition, his role in the Qs' functioning was, by design, extremely *low profile*. Far from avoiding the public's attention, the old folks of the Qs were known for public clamoring, when a matter of their interest was at issue. Only a select few in the city, outside of Qs and prospective

Qs, knew of DeMendt's affiliation with them. No one but the Qs knew *exactly* what his role was in relation to them.

Onto the Rolling estate, three very ordinary minivans steered carefully. To a back area of the grounds and out of sight, the vehicles came to rest. From them had emerged twenty elder members of Mount Pleasant's most noted families. Following not far behind, F. L. DeMendt eventually made the same maneuvering in his own aging automobile. Seated altogether now in the Rollings' clubroom, the group of twenty-two very privately addressed their concerns.

Seventeen names were submitted for possible consideration as Q nominees. Eventually the Qs and DeMendt would whittle them down to six, four, and then three to undergo extensive interview. It would all accord with special processes long ago established.

Early, the group put in order their planned topics of focus. First, they anticipated serious discussions of how best to debate a fiscal matter with the municipal government. Recently, DeMendt and the Qs calculated the amount of money local government saved from having no need to build new jails, for decades. They thought they should like to have a say in how that money might be used.

Finally, on the evening's agenda, was the Chilton boy's alleged involvement in the incident at Mr. Fiker's, a month prior. The sole witness to Mr. Fiker's laudable scare-shooting had made the identification. In an odd twist, she had not trusted reporting it to the police. Tentatively, the Qs concluded that one of the teens involved had taken on the role of the proverbial *bad apple* of the neighborhood.

Dan gave much thought to how he might approach DeMendt. Time-wise, it needed to be a little beyond the end of his shift on an evening he didn't have class. The choice of an *initial-exchange topic* was obvious: something about the operation of microfiche. Then, if he could bring it in smoothly enough, he would mention his desire to *build* something in his backyard. It should be something nature-related and something to entertain his girls. What Dan hadn't reckoned on was DeMendt's having taken a quiet interest in him, also.

In spite of DeMendt's preference for social non-engagement, he showed a little less of that propensity, the day Dan Kopochek approached. There was something *stark* about Kopochek, from his viewpoint. No doubt, he calculated, the impression was influenced by the officer's highly publicized exploits. But, there, in person, up close, and talking, DeMendt felt the "legend" to be confirmed.

In Dan, DeMendt saw no example of a *mindless sheep in human form*, or what he alternately deemed a *societal myrmidon*. Those descriptions he reserved for "average" human beings, applying them with bitter distain.

Among DeMendt's offspring, and offspring of offspring, he had two sons and five grandsons. Not a single one of them, in his estimation, had inherited his austere vision, his dark values, his veiled audacity. Almost from the beginning, DeMendt saw, in Officer Kopochek, the model of the son or grandson *that might have been*.

F. L. DeMendt took pride in his own resolve never to waste time with fools. Toward that objective, he made quick assessment of those with whom he had dealings of one sort or another. Outside of the Qs, whose perspectives he and predecessors helped to shape, there were few who shared his *world view*. Among those few, less than a "handful" was being groomed to take over when he succumbed to *time*. How he'd hoped it would be progeny, to keep a tradition that stretched back five generations, of his awareness.

Just as Julie was adapting to the schedule Dan settled into for summer, another incident marred her composure. One evening Dan brought this old stranger to their home's back yard. How, she wondered, could he justify interest in building a *birdhouse* back there, with so much school work to do? Thankfully, from her perspective, the unexpected visit occurred just that once. And no further indication emerged that Dan was sacrificing critical study time, in his oddly newfound interest.

Dan's invitation to DeMendt to visit his backyard occurred on a day that was also a school night for him. During class, it had been a struggle for him to push thoughts of DeMendt and the Qs to a back area of this mind. At a break between classes, Dan and Jennifer found time to chat:

"So, how's ol' *F. Laek* working out? Is he providing what you hoped?"

"Jen, if there was a prize to be given for the most valuable *find* of the year, you'd get it. The guy's the *key* to my mystery. I can *feel* it. And guess what. Laek—that's what his friends call him—Laek's invited me to a Qs' meeting! How's that for standing on the edge of discovery?!"

"Incredible, Dan! You would have made a great *detective* within our police force."

"I wonder if Julie would have any problems with me branching off, into *that* area."

"Based on what you've told me—I'd say, probably not. I think she wants you out of law enforcement...away from guns...away from bad guys...away from fistfights. Maybe you should consider becoming a *civil engineer*. It requires a lot of study, but the pay is good, if you can complete the program."

"Good one, Jen. Good one."

For two weeks, Dan prepared mentally for the Q-meeting to which he was invited. Within that period, Dan and DeMendt had many conversations, which aided that preparation. Gradually, the older man introduced an intriguing philosophy he held. All tenets associated with it were based on a central, underlying theme. It was that human beings are incapable of what he called "true sight," for most of their lives.

The minds of humans, DeMendt explained, are, over an extended period, lost in a *physical-psychological* turmoil. The body and mind collude to render humans incapable of achieving levels of objectivity not tainted by learned or fabricated delusion. As, slowly, he unveiled his ideas, DeMendt watched Dan's reaction. The least sign of cynicism, derisiveness, amusement, or offense would have terminated the elucidations.

It was DeMendt who introduced the topic of Mount Pleasant's *Q Society*: "You may not yet realize it, son," DeMendt said on more than one occasion, "but a community not guided by those with age, wisdom and experience is a *feral* community." At these times he intimated that the Qs made Mount Pleasant the special town it was.

With confidence, DeMendt commented: "No doubt you've noticed how our city differs from any other place you've been to." Dan expressed concurrence.

"It's the Qs' *philosophy* at work," informed DeMendt. "It's the Qs' philosophy that underlies the *order* that characterizes Mount Pleasant."

It was a statement of the latter sort that brought to DeMendt's mind Dan's brazen brand of policing.

"The Society has taken note of your...particular way of *enforcing the law*, in the time that you've been here," DeMendt conveyed. In response, Dan showed genuine surprise, as the older man continued.

"I can tell you that they find the, let's say, *quality of your work* pleasing—just what is needed around here."

In fact, Dan was unsure as to whether or not he should be gratified, given his suspicions about surface appearances. But he tried to sound as though he was honored.

For the first day of August, a Sunday, the Qs' next meeting was planned. Its duration was expected to be no more than ninety or so minutes. The home chosen on this occasion for convention resembled an old Southern mansion, resting on 15,000 square feet of land. No recording, electronic, or other mechanical devices were allowed. DeMendt had apparatuses set up to assure that condition.

He didn't know exactly why, but Dan felt, almost, as though he was going before a board of mutants, of a sort. He hoped it wasn't a sign of some latent prejudice he held against elderly people.

Entering the conference room, Dan saw the half circle composed of five adjacent tables, each three yards in length. By design, each table had a seating capacity of five. Facing the inside of the tabular arc were two huge leather chairs, with wheels. These had been provided to accommodate the two men whom the Qs had reverently dubbed "the Officer and Gentleman." Once seated therein, Dan, like the rest of the attendants, was offered refreshments by servants who appeared from the shadows, now and again.

Following friendly introductions and small talk, the convention's business commenced. Seventy-seven-year-old Mrs. Stepon began with an inquiry, to Dan. By her expression he could tell this was not an extension of the meeting's earlier chitchat phase.

"How do like our town, Officer Kopochek? And would you be so kind as to add your impressions of what it's like to raise a family here?"

"In short, ma'am, Mount Pleasant is the quietest, most peaceful town I've ever been in. It seems a great place to raise a family."

"The difference in *our* town and most any other place you visit," spoke Mr. Caransino, "is a matter of *selection*."

"*Selection*...sir?"

Mrs. Fallon gave an aged impish smile and cut in: "Yes—who has been *selected* to stay and who hasn't. Oh, but it's a process that has been in effect for years and years."

"We assume, Officer, that you intend to stay in Mount Pleasant, raise your family here, grow old here, you and the Mrs.?" It was seventy-nine-year-old Mr. Shovelton's question.

"My wife and I are hoping to." Dan thought he should play along since he had gone this far.

"Everyone planning to grow old should come to terms with certain ...realities, Officer," spoke Mrs. Stepon. "What every one of us in this room has come to understand is the *true nature* of youth."

Mrs. Bluecastle, sitting imperiously beside her husband took up the dialogue: "Officer, you probably think of *nature* as perhaps a *neutral* thing that aims to harm no one. You may even sometimes think of it as a loving, giving *force*, like *Mother Nature*. Well, if so, we've got unsettling news for you. Officer...*nature* is, in fact, one of the worst examples of a *mother* that one can imagine."

Dan raised his eyebrows but kept silent, signaling attentiveness and willingness to listen. Beside him, DeMendt sat, relaxed, sipping a drink supplied him by a server.

Next, Mrs. Grizolene added: "Each of us comes into the world with a wild, unrefined, self-centered *nature*. Through good parenting, a measure of refinement is imposed. But it is always in opposition to one's *true nature*. Under the surface of every person is someone who desires to have her and his *own way*, in spite of society.

"Officer, there's a *monster* inside every human being, at every age. Babies, you control by learning how to appease. Children, you control by skillful manipulations, wise punishments and threats of wise punishment. As most everyone knows, when children are not properly subdued before adolescence, the 'monster' becomes fully unleashed, at such time that they reach it. That's opposed to *partially* unleashed, when they *are* properly subdued."

Dan looked around placidly at the old faces. *I'm getting a lesson in childhood development,* he mused to himself. Notwithstanding his nonchalant mood he could sense a sinister outlook underlying the discussion. With genuine interest he resolved to hear it through to the end. He offered a prompting question:

"Young or old, you say, we've all got...*monsters?*"

"Damn good question!" intoned Mr. Keye. "Damn good. It shows you're listening. The answer is a fat, resounding, ass-kickin' *yes*. And that's where a big issue is raised. Who in society is less under self-control and who is more? Now, law officers like yourself are hired to be on the lookout for folks who can't control themselves. And thank God for that. But it's not enough, Officer. We're going to tell you today, it's not enough!"

"Catching the *monster* after it shows itself by committing crimes," added Mrs. Skiewumble, "is good but woefully inefficient. But before anything else is said, I think we want to make, thoroughly, the *original* case.

"As was said, nature *deposits* in each person a *monster*, at birth. If that is not clear, then no arguments to follow will make sense. We will have planted a null seed from which no fruit can be borne. And remember, Officer, we're old people. We'll know if you don't really see what we'd like you to see. Collectively, you're looking at over seventeen hundred years of wisdom."

Ninety-one-year-old Mr. Houte spoke next: "It is generally not in our nature to see, or acknowledge, things in ourselves that are unflattering or unpleasant. It takes a special sort of insight to do so. Human beings are, in the final analysis, like other animals: pleasure seekers. Points of view that don't bring pleasure or gratification of some sort, we shy or slink away from."

Dan thought it best to maintain a show of complete interest. Careful not to appear mocking, he stated succinctly the old people's proposition:

"A pleasure-seeking monster...you're saying that summarizes our make-up."

"The two are major underlying factors of human nature," clarified the younger of the three Pineneedle brothers present. "Of course, there are more:

"There's the need *to belong, to feel loved*, the need to be *looked upon favorably by peers*—all that kind of crap. And then there's that *big* one, of youth—the need to fulfill *sexual* desires. All of that is in the mix within us—some much more so in youth than in later years, but *there* nonetheless."

"But this is the thing, Officer," joined Mrs. Swayer, in a seemingly testy tone, "Our concern is not people's *needs*. It's about knowing that we got a problem. There's a *monster* in every human, Officer, as well as a *pleasure seeker*. Those without enough perception to see it are virtually *blind*."

Dan responded: "Well, I understand your premise. As you may suspect, I've seen more than my share of the *monstrous* things people do. Of course, we all know that not everyone does monstrous things.

"On the other hand, philosophers and social scientists kind of substantiate your point. They point out and sometimes demonstrate that *situation* is more determinant of human behavior than one's stated morals. So, I wouldn't say your premise is unsound. With people, everything depends on whether or not we're under self control, at any given time."

"Excellent addition!" averred the middle Pineneedle, age-wise. "Extreme or extraordinary circumstances might bring out the *monster* in any one of us. So, yes, we see a problem with individuals who, *under the usual conditions of life*, can't keep their '*monsters*' in check. Excellent!

"Laek, leave it to you to find a young man of such insight, to bring before us!"

DeMendt smiled, nodded, and drank of his praise, while he took notes.

It wasn't just Sturgis Pineneedle that showed favor with Dan's commentary. All the old faces and stern expressions they bore seemed to lighten in intensity. Next, Vorst Pineneedle, the elder brother, spoke:

"I'd like to introduce a discussion about the so-called *free society*. We all talk about a *free society* and how good it is to live in one. What do you think, Officer? How damned free *should* a society be? Can a society be *too* free?"

Dan responded: "It's important, I think, to live where you can speak your mind. It seems to me that that's often what people refer to, when they use '*free society*.'"

"Alright—fair enough," responded eighty-eight year old Mrs. Gertha Hogmatee. "So, let's try this: What place do *monsters without self control* have in a *free society*?"

"If you were trying to pose a tough question, ma'am," Dan replied, "consider that you're asking someone who helps put away bad guys for a living."

"Good point, young man," responded the older Hawmawtee sister. "Again, about the free society, most just assume it applies more to the youthful, energetic element of communities. The consensus is that *that* group must be free to become what they choose, to achieve according to ability. Well, we say it must apply also to us—the *aged with wisdom and experience*. Sometimes, we refer to our group, accordingly, as AWEs. Perhaps you have noticed, Officer, that Mount Pleasant is a model town for *AWEs*. We don't tolerate being shut away as is the case in other places."

Dan responded: "I *have* noticed. My wife and I sometimes talk about it. We think it's great—and amazing."

"Usually, young people don't realize where they're headed. Here the youth can look at us and see their future. In other places, they look at the old people and are forced into a self imposed blindness. They don't want to see what is in store, if they live long enough. In Mount Pleasant, getting old is not to be feared, but welcomed."

Grace Hogmatee took a sip from her cup and then continued: "Long ago a cancer that exists in all cities was identified, *here*, and a cure developed. So, think about how it will be to grow older and not be shuffled to the back, out of sight, but to stand in the forefront of the community."

Dan responded: "It sounds great. But I guess my question is: What is it that you do to bring about this kind of condition? Is there a relation to that 'cancer' you spoke of?"

"That, you will understand better as you continue to work with us. When you think about it, no one in the community should ever work *against* us. Everyone here is actually on the road to *becoming* us. Our faces are the faces all the younger folks will see in their mirrors, in time."

It was eighty-six year old Mr. Rolling that picked up the dialogue: "We invited you here to begin a process, a slow un-pressured process of asking your support of our cause. We are for everyone in this town who is *becoming* us, in the future.

"Sometimes we work in the open, other times we work in pure private. But we are always working for those who have *become* us and who are *becoming* us in the future. As is obvious, that should include everyone."

Not long after Mr. Rolling's last statement, the Q's interview was adjourned. The old people made clear their preference that Dan keep confidential all that was said in the session. That was the condition only if he, Dan, wanted to remain in the confidence of the Qs and Mr. DeMendt. To have *no* further dealing with them, he might follow either of two courses. One was to ignore subsequent attempts to engage him. The other was to betray their trust.

To Dan, being in the company of the Qs had brought an odd sensation. They actually seemed to emanate a sort of *power*. It had everything to do with power of *knowing*. The example he conjured was of a victim being held at gunpoint with a weapon he knows is rigged to backfire. Regardless of appearances, the power resides with the "victim."

Later that same evening, Dan confided with Julie his amazing success. The audience he'd managed to get with the mysterious Qs, he conveyed, had been a major adrenalin rush. He was careful, however, to describe the experience as essentially one of political intrigue. To prevent her predictable alarm, he omitted the more nonpolitical, sinister impressions he had gotten.

Four days later, two 17-year-olds were found floating, dead, in a creek located off Landstone Way. That was the road bearing the address to which Dan arrived that day to investigate the gunshot report. Death by drowning is all the coroner could come up with, after thorough examination of the bodies.

At just this time, Dan began plotting a course he was not at all sure could be justified. But his *need to know* overwhelmed all his sense of caution and better judgment. He had been informed that elderly folks in a nursing home had made sketchy but tantalizing reports concerning the Qs. Because the potential leads had been provided by *Sonja Spark*, he saw no other way to access them, except through *her*.

Although he agonized over the decision to make new contact with Spark, after several days he gave in to the idea. He also thought about telling Julie of his intention, but in the end he knew he couldn't. Aware of his wife's period of agony over misplaced suspicions, he had no desire to reanimate them.

When his shift was over this particular Thursday, Dan pulled up to the *Norris Assisted Living Community* in his private car. Days earlier, he had received Sonja's reluctant agreement to take part in a scheme he concocted. The design was for her to take to work a written set of questions for which to jot responses from patients who had mentioned the Qs.

Of all the patients at *Norris* who spoke cautiously to Sonja about the Qs, Ms. Blebbins had seemed the most eager to communicate her impressions. But the elderly woman did not speak very clearly, even when she was in a relaxed state. When trying to convey a report on the Qs, nervousness rendered her nearly incomprehensible. On the other hand, if she needed only to give brief answers to pre-designated questions, it would be a lot easier for her.

Sonja could rationalize, now, that she was giving Mrs. Blebbins an opportunity to vent facilely, to an interested ear. She waited until Ms. Pointer, who rested in a recliner nearby drifted off to sleep, to begin her inquiries. After the notes were taken and Sonja left the room, Mrs. Pointer, sat, with eyes still closed, considering all she'd heard.

That had been Wednesday—the day before. Dan waited, now, in a parking space of *Norris's* lot, having arrived to collect his eagerly anticipated prize. Right on schedule, he saw the approach of his collaborator, from one of the building's exit points. He saw how stunningly the nurse's uniform emphasized her flawless figure. From Sonja's quick, smooth and quiet passage of the jotted notes to him, Dan read her strictly-business frame of mind.

The information access and transfer had transpired without error or delays. Given the intriguing quality of Mrs. Blebbins' responses, it could have been deemed an unqualified success. However, one development subtracted from the elegance of the completed task. The following Monday, between three and four a.m., Ms. Blebbins succumbed to sudden heart failure, of uncertain cause.

As days passed, Dan's mind slipped into a semblance of "alarm mode." That interview with the Qs had left him with heightened apprehension about their role within the city he patrolled. Mrs. Blebbins had made nebulous mention of a "dark side" the Qs possessed. And now, she was dead. Suddenly, Dan found himself hypersensitive to any event or occurrence in town with the least peculiarity.

It was in this state that Dan took note of a vehicle with *out-of-town* tags. Tinted windows on a personal vehicle always irritated him as a law officer, but he'd learned to live with it. They were, after all, legal in his state. Now, however, something in the *feel* he got from the car instilled a shuddery, ominous regard for whomever might be inside. With a policeman's instinct he decided to follow behind discreetly.

For nearly a mile, Dan kept the "tail," until the car he followed stopped suddenly. It dawned on him that the location was very near the home he knew belonged to F. L. DeMendt. In his mind, a number of considerations were formulating:

Had the driver taken note of the police car trailing inconspicuously, more than a hundred yards behind? Maybe he, or she, didn't want an officer to know where the vehicle was headed. Was the nearness of the stop to DeMendt's home merely a *chance* condition?

Now, Dan had to decide whether or not to cruise nonchalantly pass the stopped car as though he had no interest in it. The other choice was to find a pretext for having "a word" with the driver, providing him an opportunity to scan the car's inside.

Activating the police-emergency strobe, Dan stepped outside his patrol car, just behind the stopped vehicle. As he approached, he saw the tinted driver window lowering. The man inside had a stern face but seemed to try to lighten his expression for the impending exchange. In information-gathering mode, Dan assessed the man's suit to be of good quality, matched by that of his dress-shirt and tie. Beside the driver, the lone passenger looked straight ahead, in a dispassionate stare.

"I noticed that your tags suggest you are not from Mount Pleasant." Dan stated it to the driver in an officer's business-like tone. "When you stopped I wondered if you may have lost your way."

"Oh, no, no. We were just checking some documents before moving on."

"You mind if I ask where you're headed?"

"We're attending a business meeting, at a location down the road. We have a few minutes to spare, so we thought looking over these reports would be a good idea."

"I see. Oh, and just so you know, I noticed you didn't put on a signal when you pulled over to the side of the road. Technically, that's a moving violation with potential to contribute to an accident. It may seem a minor point, but it's something you want to be careful about in the future."

"Yes, sir. I appreciate the warning. Is it all right to be here for a minute, or should I find another place to look over our notes?"

"A few minutes won't hurt. You're not in violation of any statutes right now."

"Well, thank you, Officer. I appreciate the warning."

Dan wondered if his growing apprehension about the Qs was making him suspicious of even *the ordinary*. Even while he saw absolutely nothing unusual in that last encounter, he sensed *red flag*, from hood to trunk of the car. Nevertheless, he reentered the patrol car, made a u-turn behind the Lexus and headed back toward town-center.

After a few minutes, though, he u-turned again. An inexplicable whim suggested, against all odds, a connection between the men in the car and the DeMendt house. He could just barely see the front of what looked like the Lexus in back of the home in question, as he passed by.

At this point another instinct compelled Dan. This one urged him to take an out of the way side street back—one *out* of proximity to DeMendt's residence. For now, he had no further desire for—or to be seen attempting—exploration.

It didn't take Dan long to realize he needed to put his Mount Pleasant mystery aside and focus solely on school. The question was, would knowledge of things he'd seen and heard recently allow it? Dan kept recalling the woman at *Norris Assisted Living*.

To Sonja Spark, her patient, Ms. Blebbins, had spoken weakly, vaguely, disjointedly, of "hunters" loose in Mount Pleasant. She intimated that, in spite of outward shows, the Qs were "Godless." The only *force* they recognized was *manmade* law, self control and something they called "selection."

As with any death, Mrs. Blebbins' demise had been given a coroner's proper address. Absolutely no foul play had been determined or even suspected. Although Dan could make no definite connection between Ms. Blebbins' sudden death and her unflattering commentary on the Qs, he still speculated.

For their last CE assignment, Dan and Jennifer had chosen the task of planning development of a *water treatment* facility. An imaginary town of specific size, location and geography was presented. Required was a detailed description of conditions for providing clean water to various communities and businesses. For project-completion and course credit, the two depended on one another, as before.

Three weeks now remained, to the end of the summer session. It was comforting to Dan to know that success in this last one would mean graduation. Patrolling Mount Pleasant just before 3:00, his thoughts settled, suddenly, on a critical part of the design he and Jennifer were constructing. It involved information to be acquired from the central office of City Planning, which closed at 4:00. Dan's shift didn't end until five. He had been advised by the worker providing him the crucial project data, that the deadline to access it was this day.

For Dan, it was punishing to have to admit that an unnecessary alternate focus had caused this oversight. He'd had a week to arrange to get to the indicated office and collect the data he and Jennifer needed. Now, just hours away from the deadline, he was on duty. Other than himself the only person who understood what needed to be done was Jennifer. He knew she could, without the problems he would incur, take care of the matter, by taking off an hour early.

The problem now was that, as sometimes happened, he had left his private cell phone in his personal car. It was back at the station, a half-hour's drive away. On the other hand, Sap Tree was about five minutes away. With a little luck he might just be able to impose upon someone among his Sap Tree connections, to allow him to use a phone. In minutes he was ringing the doorbell at 234 Pine, the home of Mrs. Florn.

Dan's quick contact of Jennifer allowed her ample time to leave work to make the needed run to the City Planning office. As he handed back to Mrs. Florn her house phone, Dan recalled something that literally gave him pause. It was that he had not spoken to Mrs. Florn about conditions of her son's death since that first visit. Now, he felt he owed her at least a mention of his private inquiries.

It was likely, he thought, that Sonja Spark had already mentioned, to Mrs. Florn, his and her last "project". Accordingly, he spoke of his suspicions that the Qs had influence on his department's priorities. He commented, in short, that he thought the Mount Pleasant police had put certain investigations on a "back burner," to appease the Qs.

To avoid alarming, Mrs. Florn, he said he believed the Q Society to be just what everyone perceived. They were colossal advocates for the aging population of Mount Pleasant. Their only fault, he told her, seemed to be their singularity of purpose. They appeared content, he added, to promote disproportionate focus on their own issues at the expense others. As for his department, Dan said some officers had recently formed a coalition. Their mission was that of refocusing on mysterious and unsolved cases. In fact, it was a partial truth, to the extent that *Dan* was that "coalition."

In order to dine with her husband this evening, Julie had delayed her own indulgence in the meal she prepared. Thus, she had earlier sat at the table, plate-less, as the girls enjoyed dinner. Later, Dan arrived home at the expected time. With their daughters playing upstairs, the two savored their alone-time. One whole week, and one partial, remained before freedom from academic pressures. She thought it a sign of Dan's relaxed mood, when he asked a question totally unrelated to his studies:

"Julie, remember that school board election they were making so much over when we first came to Mount Pleasant?"

"I certainly do."

The issue just came suddenly to mind. It was the first time he had given it thought since the talk with Officer Ezey the past October. Suddenly he felt the need to recall the name of the truancy officer incumbent.

"Do you know the name of the lady who won in the re-count?"

"Graves...Jill Graves. She's still the truancy overseer for the schools—at least until the next election, which I think is next year. What makes you ask?"

"Who knows?" Dan answered shaking his head. "I wind-down from an assignment and rogue thoughts just pop up out of nowhere. Call it random *synapse-firing* from overload. What I should be asking is: May I have the honor of being an equal partner in the kitchen clean-up this evening? You have been a true *wonder woman*, taking care of everything at home, while I *zone out* in a world of books, research, and papers."

"You're the real superhero, honey pot. Just a little more to go, and you will have completed a terribly rigorous program."

The following day, on the Mount Pleasant School Board website, Dan found the page that featured the current truancy officer. There was the usual "mission statement" and a small *bio* segment running to a second page. There, Dan found what he was looking for. Indicated incidentally with Graves' educational history was her maiden name: Jill Fallon. It suggested blood relation to a member of the Qs.

All through the following day, Dan's mind was in "automatic contemplation" mode. Trial after trial, he endeavored to fit together bits of his knowledge, such as to construct a picture. At present, only a fuzzy hodgepodge of data arranged and rearranged, to suggest solution to his mystery. Finally, something inside told him he had to pay a visit to the Mount Pleasant Schools truancy officer. He felt certain that if she was a key player in the mystery, he would somehow detect it in a face-to-face encounter.

The next day, Dan found the pretext that would provide him duty-related audience with Dr. Graves. Typically, truancy offices of schools work with the local police. Dan knew there was a contingent of the Mount Pleasant force dedicated to that function. He thought it would not seem out of place to ask how he might be of aid, in the course of his usual patrols. Through an arrangement made by his captain, Dan obtained permission to speak directly with the elected truancy officer.

After meeting with Mrs. Graves, Dan was gladder than ever to be so close to semester's end. From her, just in terms of *vibes* she emitted, he got more than he bargained for. It was clear to him that she had *informed* knowledge of him before he walked into her office. While her words conveyed professional neutrality, her affect suggested cryptic, perhaps ominous, intent. Now the telltale "picture" his mind so diligently sought to conjure, concerning his Mount Pleasant mystery, was starting to crystallize. At one and same time, he simply couldn't believe what he was seeing.

By the coming Friday, Dan was making the decision to abandon the "Mount Pleasant mystery." If the truth regarding it was even close to what he was imagining, it was too disturbing to deal with, alone. On the other hand, he posited, if conclusions he drew were accurate, how could he *not report* it? How could he not, at least, *begin* the dreaded task of making his suspicions known to the appropriate authorities?

Such was the state of his mixed emotions when Dan returned to the station at shift's end, to clock out. Waiting for him was F. L. DeMendt. Dan noted that the man's usually staid expression showed a degree of liveliness. It was in his eyes, Dan thought—they seemed more infused with excitement than before. He spoke to Dan in private:

"They want you," announced DeMendt, low but emphatically. "The Q Society wants to make you their point of contact with the police department. You see, each newest version of the Society has its favored member of the police force. That's the person they confide in, whenever they have matters they'd like 'the force' to address."

"I see. So, who do they have now?"

"Well, that's the problem, Dan. Lately, they haven't been able to decide on a special liaison. As you've heard—and seen—the Qs stake a *claim*, kind of, to Mount Pleasant. Their influence makes this a unique town. It's been that way, oh, for over a hundred years now. From what I know of the history, I'd say most of that time, they had a special police *go-between*. You see, it's someone the police can trust to give them an understanding of the Qs' agenda and concerns. It's someone the Qs can trust to convey concerns accurately and unbiased, in both directions."

Within the space of a minute, DeMendt had seemed to offer Dan all he'd hoped for, up to this time. Access to the inside workings of the Qs was being handed over on the proverbial silver platter. Suppose, Dan thought, his lurid summation of the Q's doings was in error. How would he ever know, if he didn't at least find out more about what they wanted from him?

"So, what are they proposing?" Dan was trying to lighten his tone—not sound so apprehensive.

"Another meeting…for Wednesday, next week. You might say they're an *overindulged* group, Dan. Usually things of this sort happen on their schedule or it doesn't happen. If you're uncertain, better to have me tell them to cancel."

"No…I'm in. What time and where?"

"That, they'll have to work out based on their obligations and all. Obviously it has to be after the end of your shift, since it is on a weekday. I'm sure they'll have it pinned down by early next week. I can let you know then."

Saturated was the word Dan came up with to describe his mental state. He had final exams for which to cram, starting this very evening and continuing through the weekend. His final portion of the project assigned him and Jennifer needed completion by the coming Wednesday.

In some ways, he knew he'd been neglecting, even avoiding sometimes, Julie and girls, for schoolwork sake. It was all for a good cause, but it made him feel like some sort of "stone god" in the household—cool, sometimes commanding and unapproachable. Now, as if he needed an added component to his emotional state, the Qs seemed ready to help solve his mystery.

It was almost with relief that Dan saw no sign of DeMendt upon shift's end, the following Monday. To his surprise, *final-exam-*Tuesday was also spared DeMendt's possibly disorienting effect. At the end of classes that Tuesday, Dan was, at last, free of his college-related burden. Accordingly, he felt more and more able to handle whatever were the Qs' intentions. The sentiment was a timely one. When Dan returned to the department at shift's end, Wednesday, DeMendt was waiting with updates in the clock-out room.

At just after 5:00 p.m., that same Wednesday, Mr. Pathwinder dozed off in his wheelchair on his daughter-in-law's front porch. After several minutes, he awoke from a dream, clearly shaken and unsettled. He sat still and staring, as if into oblivion, even as Mrs. Florn made her way toward the front door, to investigate his gasp. In fact, she suspected that Pathwinder had been visited by another of his "portents." Quite familiar with the distressed murmurings they caused, she wondered what and whom he had "seen" this time.

About half an hour later Sonja Spark took notice of something peculiar among some of those whose health she monitored. They were at it again, she mused. Watching the clock, a number of the residents began to get fidgety. They looked around, warily, and acted as though they were in possession of some tantalizingly dark secret.

It brought back to Sonja an earlier determination she'd made. At times, she thought, the old people became like children, unable to conceal their sentiments with much sophistication. Something was "up" it seemed, but she had no idea what it might be. Another fifteen minutes would pass before she got the strange call from Mrs. Florn.

Meanwhile, Dan was on his way to the Bluecastle estate. According to the plan DeMendt laid out minutes earlier, DeMendt would arrive, as before, sometime later. It was with some feeling of guilt that Dan made the decision to meet with the Qs again—without Julie's thoughts on the matter. It was, perhaps, that same emotion which compelled Dan's call to Julie, finally and quite after-the-fact, during his drive.

In their talk, Dan informed her of his destination. He tried, also, to assure her it would be the last of such unilateral undertakings, on his part. If, he announced, she indulged him this final *lark*, fitting together remaining pieces of the Q puzzle—that would be the end of it. Afterward, they were free to plan the next phase of their lives unencumbered by his obsession with the Mount Pleasant mystery.

To Julie, he had sounded very convincing. Maybe she just wanted to believe him and refrain from protesting. Privately, she balanced two contrasting sentiments: She felt a bit of unease about Dan's having taken up an assignment, of sorts, without consulting with her. But she was still brimming with joy over his having completed the civil engineering program. In the end, she concluded there was nothing to do but let it be.

Aware of the Qs' insistence on secrecy, Dan's talk with Julie was brief and spare of information conveyed, regarding the visit. Ending the phone call, he continued his course with only mild reservation. *The old gambler's compulsion*, he reflected with some lament, induced him to take certain risks. At the same time, he relied on merits of the aphorism: "Nothing ventured, nothing gained."

Regarding his *policeman's instinct*, Dan felt more than mild apprehension. But he assuaged himself with the thought that, so far, he had more to be thankful for, in trusting it, than to regret.

Driving along a road toward his destination, Dan glanced periodically at his service revolver. It rested on the seat beside him. It was just like him, he thought, to consider taking it, unseen, into the Q meeting. Typically, at the end of a shift, he checked it back in with the duty firearms dispenser, at the department.

DeMendt had been with him, as he walked to the submission desk. But, as they saw, no one was manning the station, at just that time. Whenever that happened, officers simply took their service revolvers home. The older man's comment stayed in Dan's mind:

"Dan," he said, "if you're going to be working with the Q Society, carrying your service weapon is going to be a *given* on most occasions." With that advice, Dan considered wearing it, inside his present civilian attire. Or maybe, he thought, in contrast, he'd better keep the earlier agenda of entering the meeting without a firearm. *Decisions, decisions....*

Dan was finally at the edge of the Bluecastle estate, and he parked in a space to the side of the large home. Walking to the pillared front entrance, he saw that the front door was open, as if inviting him in. As a courtesy, he knocked and rang lightly the doorbell before entering and calling out his arrival. The living room, when he walked inside, was brightly lit by sunlight through translucent curtains. Wafting heavily detectable in the air was the smell of pine. The strength of it made Dan wonder if its design was to cover a less attractive odor. Whatever the source and purpose, he wouldn't have described it as, at all, offensive.

Suddenly, a voice reflecting eight decades of use rang out, through an unseen intercom: "Do come this way, Officer Kopochek. Walk straight ahead, into the dining room and down the stairs."

Dan spoke loudly his compliance: "Okay. ...Oh, it just occurred to me that I'm still carrying my service revolver. Habit, you know. If you like, I'll return it to my car."

"Well, no, that's not a problem. You were not advised, this time, to leave it behind. I guessed that you tend to carry it, off-duty, when there's no restriction."

Upon opening the door leading to a lower level, Dan was met by a combined odor of pine and gunpowder. As he descended the stairs, the earlier voice continued, this time without the aid of electronic conveyance.

"Actually," it was announced, "the presence of it will make our talk that much more interesting."

When Dan arrived at the bottom of the stairs, it was clear the direction from which the voice came. Mrs. Bluecastle caught his attention immediately, sitting, as she was, in an oversized chair that required small ascension and dissension steps. As it sat on a small, raised portion of the floor, the chair seemed designed to invite an address of its occupant as "your Highness." The apparent fineness of her garb and shawl reminded Dan of pictures he'd seen of a past British queen.

"Officer," spoke Mrs. Bluecastle regally, "I'd like you to be so accommodating as to stand, at center, on the Persian rug before me."

Stepping onto the designated spot, Dan noticed that it was half of ten yards distance between the stairs and chair-throne. On the wall behind Mrs. Bluecastle, oval mirrors showed a reflection of a draw curtain behind him. The thick drape concealed an area of the cellar that was on the other side of the staircase.

"I'm not one to beat around the bush, Mr. Kopochek. We've been deciding for several days, now, just how to deal with you."

Receiving the elderly woman's lofty tone, Dan wondered just what to make of her puzzling words. He decided not to interrupt, but to listen farther.

"The 'verdict' finally came down just hours ago. You can't be trusted and must be—how shall I say?—*done away with*. With some regret, we find that we may have to apply that to your family here in Mount Pleasant, also."

Dan paused for some seconds, waiting to hear a subsequent remark designed to offset the impropriety of what was just said. When it was conveyed in the old woman's expression that none would be forthcoming, Dan quickly concluded that Mrs. Bluecastle was insane. Without the slightest intention of responding to the report, Dan turned to leave.

"You'll never make it to the stairs in time, Officer!" As she spoke, Mrs. Bluecastle threw aside her shawl exposing a hair-trigger automatic *Glock*, with tracker beam. When he saw her posturing to take up the arm, Dan went automatically into officer "defensive mode." Guided by extensive police training and experience, he reached around and whipped out the service revolver. He adopted the classic police stance for preparing to shoot.

By this time, Mrs. Bluecastle had the *Glock* firmly in hand, although she rested both in her lap. The barrel pointed, Dan could see, quite leisurely and quite squarely at him. Notwithstanding the woman's relaxed state, the weapon, he knew, could go off with the slightest pressure. Trusting his impressions about the pistol's magazine, he determined that it was of 6-rounds capacity.

Dan was able to remain amazingly cool. But he spoke loud and clear:

"Ma'am, you should know better than to point a gun at a police officer. Now, why don't you very slowly and carefully place it on the floor, to the side." Dan's notice of the gun's target-tracker beam was increasing his apprehension.

"Why don't I? Well, let's see. …Mainly, because *I intend to kill you with it!* Oh, if I had a hundred dollars for every shot I've fired into the *shock absorption* wall behind you, Mr. Bluecastle and I would be a lot wealthier." With that remark, Mrs. Bluecastle pressed a button to her left that drew open the curtain positioned behind Dan.

"Ah-ah-ah, Officer! I wouldn't advise you turning around to get an appreciation of it. As soon as you drop your guard, I swear I'll shoot to kill. Right now, you'd better use all your instincts for *sensing* when someone eighty years of age is dead serious, even during a *game*."

Watching alternately the woman's eyes and hands, Dan noted that at least she didn't appear nervous. He realized immediately, though, that it was a mixed blessing. If she was the least unsteady, the *Glock* could fire. If the bullet hit him where it was pointed, it would spill the contents of his abdomen all over the basement floor. On the other hand, the fact that Mrs. Bluecastle was so cool seemed to bode badly, also. At present she appeared an unlikely candidate for persuading to relent. He determined that the only thing he could do was play along and wait for an opportunity to break the stalemate.

With his weapon still pointed at the old lady, Dan spoke:

"And just what is the purpose of this ma'am? If this is some kind of bizarre initiation, you've chosen totally the wrong method and totally the wrong man. I strongly suggest that you end....."

"They *say*...I'm a little *eccentric*, Officer." When the woman spoke, Dan thought he saw a hint of "unbalance" in her aged eyes and expression.

"I do love my *games*, though. Oh, but if loving *games*—exotic games—is eccentric, Mr. Kopochek, then lock me away and throw away the key. You think about this, Officer: How often does an old woman like me get to enjoy a match of this *caliber*—no pun intended. Why, I've been waiting for something like this, practically all my life."

"You think this is a *game*, ma'am? *This is no game*. Do you realize I will be forced to shoot you, if you don't drop your weapon? You can put an end to this insanity right now, just by....."

"You silly policeman—I wouldn't *dream* of it. Obviously you have no idea how much I relish this. Over the years I've had the opportunity to shoot a few *acorn-heads*—good fun, for sure. But I've *never* engineered a standoff with a policeman!

"This kind of drama, Officer Kopockek, *is an old woman's dream*. I know what you're thinking: the dream of only a *crazy* old woman. Well... if you want to be nasty about it—just remember, you started the name calling."

More than ever, now, Dan was convinced that this was not a case of *misguided initiation*. Mrs. Bluecastle, he determined, *is really, and truly, a nut.*

"I see you're relaxing your grip, Officer—big mistake. I've already told you the verdict is for you to die. And you're *going* to die. I just want to enjoy a 'cat and mouse' first. You'll forgive my mixing metaphors. From my point of view, I've set up the ultimate poker game, with the highest stakes of all—not money, but *life.*

"I'm convinced my *hand* is better than yours, Officer. In fact I *know* I'm going to win. Most likely you'll fold before I can show off the extent of my *gaming* skill. Either way, I shall *flush out*, royally, upon you."

As Dan could see, the old woman's "poker face" was impenetrable, except for what looked like *regal* madness.

A disturbing series of thoughts entered Dan's mind, just at that time. As Mrs. Bluecastle diminished her focus, at least seemingly, with insane talk, he could fire his weapon. But would the bullet's impact cause just enough movement of her trigger-finger to make the *Glock* fire, in return? Maybe he could aim at the *Glock* itself, hoping at least to alter its line of fire. But what if he missed?

But, then, suppose he managed to kill the old woman and survive, himself. How ever would he explain it to…anyone? It seemed the eighty-year-old had him over a barrel, as they say. Maybe, he thought, he should just try to keep her talking.

Slowly, Dan went into a squatting position, keeping the aim of his weapon in place. Holding a .357 magnum for a long period, even with both hands, was tiring. In a kneeling position, he could rest the gun on his leg and still be in good firing position. As he spoke, it didn't escape his notice that the *Glock* now pointed at his head.

"What is this *verdict* you spoke of, earlier? I don't think, under the circumstances, the inquiry is asking too much."

"You scoundrel! You deceived the Q Society! Luckily for us, you showed your *hand* within an environment that is loyal to us. Who do you think *foots the bill* for most of those *old soldiers* over there at *Norris Assisted Living?*

"We don't appreciate your *probing, Mr.* Kopochek—asking lurid questions about us, to members of our outer circle. When you do, you should do more to cover your identity. You didn't—at least not enough. People talk, Officer, you should know that, as well as anyone."

"Nobody can ask questions about the Q Society without you-all casting a verdict...*to kill?*"

"It's not us, it's you! Unfortunately, you are as dangerous to us, now, as you would have been helpful. We liked your brash , *maverick* reputation and style. We appreciated what we interpreted as a *flexible* morality you hold. But we misjudged your loyalty. We now think you're just another blind cop with an *equal justice for all* philosophy."

Dan allowed his eyes to shift to one of the mirrors on the wall behind Mrs. Bluecastle's chair. In it, he could discern a wall at the far end of an adjoining room, behind him. Earlier, it had been hidden from view by the draw-curtain. The wall had a greenish gray appearance and seemed to have a leathery texture. It also looked as though it might be layered, ideal for bullet impact absorption.

Dan had noted that the smell of spent gunpowder increased a little when Mrs. Bluecastle opened the curtain behind him. What he didn't know was that the home had a ventilation system installed, that constantly replenished the basement air. Thus, scents in the environment waxed and waned alternately, with shifting air currents.

"I've never seen anyone your age," Dan offered, "so disregardful of their own life. I have a wife and three little girls. I can't afford to allow you to fire that weapon, whether by mistake or intention."

"You're a pretty smart fellow—once I factor out your *fault of over-curiosity*, at least in this case. But, you, like most of the rest, miss something very important that's right in front of your face. One's last years on earth are dear, when you *know* they're the last years. We old folks *know* we're near the end.

"Now, imagine being able to live those final years, not the *least-*regarded in society, but the *highest* regarded. It's *intoxicating*—that's what it is. I...*crazy?!* No, I'm *drunk* with power! Younger people of this town don't shove me aside. They walk *around* me. And if they don't, I'm likely to *outlive them*, here in *Mount Pleasant*. Our town is a paradise for the old. What you apparently didn't, and don't, appreciate *enough*, is—that fact alone makes it a paradise for *everyone*.

"Why wouldn't you want to work," Mrs. Bluecastle continued, "in the service of your *future?* Why would you question a society dedicated to handing down to you a rich *quality of life*, in your final years? Why couldn't you switch loyalties from 'equal justice for all' to *preferred justice*...for 'old'?

"Why, you're a fool, like the rest," continued Mrs. Bluecastle, "not realizing or appreciating the gift we've bestowed. And for that failure to live up to the Society's, and Mr. DeMendt's, high expectation, you must be *eliminated*."

Dan resumed his review of options: *Kill her or call her bluff.* Would she really shoot if he stood, to walk away? If he turned his back and she shot, it would be difficult for her to prove *self defense*. But then he'd be just as dead, whether she proved it or not. If he survived her gunshot, killing the old lady, in return-fire, what would *that* look like? How would he explain being involved in a gunfight with Mrs. Bluecastle, in her own home?

He had no evidence to present, that the Q Society was evil. How would he even explain *his presence* at the Bluecastle home? How would his arrest and a long, drawn-out trial affect Julie and the girls? *Wait*, he thought. This *senior maniac* had spoken of harming his family, too.

Something, in his estimation, *had to give*. He had to *do* something that altered the circumstances, and soon. But...what? Suddenly, he had an alternate thought. As the old woman had indicated, there were two of them. A Mrs. *and Mr.* Bluecastle—DeMendt had, in fact, referenced them both. Maybe *Mr.* Bluecastle would come on the scene—and be the *sane* one of the couple.

Back at *Norris Assisted Living*, Sonja Spark answered a personal call on her "cell." On the other end was the decade-older friend who, in earlier years, she thought would be her sister-in-law. As Mayzie Florn informed, her father-in-law had suffered one of his nervous spells. It had necessitated his immediate return to his own home for supervised medication. Sonja inquired farther into Mr. Pathwinder's state.

"He had another one of those dreams," answered Mayzie. "You know he has these... premonitions. I swear—this sure takes me back to the one he had about Lonnie. I could have done without being reminded of that. Before, Gumpy had that spell, I was havin' myself a real good day."

"What was the dream?"

"It was that policeman—the one we call 'Kops.'"

"Yeah, you mean Kopochek. What in the world did he dream about *him?*"

"He says he saw him in a big, scary old house. He was chained to the floor at the center and two lions coming at him. Then the house blew all apart, like in a fiery explosion. And from it, in the air, he could see bits and pieces of little children flyin' and falling to the ground. It upset him bad.

"The bad part about Gumpy's dreams—the really *messed-up* ones he gets and *remembers*—usually some'em happens, and it ain't good."

"Yeah, May, I know. ...You know I know."

"And you know Gumpy don't much care for no police, but he looks at that one as halfway decent. We all do."

Sonja whispered audibly: "Listen. He gave me some questions to ask Mrs. Blebbins, the one that died a couple of weeks ago? He was asking about the Qs. I let her know it was from a new policeman on the force who was interested in them. A few days later she was gone."

"Umph. That don't sound good. I'm startin' to get a bad feeling myself, now, Sonja. But I don't guess there's anything we can do. Just wait and see and hope, right?"

"That's all. At this hour, Kops is probably home with his family. Maybe Gumpy's wrong this time. Maybe...right?"

"I don't know, Sonja. I just keep gettin' the feeling it would be good to warn him, this evening. Don't you feel it?"

"Even if I did, there's no way to—. I don't have any numbers, and I sure don't know where he lives. Not that I'd go to his house anyway. I told you about his wife coming by, that day."

"Yeah, that was *off the hook.* ...But you know what? Remember I told you he made a call from here, to somebody he knows, some friend. I think he said somebody he was working on a class project with, or some'em. It should be in my phone's *call list.* Maybe *you* could call it—."

"I don't know, May. I.... Why don't *you* call?"

"You're friendlier with him than I am. ...You know what I mean. You say you worked with him—you know, getting that information he wanted."

"Suppose I did call the number. What would I say to whoever answers?"

"Just ask that person...to ask him to call...one of us. Then we'll tell him that there's something *in the air*. And he'd better watch his 'Ps and Qs,' especially, his...*Qs*."

Sonja reflected on the strange attitude, of some of the residents, that persisted even to the present time. Many of the old folks at *Norris* had affiliation with the Qs in one way or another, she knew. Was this all coincidence or was something ominous in the works, even as she and Mayzie spoke?

"You can give me the number, May. But I don't know whether I'll call or not. It just seems too weird to be calling people *I don't know* and asking about somebody I *barely* know. And then, if by some miracle someone *did* reach him—and he called one of us—what then? I'm supposed to say: 'Hey, watch your back. Mr. Pathwinder—Gumpy—had a wild *premo* and you were in it'."

"I know if something *does* happen and I could have done something, maybe—then, I'll feel like *dirt*, Sonja. I'll feel just like *dirt*."

"I don't know. This is crazy. Give me the number. I may call and I may not. Suppose it gets back to his wife that I'm calling around for him. She'll be back at my door and next time maybe with a gun."

"I see your point, Sonja. I feel what you're sayin'."

To the present time, the situation back at the Bluecastle home remained unchanged. But, in fact, Dan had had enough. His legs now ached from maintaining the awkward kneeling position so long. He began to straighten up. As he did, he spoke:

"You know what, Mrs. Bluecastle? You're just going to have to kill me. I'm not playing your game anymore. You would have shot by now, if you had really planned to." With police revolver pointed upward he looked squarely at the aged face in front of him. In her eyes he saw the seeming hollowness of her soul. To him, they may as well have been nickel-sized openings to caverns of hell.

Glancing downward at the *Glock*, he saw its barrel being raised. He saw the old woman's finger nudge the trigger just before the sense-shattering blast.

The feeling was like having been shot in the face, with hot particles, of no *mass*. The *Glock's* round actually grazed Dan's right cheekbone, just under his eye. But it was the rush of the air exploding about his face that gave the surreal feeling of having been shot. The experience was both humbling and enraging, all at once. It was *fight and flight* occurring simultaneously.

"The next round's going right between your eyes," the old woman conveyed. "I'm one *hell of a* shot—always have been. Of course, as you must have noticed, this *Glock* has laser. At this range, I could shoot your ear off."

Etched in Dan's expression was a mixture of fury and utter incredulity. The sight of it delighted Mrs. Bluecastle.

"You were half right" the old woman confessed, "when you guessed I have reason for *prolonging* the game. I want to give you the full answer you sought. I want to see your face when you hear it. And I must say, I get the greatest kick out of seeing you, biding your time, thinking you'll find a way out of this."

Instinctively, Dan brought his left hand to his face, to feel where he had been grazed. He kept his right in a snug grip of the service revolver. Nearly every "fiber" of compulsion, urged *taking the old woman out*, right then, right there—even if she fired, killing him in return. Somehow, though, he just couldn't. He was all too aware that she could just as easily have shot to kill, but hadn't. So far they were both still very much alive and intact. And maybe, just maybe, a solution would surface in upcoming minutes. It would *have* to, he thought. Because if not, then what?

As if in answer to Dan's desperate hope, a sound from outside filtered into the basement. It was a vehicle pulling around to the back of the property. After some minutes, Dan heard someone's entry into the house. Moving through rooms, the footsteps made the floor wood above groan slightly.

"Millicent!" an old man's voice called out. "Why is the front door wide open?"

"If you so much as turn, *Mr. Officer*, in a second you'll be among those who know what it feels like to have a bullet crash through their skull. Think about the family, Officer, think about the family—yours!"

Dan could hear the creak of the stairs behind him. In the mirror he could see the old man making his way ever so slowly down the steps. Trying to come to grips with the scene to his left, Mr. Bluecastle spoke:

"What in God's name—?!"

Dan didn't know whether he should attempt explanation or wait to see what the woman across from him might offer.

"Didn't you hear," rattled Mrs. Bluecastle. "The decision was made. The officer here has to die. I've been having great fun with him, heretofore. He's a feisty one—nerves of steel, too. He would have made a good ally."

"Mr. Bluecastle...." Dan had half-turned to address the elder man.

"Shoot him, Millicent! Don't let him make another move!" In reply Mrs. Bluecastle fired another round, once again to Dan's right side. Unlike, the previous one, this missile passed a few inches from Dan's ear.

"Turn back this way, Officer! *This way!* I'm going to fire a shot every three seconds that you don't comply. Either time could be the one to lodge into your brain!"

It was like some extraordinary test of endurance, as in the military—shots being fired every three or four seconds, even as he stood still. His mind in *survival mode*, Dan counted the rounds as he watched the aged, sadistic face, between shots. Four in slow succession he counted, to the extent that his mind was clear enough for accuracy. Whatever the case, he was still alive and except for the burning at his cheek, he was in one piece. But if he'd counted correctly, there was a single round left, in the *Glock*.

More bad news, though, was *in the mirrors*, mounted behind Mrs. Bluecastle. Mr. Bluecastle had retrieved a rifle during the shots and, now, held it pointing squarely at Dan's back. He shouted:

"You didn't have to arrange things in this way, Millicent! You didn't have to!"

"I'm going to see an opportunity like this and let it go—never!" The old woman was indignant.

"You should have gotten it over with, before I got back, then, damn-it—if you were gonna' take this route."

"It's the *game*, Heinrik, it's the *game*."

"Oh, you and your *games!* You should have killed him already. Have you lost *all* your marbles, woman?! You've been playing *movie-westerns* with an *armed policeman!* ...What if you're out of bullets? Did you think about *that?!* If he raises that gun to shoot you, and you can't hit him first, I'll have to shoot from here! Do you know what that means, Millicent?! You're going to get hit, too! This is buckshot, damn-it! Slugs'll spread out seven or eight feet!"

"Don't you want to satisfy his curiosity about...*our methods,* before he dies, Heinrik?"

"No! Hell, no! I don't care anything about his *curiosity*! Kill him!"

"You never were a good *gamesman,* Heinrik. Officer Kopochek here needs to know how the *Society* hires *outside help* to dispose of Mount Pleasants' undesirables.

"It's an *investment,* Officer. The Society's got the money and Mr. DeMendt's got the connections."

"Millicent, I swear, if you don't take care of this right now, I'll *have* to! You're giving him time to wiggle out. He'll do it, too, Millicent! He'll do it! Damn it, this is the one that crashed his police car through a store window—on purpose!"

"Like I don't know that—. Look. He *wants* to *know.* You can't see his face, like I can. He's a *curious cat.* So, here you are, *Mr. Curious Cat:* I'm unraveling the whole ball of string for you. You obviously figured some of it out on your own, though. That's why you visited Jill's office, isn't it? But in case you didn't quite put it *all* together, I'll illustrate for you how *connected* we are."

"Millicent, for God's sake...*will you kill him and get it over with?!* What is the point of this? I swear, woman, when this is over, I'm taking you to see somebody!"

"Tsk-tsk...no sense of gamesmanship, whatsoever. Anyway, our Truancy Officer keeps us abreast of all the school dropouts and school trouble-makers. I don't know if, as an officer of the law, you discovered it or not, but that is the major source of a city's crime. School dropouts, that cannot seem to get back on the right track, are a society's bane. Dispose of them properly and you dispose of most of your city's future problems."

Dan stood motionless and nearly without emotion. With each second, his mind fought to come to grips with a nightmare that had escaped into wakefulness.

"Oh, I know what you're thinking: *All* of a city's *criminals* aren't young dropouts. Well, most of its criminals *start* that way. Don't you see? You have to *nip* the problem *in the bud* before it sprouts. Mount Pleasant has been nipping and weeding its would-be *city-terrorizers,* since before I was born. I'm talking over a century—a damned long time."

Mrs. Florn could understand Sonja's reluctance to do a phone-call search of the officer for whose safety they feared. She, therefore, took on the task herself. Hesitantly, she pressed the "dial" function, for the number she located in her directory, belonging to Jennifer Plaetonik. Dan's school project workmate was actually browsing through a shopping mall when the call came.

"Hi, I'm calling about a police officer who called your number from my phone. It was a couple or so weeks ago. He said it was an important call—something about a class—so I let him make it."

"You're talking about Officer Kopochek?"

"Yes, that's him. I live in Sap Tree and he drives by to check on the neighborhood sometimes? That's how we know him over here."

"Okay…. Is there anything wrong?"

"Well, I don't really know. But there're some things happening that we thought maybe he should know about. I guess I wanted to get a message to him…for him to call, so I can explain better, directly to him."

"I imagine he's home now. I can call his home…that's not a problem. What would you like for me to say? Oh, and what is your name?"

"I'm sorry. I'm Mrs. Florn at 234 Piney. There are some people who think that either he might be in some trouble or needs to be careful over the next few days. That's really all I can say, because I don't—. It's just one of those things where we don't have any evidence, but it still seems important."

"Well, I can take your number and ask him to call you. Will that be okay?"

"Sure. We can do that."

Immediately, Jennifer called Dan's home number and got Julie. Her tone was the same one she'd used on scores of previous occasions:

"Hi, Julie. Can I speak to Dan a second? …He's not home? …No, it's not about school this time. Someone just called me from the Sap Tree area—a Mrs. Florn? She seemed to think Dan might be in some… trouble or something. She was real vague about it, but she did sound serious. …At one of the Q residences? …No cell phone calls at their meetings…I see. …Do you want to call this Mrs. Florn and find out what it is she's trying to say? …Okay, here's the number."

Situated between two deadly firearms, five yards of distance each, Dan wondered how his situation could be *real*. A mere hour ago he was an ordinary uniformed policeman, ending his day watch. He was a college student completing a two-year program, condensed into four grueling semester-quarters, that would open new career doors. He was, then, a husband and father not in the least threatened by total ruin and catastrophe.

Somehow an hour later, he was at the edge of doom. There appeared no good outcome to be achieved, from action on his part. To the present minute he had kept himself alive, and avoided killing, only by inaction. There still seemed nothing to do at this point—but *nothing* itself.

Looking into the mirrors on the wall behind Mrs. Bluecastle's chair, Dan could see the shotgun pointing straight at him from behind. In the face of the old man holding it he saw dead seriousness, but also worry and even fear. He shouted yet again to his wife who was the essence of antiquated cool.

"Millicent, goddamn-it, I've had enough! I'm giving you a minute to get up and move out of the buckshot spray-line."

"You could inch your way around the good officer and then shoot from another angle, dear."

"Hell-no! You know I don't move that well, Millicent. I'm not going to chance getting too close to this guy. Right now, if he spun around to shoot, I think I could get him first. But, changing my position would make me an easier target for him. He's got nothing to lose. He'll shoot me, if he can."

"I don't know, dear—he hasn't shot *me* yet."

"Millicent, *I swear*...I swear I think you've finally *lost it!* I mean it, Millicent. You see that clock? One minute more and I *blast*. ...I hate to do it, but you're gambling *too hard!* You'll give him an escape! I know it!"

"You have always *respected* my gambler's nerve—up to now, that is. Now, just hold on a second, Heinrick. I'm going to really show you something, now. I'll bet the good officer, here, knows his weapons. Maybe he determined earlier that this gun has a six-round clip. In that case, our guest probably thinks he's counted my fired bullets correctly. But has he? The question is: Did I fire four, five or all six rounds. Watch this."

The old woman's words were, to Dan, prelude to a new phase of "the game" she played. As he correctly guessed, there was yet another round to be fired. The discharge sent the bullet, again, just to the right of his head, away from Mr. Bluecastle.

"Now," breathed Mrs. Bluecastle in a bizarre sigh of relief. "Am I out of bullets, or is there one more left, with the officer's *name* on it? Is there such a thing as a seven-round magazine for *Glocks*? There didn't used to be, but maybe this is something new." She gripped the *Glock* in a way that suggested she would attempt one last shot.

Were there five shots fired, or six? Maybe, Dan considered, he had misjudged the magazine capacity. For that matter, what if it was of nine- or ten-round capacity?

Mrs. Bluecastle spoke as if reading Dan's thoughts: "We're all about to find out in a minute."

"Damn you, woman! Damn you! You're putting it all on me, now! Before she died, *Mother* always said we'd have to put you away, someday!"

At just that moment there was the sound of an automobile pulling onto the front of the property.

"Who the hell could that be?!" questioned Mr. Bluecastle, nervously. By the change of expression on his wife's face, he could tell she wasn't happy with the new development. In the passing of several quiet seconds, the sound of footsteps across the porch heightened the suspense. Finally, a frightened voice called into the cracked front door:

"Dan…Dan…." At that moment, Mr. Bluecastle remembered that he had left the front door, still ajar.

Whether intuition or whatever, Julie had gotten a bad, ominous feeling after Dan's call home. His words had elated her and she believed a new dawn had arrived to push the dimness of two-years-pass, into the past. But soon afterward came the feeling of foreboding. She had dismissed it as a case of *doubt and misgiving* trying to linger on, even after justification for it was gone. Then she got the phone call from Jennifer.

She found the Bluecastle address in phonebook listings. As though it were a matter of life and death, she packed up the girls and drove to the estate to which Dan had given sketchy mention, in that last call.

When Julie's minivan pulled onto the Bluecastle property one of the first things to catch her eye was Dan's old clunker. But it wasn't just that. It was clear she had surprised someone who was doing something beneath the car, near the front. When, at the sound of the minivan's approach, the man peered out to see, Julie could tell he was startled. She watched, mystified, as he got to his feet, moving hurriedly in a direction that took him out of her line of sight.

Casting issues of *respect for property* aside, Julie drove right up to the front porch steps. The girls, secured in their seats, were exhorted to *stay put* a minute, while she went to ask for Dan, at the door. Apparently, in her mounting distress, she forgot even the protocol of knocking and ringing for occupant attention. "Dan…Dan…" she called out.

Though elderly, Mrs. Bluecastle had her wits about her. She knew she had to get Dan to fire his service revolver, if at all possible. Up to now, she had toyed with him and played her "game" and, from it, derived great amusement and satisfaction. But now an unforeseen presence was corrupting the playing field. There could be no more delay. In order for the game to end, in accord with her design, it was crucial that he *fire his weapon*. In a flash of inspiration and perceptiveness, the answer came.

"That's his wife, Heinrick! Kill her! Go—now! Up the stairs. Go now—and kill her!"

If Dan knew little else in the final minutes of this anomalous and surreal episode, he knew his wife's voice. Now, in an incredible extension of the horror, Julie had entered the dream! To this very second, he had held out hope that *waiting* and *inaction* were the key. Within this nightmare scenario, he was like a body in quicksand. Avoidance of extreme maneuvers prevented his sinking irretrievably into an abyss. But now conditions of the nightmare had taken a terrible turn. Somehow Julie had entered it, and her life was clearly, undeniably, under threat.

Reflexively, Dan spun around, calling out, "Julie! Get away! Quickly!"

As he did, he aimed and fired his weapon at Mr. Bluecastle's heart. In a compact but potent explosion, Dan's gun flew apart, the fiery shock and impact knocking him, barely conscious, to the floor. As he fell, only dimly did he take note of Mr. Bluecastle collapsing, still clutching his shotgun in a sort of death grip.

Dan had no way of knowing that the old man's distress was solely the result of emotional shock. Enhancing the grotesqueness of the nightmare, Dan could hear the sound of Mrs. Bluecastle laughing in unrestrained shouts.

Julie had stood on the Bluecastle's porch, where she could peer into the living room and keep an eye on the minivan. Suddenly she was sure she heard Dan's voice. The sudden sound of the backfiring gun took her feeling of apprehension and foreboding to a new level. She called out:

"Dan!…Dan! …Hello…is everyone all right?! I heard an explosion… is everyone all right?!"

Julie thought about phoning for the police, but her cell phone was in the minivan. In any case, at just this time, conditions within the house held her captive. She just wasn't quite ready to abandon her monitoring of the sounds that reached her from somewhere inside. A feeling of urgency compelled her to shout once more into the house: "Dan!"

Finally, the "game," from Mrs. Bluecastle's point of view, was to be given a whole new direction. It had been her original intention to goad Dan into firing the *changeling* weapon and then silence him forever, with hers. She was, after all, armed with an important piece of information. Monday, two days earlier, DeMendt had engineered the "fixing" of Dan's service revolver, while it lie in the department dispensary.

But, here and now, as it turned out, Mrs. Bluecastle had dragged out the entertainment a tad too far. Now, out of nowhere, it seemed, had entered a *new* and "deal-breaking" *player*.

Some quality in Julie's voice prompted the decision to alter the game's *objective* in mid stream. Maybe the murders planned weren't necessary, supposed Mrs. Bluecastle. Everything now hinged on a hunch she conceived currently. It was possible, she thought, that the Kopocheks were smart enough to "cut their losses," "fold their hand," and *leave* the game, utterly, without looking back.

"Is that Mrs. Kopochek?" the old woman called, while helping Mr. Bluecastle to his feet. "…Good! You must come down immediately! … No! You don't have time to get the children from the car! Come and get your husband *out of my house*—immediately!"

Looking back once more at the locked minivan, Julie made the hasty determination. She could likely devote a *minute* to investigating the situation in the house. A second beyond that minute, she would hurry back to the children. For now, they knew to stay *put* and keep the doors locked. Following the sound of the elderly voice, Julie passed into the dining room and began descending the stairs there. The sight of Dan reeling on his knees, his face red with blood, sent her into near panic.

Mrs. Bluecastle spoke: "Your husband has worn out your family's welcome in this town. Don't think about calling for help. Just get him *out of my home!* If you're smart, you'll get him—and your family—*out of Mount Pleasant.* You've been given a second chance that only comes once in a lifetime. You'd better take it. Your husband will explain it all to you when he can, I'm sure."

The chill of the Bluecastle basement was, for Julie, nothing compared to the chill she got from the old woman's tone. If asked at a less stressful time, Julie might have said there are times when a totally ghastly situation does not warrant demand for immediate explanation. She would have identified this as one of them.

Spurred by the need to get back to the children, Julie summoned extra strength in helping Dan up the stairs. All the time that she struggled desperately, Mrs. Bluecastle shouted her ill-omened warning:

"*Leave Mount Pleasant, immediately!* Do not bother to go home! You no longer have a home here. There is nothing left for you but to get out of Mount Pleasant!"

As Millicent Bluecastle was well aware, she held all the good "cards" left in the deck, in this game. Armed, in her acute analysis, with incontrovertible "proof" that Dan had gone to her home with robbery intentions, she was untouchable. That would be the story she and her husband would tell, if it became necessary. For now, she felt certain they wouldn't have to. In her calculation, the Kopocheks had only two "game" options left: concede unconditional defeat to the superior player—or face ruin.

For effect, the old couple followed Julie and Dan up the stairs and through the living room to the front door, spewing their warnings. In addition to Dan's incapacitated state, Mr. Bluecastle was further emboldened by his continued grasp of the shotgun. His wife decided to hold off telling him it presently contained a blank shell and was incapable of firing.

Even as Julie frenetically motioned Dan down the porch steps to the grass, the old man issued his final caveat:

"Get him the hell out of here, Mrs. Kopochek!" he shouted to Julie. "Get him the hell out of Mount Pleasant!"

Julie steered the minivan and its five occupants in a sharp arc on the Bluecastle property, the girls scared and crying. As she did, she could see that Dan's old car was smoking and just catching fire. That seemed the *last straw* for her. Not only the present scenario but perhaps the *whole town* reflected an evil, of unfathomable proportion. Revisiting Dan's often stated belief that Mount Pleasant held an ominous secret, she felt certain that he had uncovered it. Now, by all appearances, the town was rising up like some hideous leviathan, chasing them out its domain.

Julie felt she was *ready and willing* to heed the warnings of the old couple from whose daunting presence she'd fled, with family in tow. But she wondered how they could all just head straight for the safety and sanity of Grafton, without going, first, to their Mount Pleasant home, to make preparations.

Beside her, Dan seemed to be coming around. It was revealing of how incredible had been his experience at the Bluecastle estate, when he asked: "Did I *dream* a nightmare, Julie, or did I just *live* one?"

Julie's reply: "It wasn't a dream, Dan. And it won't be over until we get out of Mount Pleasant, for good—which is just what we're going to do."

Once the minivan and its occupants were out of the old couple's sights, Mr. Bluecastle started fussing. How could she subject him to all she'd just put him through, knowing he had a bad heart? Was she trying to kill him? If that was the case, why didn't she just shoot him with one of the bullets she fired into the slug-absorption wall?

And what would the other *Q Society* members think about them letting Kopochek go free? How would DeMendt take the news, given his trust in the Q Society's dedication to *elimination?* At a point, he began to use a railing tone: Was she aware that she was carrying her love of "games" way too far?

A whole half hour expired during the time of his frantic, accusative questioning. At the end of that period, he made a final inquiry, with exasperation. Had she even listened to a word he'd said?

From Mrs. Bluecastle's point of view, something she kept from her husband might be viewed as an *affectionate* gesture, on her part. Unbeknownst to him she *regularly* kept his shotgun loaded with a dud shell. As far as she was concerned, she was the *firearms* person in their family. Her husband just wasn't strong or level headed enough, in her estimation, for properly handling a deadly weapon. She thought it far more important that he *believe* he had recourse to firepower, than it be the actual case.

Even after the passing of ten minutes in their drive, Dan's vision was still blurred. He felt also bereft of strength but assured Julie he didn't need hospital care. Tilted back in the adjustable front seat, he rested, trying to regain his senses.

In the relative cool of the waning summer evening, the ride home was quiet and comfortable but nevertheless eerie. To Julie, the feeling was one of being *in the sights* of a predator that was perfectly still and awaiting its time to strike. Gone, even, was the routine chirping of birds along the stretch of back road she took. The absence of their various calls seemed, to Julie, an omen of something bad and imminent.

Sitting in the driveway of their home, Julie paused. The old people's words began to replay clearly in her mind. *Get out of Mount Pleasant right away! Do not pause or delay for any reason!* Yet, there she and the family sat, in ongoing delay. An odd state of indecision held her captive.

Through the ride home, the Kopochek girls maintained a precocious compliance and quiescence. Now, however, after sitting idly in the minivan, awaiting their parents' next decision, they were starting to get upset. But that was only until the explosion erupted, brightly visible from the vehicle's side and front windows. Observing the scene from the relative safety of the minivan, the family witnessed a house coming apart in a series of brilliant and thunderous flashes.

Within seconds, Julie steered back to the road and headed for Grafton. Behind her, in time, the grounds around their home became littered with falling pieces of burning furniture, clothes, doll parts, and other toys.

All the way to Grafton, Dan drifted in and out of a dream that replayed segments of his recent nightmare. Who would have thought, he reflected, in a moment of mental clarity, that solving the Mount Pleasant "mystery" would have become such a deadly enterprise. Later, when he looked back over this evening, he would have a significant realization. The concussion he suffered from the gun blast and his consequent diminished lucidness shielded him from a horrendous awareness of all that was happening.

Marginally aware that his thinking lacked continuity, Dan accepted the series of abrupt shifts in his focus. In one of them, he reflected on his and Jennifer Plaetonik's final project for the semester. The finished product was in her possession. He had no doubt that, by now, she had turned it in to their professor.

Partly reclined in the vehicle's front seat, Dan took in the soothing sensation of Julie's hand clasping his. It also gave him deep comfort to consider how pleased Julie must be that his days of *police patrol* were over. She would finally have the contentment she deserved, he concluded, married to a man determined to be the best *civil engineer* possible.

Creature Faith

Sid Seine's two brothers and sister made it their business to come out and stand with him, through the public scrutiny. They were well aware of his past emotional turmoil and present signs of diminished passion. Taking a positive outlook, they hoped all the interest, in Sid, generated in the community, of late, was therapeutic for him.

Even as the crowd gathered, Sid acted as though he was an unconcerned bystander amid a throng there to see someone else. In fact, though, amblers departed from their usual activities—to see him. At the very least they were there to witness what would be his responses to the news reporter known to be arriving.

Albert and *Wine* was the street corner at which Sid made his, sort of, "official" location. Anyone with a special need to see him had but to drive by that downtown intersection occasionally. At some point in the course of a typical day, Sid could be seen in characteristic form. That would be standing somewhere along the block of storefronts for long periods, deep in thought. Or he might be sitting on a cushioned buffer he placed atop a fire hydrant, blankly watching the flow of traffic.

It was that routine, that level of predictability, which had given the *Order of Neo-Euthenics Strategists (ONES)* their opportunity. That group had a special interest in Sid. In short, they designed for him to play a central role in an elaborate agenda of their making. It was key to know what motivated Sid to do or not do a thing. As he was given to belief in "otherworldly" affairs, talking along those lines often got his attention. The challenge, for those who, earlier, sought secret business with him, was keeping the "spiriting away" of Sid a thing unnoticed.

Choosing the perfect time of day or evening for both the acquisition and the return of Sid was important. That he was "detained" for no more than a few days at a time helped keep concerns about him to a minimum. After all, he was for the most part an indigent; but even they can raise eyebrows if absent too long. It was upon his return from one of those "secret sabbaticals" that Sid began to say things that, more than ever before, got people's attention.

As noted, a small audience now gathered slowly around the usually reticent homeless man and his siblings. Passersby, pausing momentarily and then passing on, alternately swelled and diminished the numbers. In this way, the crowd near him ranged from a mere fifteen to nearly double that amount when the *ambling curious* lingered.

Across large, downtown Albert Street, ONES workers watched clandestinely from a second floor window. Within the big, high-ceilinged room from which they made observations were some of the most sophisticated devices of technology, to date. Present in the spacious enclosure were machines for receiving, recording, and transmitting brain-wave data—all remotely.

Cameras attached to the front of their building provided zoomed-in pictures of the scene across the street in real time. Others were mounted on the side of buildings on Wine Street and its parallel counterpart, Tilman Avenue. These showed scenes occurring at those intersections with Albert, and beyond. In addition, highly sensitive microphones motioned about at the site of interest across the street. But it wasn't *locomotion*. They were fitted within hats, vests, sweaters and other outerwear of ONES "plants."

Finally, the news-van from local station WNSY came cruising down Albert to the corner of Wine. Conveniently, it parked at a corner "no parking" zone in front of Sid's hydrant, at the edge of milling onlookers. Inside, the roving news gatherer and her cameraman exchanged amused glances. The message each conveyed to the other: *This ought to be interesting.*

The little crowd at the corner of Albert and Wine proved rather accommodating. When the van driver politely requested that the curious onlookers make room for the reporter's set-up, they complied. It was in fact due mainly to excitement each felt at being a part of a televised event. Who knew but that any of them might have her or his face featured in the evening news? There was also the chance that the guy at the center of interest might actually say something worth witnessing.

In point of fact, Sid *had* amazed a number of the regulars of his milieu with uncanny predictions and displays of knowledge. As for the merely "browsing curious" who'd heard about Sid, some had, likewise, been made privy to feats of the kind. Often, these latter had gotten responses that left them hang-jawed.

Within roughly a three-week period, word of these marvelous deeds ultimately spread. And so did people's interest in Sid's unfathomable insights and apparent auguring. Eventually, it all came to the notice of the brash and scoop-hungry young reporter setting up for the present interview.

Tamia Earlson, twenty-three, smart, and enterprising, knew she should do some preliminary maneuvering prior to this venture. Acting on tips from "sources," she located Sid. That was three days earlier. After a mainly one-sided chat, Tamia coaxed Sid to sign a simple form allowing a public exchange that might later be aired on TV. She explained that his story may warrant a small *human interest* segment in a news program.

Finally, Earlson's cameraman and his equipment were in place and the microphones activated. As she had been trained to do, Tamia spoke articulately, glancing alternately at the camera and Sid.

Tamia:	"And so the talk, among folks who frequent this section of downtown Crystal, is that Mr. Seine, here, displays some interesting talents of late.
	[Turning to Sid] "Quite frankly sir, I'm hearing everything from *psychic* to modern-day *prophet*.
	"Just to inform the folks at home watching, I spoke to Mr. Seine briefly a few days ago. He said I could address him as his friends and associates in the neighborhood do—that is, as 'Sid.'
	"So, Sid, what do you have to say...with regard to what folks are saying about you?"
Sid:	"People say what they see. Sometimes they say what they don't see. And...what about you? You see news and you report it. Do you, in turn, report what has *not* occurred?"
Tamia:	"Well, I sure try *not* to, Sid. ...Okay, let me approach this

	a different way. Do you consider yourself to be psychic or to be a prophet?"
Sid:	"I speak in behalf of the *true God*. You will have your own ideas about what I am."
Tamia:	"Another *good* one, Sid. Alright. Well, the word out here is that you've made some predictions that have come true. Could you spare one for a novelty-news geek, like me?"
Sid:	"You are asking for a forecast of future events. I can only speak on what the *true God* reveals to me."
Tamia:	"Okay. You're not going to make this easy for me, are you Sid? Alright, then—how about your reputed gift of knowing *current* things the average *Joe* wouldn't ordinarily know?"
Sid:	"If the *true God* chooses to acknowledge your inquiry, then that which you seek may be provided through me."
Tamia:	"You're a hard man, Sid. It's going to be *tough love* from start to finish, isn't it? Okay—let's start with the simple. How old am I? I'd like the 'true God' to tell you how old I am?"

The ONES monitoring the scene across the street from their building had guessed something correctly. It concerned the kinds of questions that might be asked by the reporter to whom they had Sid's story leaked. Owing to careful research by certain members, just the right reporter had been sought, discovered and alerted. Anticipating that she might use herself as a test of Sid's "knowing," they had collected extensive data on her.

Trusting wholly in their preparedness for challenges, the ONES were ready to take on Sid's mission. Employed were a number of state of the art technologies playing a role in an essential purpose: remote mind communication through wave-transmission. In short, the ONES were going to employ processes that allowed them both to influence and to loosely perceive Sid's thoughts.

Sid:	"You are twenty-three...three older sisters. The yellow Mazda you drive sits in the employee lot at your station. You...."
Tamia:	"Whoa! Hold on, there, Sid. Alright, alright. So either

you've got 'gifts' or some pretty darned good connections. Let's just change directions a little and try something that doesn't involve... *me*.

"Uhh ...okay, maybe we can explore any ability you have to predict or forecast, I don't know, conditions in the environment. There are at least six buses with different routes and numbers that run up and down Albert. Don't look but there's one coming from east. Which is it?"

On the outer wall of the building across from the reporter, the camera swiveled to catch the desired bus image.

Sid: "The *true God* shows me that it is the #17 to Wilston."

Tamia: "Well, this will be easy enough to.... Oh, my God! I believe it is. What've you got...a *bus schedule* in your head, Sid? You've got 'em timed, don't you?

"You're not wearing a watch, though—maybe there's a street clock somewhere that I'm not seeing."

Sid: "The *true God* shows me that behind the #17 is the #31 to Oglethorpe. ...Coming east from west is the #2 to Fattsburg. There's a *Continental Furniture* truck coming north on Wine. In less than a minute, it'll be at this intersection. ...Tomorrow the Nevada Desert will give up a long held secret."

Tamia: "Sean, get a shot at those buses coming this way! ...Folks, as you can see, Sid really knows his public transportation! Here they are, apparently right on schedule...the 17, the 31—and across the street the #2 to Fattsburg!

"Now, Sean, if a *Continental* truck rolls up, you're going to wind up with a shot of me fainting modestly on the sidewalk. ...*Oh, my God!* Catch it Sean—now back and forth between the truck and Sid!

"*News-14 viewers out there—you saw it first, right here.* We have a local man who sees without looking. Was it some kind of trick? I don't know. You be the judge. I'll say this much: Ol' Sid here's got my attention.

"Oh, and before I wrap up, let's not forget: Sid's 'true God' told him something about a secret of some sort to be revealed in the Nevada Desert. I think that's how he said it.

"Am I quoting you correctly, Sid?"

Sid: "The *true God* has said so."

Tamia: "Well, you can't get better confirmation than that! Alrighty, then—.

"*So, viewers, we'll just have to wait until tomorrow to see if Sid bats that last one out of the park.* ...Hey, I don't know about the rest of you standing right out here with me, but I've had a blast.

"And, Sid, you've been a real *class act* for us today. If you ever run for any local offices, you got my vote. You are one *ace augur*, my man.

"Seriously, though: thank you, again. We appreciate you taking the time."

Sid: "All thanks is directed to the *true God*."

Tamia: "A-men to that, Sid. Aaa-men."

Inside of 225 Albert Street, on the second floor, the ONES workers all shouted and danced around. They were like NASA scientists celebrating a successful shuttle launch, as they watched the News-14 crew undoing the previous set-up. In their unanimous decision, the "operation" couldn't have gone better. Sid, their *symbolic* first man on Mars, had performed perfectly.

In actuality, he was the Order's *human thought-reception device*—the central figure in an elaborately engineered plan. Its ultimate goal: to bring monumental change throughout the world.

As for the Nevada Desert discovery Sid spoke of, it was *in the bag*, so to speak. The ONES would, of course, never have conveyed the thought to Sid, if they hadn't been totally certain of its imminence. Almost thirty years to the day had passed since multimillionaire, Burton Shiesler, disappeared. Most of his millions had seemed to go into hiding also, as they were never traced and located. By now, investigations of both had been placed on a far back burner.

Members of the Order of Neo-Euthenics Strategists had connections, of one sort or another, with people and groups, the world over. Those that routinely make aerial surveys of land areas were no exception.

Order members saw an opportunity to make use of plans discussed by entrepreneurs to find land suitable for a business venture. The stated desire was to hire a plane to peruse landscapes from above.

Once the "when, where, and how-to" details were worked out, the arrangement included a member of the Order as a passenger in the flight. Significantly, her ONES connection was unknown. By design, the land survey would start out from New Mexico and continue over parts of the Nevada Desert.

Back at 225 Albert Street, Order members watched the news crew depart and the slow dissipation of the crowd. With interest in aftereffects of Sid Seine's interview, ONES workers began listening again to the chatter across the street. The three "plants" carrying hidden microphones moved inconspicuously among the remaining onlookers, recording their talk. One was closest in location to Sid's three siblings, the youngest being the sister. He picked up their conversation.

For now, the ONES suspended the *wave*-transfer of ideas to Sid's brain. They were just interested in the afterthoughts of those who lingered for the chance to sop up any remaining marvels. Presently, what conveyed to them most clearly, at their operation center across the street, was the voice of Sid's younger brother:

"That was pretty good, Sid," commented Jon Seine jovially. "I'd say you really gave the people what they came for. But, now that it's over, how about the four of us making a good, quiet exit together. Wouldn't it be nice just to, kind of, get off the street for awhile?"

"The *true* God directs me. I believe I'm *home* right out here. I believe my *home* is where I stand."

"It's starting to get a little cold, Sid," Jillian Seine announced. "How can you be out here all day and all evening? You know you can always stay with one of us. Daddy still keeps a place in the basement for you. Johan says he's got an extra bedroom. And Jon's got an extra room in his new apartment."

"Sure, Sid. Why don't you come with us—even if it's just for a little while." Johan Seine showed sincerity in his tone. "You're finished here for today. You did good."

"I don't feel the cold. Just the spirit of *God*, is all."

"Well, that's nice," Jon allowed. "I'll tell you what—how about just come with us and have dinner."

"I think God would want you to come with us, Sid." Jillian sounded convinced.

"Do you know," Sid replied listlessly, "that the *family of Man* knows no special blood ties?"

"I know. You've told us before, Sid. We know that's how you feel. But can't you, just for now, acknowledge *our* family connection? You and us—we're all Seines, Sid. We grew up together. That's got to mean something. Won't you come with us on that basis?"

After pausing, Sid responded: "I shall walk with you and talk with you, in the spirit of the *true God*."

"Good enough," Johan sighed, in relief.

"Yep, we'll just be together *in the spirit* as...followers of God, for as long as you feel comfortable. No pressure." It was Jillian's comment. She watched as Sid formulated a response:

"...I wonder what they'll find in the desert tomorrow, Jill. The *true God* did not elaborate."

"Well, let's let *God* worry about that for now," Jillian responded. "You just come and let us get you in a nice warm bath and in some clean clothes."

"I bet you haven't had Kreil's Chicken and rice with rutabaga and biscuits in some time, huh, Sid?"

"No, Jon, I haven't. But I haven't missed it either. The *true God* fills me, just as well, with a slice of bread and a cup of thin soup from the shelter."

It was sixty years prior that the *Order of Neo-Euthenics Strategists* first was formed. At its inception, the group was composed of the most influential individuals on the planet. With members in top governmental and corporate positions the world over, it took on the lofty objective noted in the group's title. Aptly, *"improving the human condition by improving the environment"* was their initial aim. Driven by the prospect of favorable results, they chose their endeavors with extreme care.

The organization quickly discovered, however, that trying to operate under what amounted to governmental *restraints* was all too slow, cumbersome and uncertain. They thus set out to devise and put into effect plans lacking the benefit of official approval. Of necessity, then, *secrecy* became the hallmark of the Order's existence, in addition, of course, to its creed and objectives.

After initial formation, it took years for the Order finally to draft a mission that would "galvanize" the members into unity-of-purpose and action. But once the "Created Faith Project" was adopted, the Order immediately began channeling resources toward its fulfillment. Money and planning-time put into it, over the years, grew to enormous proportions. However, while ONES officials organizing it had ample access to both, those at the top were averse to *wasting* either a dollar or a day.

Just as the Order had foreseen—or, more accurately, *planned*—an aerial sighting was made over the Nevada Desert. It happened the very next day after Sid's taped interview. The land-survey pilot making the discovery had no knowledge of Sid or his street-corner discourses on the "true God." Thus, there was nothing to connect him with the indigent "seer." The plane's co-surveying passenger had subtly suggested the specific route taken. With seeming graciousness, she was completely willing to attribute the finding to the pilot's hawkeyed detection, while flying.

BURTON SHIESLER MYSTERY SOLVED! It was both front page headlines and the top story of *Web*-casts and TV reporters. Foreign news agencies even gave it some mention. Naturally, then, smalltime local areas, as was Sid's town, became informed, too, as events unfolded.

Sid had taken the religion taught to him as a child very seriously from the start. His preoccupation with matters spiritual contributed greatly to his leaving college after the second year. Attainment of academic knowledge conflicted, time-wise and interest-wise, with his main focuses. Chief in his thoughts was what he believed to be the "word of God;" second, was determining how to do God's bidding.

This was the state in which members of the Order found Sid, two years prior. To them, he appeared at twenty eight an archetype of the individual they sought for experimentation. A whole year they spent watching him clandestinely. They set up elaborate monitoring schedules. Dedicated members of the Order posed as indigents, themselves, for a period, to gather desired data. As evidence mounted that Sid was the man for the mission, the ONES began to purchase real estate.

The 200 block of Albert Street where Sid spent most of his time was full of boarded up abandoned storefronts. Under more cosmetically favorable conditions, even renting one would have been costly. As it was, the ONES found purchase of a number of the buildings easy to bear financially. Agreements made with city officials only required that the buyer maintain proprietary environments devoid of hazard. The municipal hope and expectation was for eventual restoration of the edifices, which were at present, a blight to downtown Albert Street.

One of the buildings purchased was transformed, internally, into a model of comfort for ONES workers living and working there. All floors of 225 were gutted and remodeled, but it was the second level that was made into a *state of the art* laboratory. Anyone taking the secret elevator to "2" ascended to an environment with an almost otherworldly sophistication, in design.

Just as members of the Order had expected, and planned, Sid started first to become a hero of the destitute. With knowledge "planted" in him by his benefactors, he told them where to find money awaiting discovery, here and there. It might be of one dollar denomination, five, ten, or even twenty. Always he added a firm caution to his fellow homeless attendants.

The *true God*, he said, was not a fan of money, in general, and was "suspicious" of monetary dole, in particular. Therefore they should not expect the *true God* ever to reveal, *reliably*, the location of lost currency. Indeed, no one should look for more than a handful of such occurrences, in total. The point of those deeds was only to foster the idea that Sid had a special knowledge of the *true God*. It was not for him to be taken as a *money genie*.

The Order had Sid to relate that caveat to help assure his safety. As the researchers knew, there were always people around who would kill, literally, to know where money could be found. To emphasize the point of the "true God's" distain for the tender, Order members always planted the bills in locations bordering on repulsive. In turn, Sid would orate condemningly about the "gift." Gain accrued but not earned, he warned, remained odious until repaid, in some way.

The "dirty" money was just the start, for Sid's homeless hangers-on. Next, he began to preach to them why they were in such a destitute condition. To the small indigent audiences he would speak loudly, almost angrily: "You were set up for failure!"

The declaration never failed to elicit full attention. Sid would elaborate:

"*You are the product of parents who were not prepared to give you the best chance in life! Yet, they brought you into this callous world anyway.*

"*Oh, you probably don't like to hear it! But it's true! The true God has given me the insight to know about you. You were set-up for failure from the beginning!*

"*But there's hope. God help us—there's hope. You just need to start thinking more clearly. In time, I will be led to show you how to go about it. But, for now, please, please, please—leave me to my thoughts and visions of the horrid state of this world!*"

Sid was typically so poorly attired and dour of facial expression, that few outside his homeless entourage ventured to engage him. When they did, he sometimes treated them like supporters of, investors in, a *world system* he abhorred:

"Why have you come to talk to me?" he might ask. "Do I look like I know anything to aid your understanding of the world you feel comfortable in? Talk to the God of the world *you* know. You're not ready for the word of the *true God.*"

Such dialogue carrying to speaker devices within 225 Albert brought the ONES to almost rowdy shouts of proud approval. To them, it showed that even without their prompting, Sid could demonstrate the kind of spiritual understanding they sought to promote.

Perhaps predictably, the station whose novice reporter taped the piece with Sid that day aired it again and again. WNSY had exclusive footage of a "street person" who had shown an ability to foresee events. Citywide, people were still trying to come to terms with Sid's electrifying prediction of the Nevada Desert discovery. It wasn't long before other local TV stations were discussing the prospect of a similar interview.

The problem was that conditions in the "field," for having the encounter, didn't appear very favorable. To those sidling up to Sid to discuss a possible taping, he was rudely indifferent. Not a single sign did he give that he might be inclined to cooperate, at such time that a "stage" was set, to do a report.

Tamia Earlson, on the other hand, felt she was probably a *shoe-in* for a second "round" with Sid. Accordingly, she finessed permission from a producer to start the ball rolling again, in obtaining a second Sid interview. She set out the very next day. Locating Sid on a side street running across Albert, Tamia got his agreement for interview, to occur forty-eight hours later.

It just so happened that ONES researchers were monitoring Sid's brain activity in the hour of the request. It was how they became knowledgeable of the planned event. Once again, all the thought and preparation put into the project paid off. It had been predicted that Sid might take up impromptu speaking engagements of his own—ones of importance to the Order. This was a *case in point*. The monitors duly directed Sid to suggest the same location for interview chosen previously.

On the day of the planned event, Tamia and her van driver visited Sid's Albert Street haunt on five occasions, within an hour. In that time, they made not a single sighting of Sid. Finally, on the sixth try they caught the image of him turning onto Albert from a side street. Upon checking her watch, Tamia saw that the time was one minute before the two o'clock hour, which she had given as the optimal one, for interview. Now, her driver and she raced to get back to the 200 block of Albert, so as to be on the scene and setting up, as Sid approached.

In due course, Sid's interview proceeded:

Tamia:	"But Sid...Mr. Seine, can you explain what it *feels* like to actually get messages from...God?"
Sid:	"It's in my head...in my thoughts. I see pictures. The *true God* has a purpose for me."
Tamia:	"But, what is it, Sid? What's the purpose? What do you think—assuming it's God's work—it *is* that *He* wants you to do with this special knowledge you're provided?"
Sid:	"The truth. ...I'm here to reveal the truth to those who *want* it...to those who are *ready* for it."
Tamia:	"I don't mean to sound like *Pontius Pilate*—but, Sid, *what is the truth?*"
Sid:	"Truth has many instances...truth is a tree with many branches."
Tamia:	"Aw, now Sid—I was afraid you were gonna' get really *deep*

116

on me. Sid, my man, I'm only twenty-three, fresh out of college. Of course, at times *I think* I know everything. But deep down, I know I don't. You're going to have to *break it down* for me.

"See, you're like a philosopher, Sid. You know what I'm sayin'? I didn't do too well in *philosophy*."

Sid: "You want the *sun* in a sandwich…and then you can take a bite and know what light is."

Tamia: "Oh, okay—good one, Sid. I get it. So…let's see. You're here to reveal the truth but not necessarily to define it, explain it or point a stick at it. Is that it? Am I on the right track?"

Sid: "Truth involves a *way of seeing*…without distraction. Not everyone can *see* without distraction. Not everyone is ready for truth."

Tamia: "Wow. *Seeing without distraction*, huh? Okay, Sid, I'm ready—I think—to make myself the guinea pig again. Are there any truths you think I'm capable of seeing?"

Sid: "Humans continue to breed like the lower-intellect animals—no regard for the future."

Tamia: "I, uh…I think I can see that. Well, no…no, I can't. Just what do you mean, Sid? I think human beings, when bringing children in the world, *do* have regard for the future."

Sid: "Look around. Look at our brother over there…and our sister over there…sitting on sidewalk steps, nodding, half conscious. Look in the alleys at the thieves and future murderers, waiting their chance.

"Look in the prisons, in hospitals for the criminally insane. Peek into the *crack houses* and other places where drugs poison the mind.

"None of us who, from birth, were set up for failure and dissociation from society should have been born."

Tamia: "Whoa, Sid. I think I just took a bite of that sandwich with the sun in it. …Ouch.

"Okay, then. …Well, before we bring our second 'round' to a close, do you think you could thrill our audience with

	a prediction? I hate to be picky, but one we wouldn't have to wait too long for would be nice—like last time."
Sid:	"I actually foresaw that you'd ask that question. The answer I prepared is this: Simply giving forecasts, on command, would distract the focus from other truths."
Tamia:	[turning to the camera] "So, there you have it. Sid, here, just made it clear he's no *garden variety* fortune teller and won't be treated as such."

Barring any unforeseen interruptions, the next phase in the Order's plan of events was set for action. To be put into effect in a day or two, it was given the title, "The Line." Members, again wearing microphones, were selected to form short lines on the sidewalk, with Sid as the center of attention. The plants would seem to represent various walks of lives, although most would, in earlier phases, present as poor or disadvantaged.

By virtue of their "euthenics" focus, a number of the ONES was knowledgeable in all areas of *social science*. Thus, they were well aware of a sociological likelihood. Indeed, they counted on its occurrence. It was this: Once *non*-planted observers made the "doling out of truth" connection, many would join in, to get a "gift." In other words, casual observers of responses given to plants would soon mimic the plants.

At the 225 headquarters, the Order operators listened in on developments across the street. As they knew, plants were poised to present to Sid the kind of questions to which he was most adept at responding. From the non planted public, Sid would likely be fielding a whole range of statements and inquiries, from the reasonable to the bizarre. Thus, it was the role of the Order's plants to set the tone for questions asked. In this way they would demonstrate how best to receive Sid's "guidance." At the very least, a "good" question should evoke a tantalizingly enigmatic answer.

Plant 1:	"Everybody's heard what you say about having babies, Sid—babies we can't afford. Well, I have two that I couldn't afford to take care of without *social services* help. What do you expect people like me to do?"
Sid:	"I have no expectations. Do the best you can…and have no more, that you can't afford."

Plant 2:	"What does the *true God* tell you about rich people? Why should *they* get to have all the children?"
Sid:	"Those not afraid of truth will tell you: One's children are a mixed blessing. You shouldn't assume that people with a lot of children are happier. ...Please...there are others behind you. You must go to the back, if you have more to ask."
Plant 3:	"So, when will I be able to afford children? How will I know when I can give them what you say they're owed, that is, the best chance for a good life?"
Sid:	"Rid yourself of selfishness...and you'll know."
Plant 4:	"What's the Pick-Four number going to be this evening, Sid?"
Sid:	"Please...there are others behind you. You must go to the back if you have something to ask that the *true God* would really answer."
Plant 5:	[Speaking low] "I'm pregnant...and single...and I have no job. What should I do?"
Sid:	"Follow your conscience. Rid yourself of selfishness. ... Find a job, if you can. Get appropriate help."
Browser:	"What's wrong with being poor? You're saying poor people can't have children?"
Sid:	"A poor person should 'purchase' that which he can afford. When a person cannot afford a million dollar home, he should not contract to purchase it. If he does, it will surely be taken away."
Plant 6:	"I want to piggyback off what that guy before me asked. In the end, it still sounds like you got something against poor people, Sid"
Sid:	"The *true God* directs me to love the poor more than the rich. Love is care. I care not to see children born with less than half a chance...."
Plant 6:	[Continuing] "Children of the poor are *God's children* just as much as their rich counterparts, no?"
Sid:	"Please...there are others behind you. You must go to the back if you have more. But as you do, I will tell you this:

The *true God* has no *flesh* offspring. The term *child of God* is used to mask the truth."

Plant 7: "I heard that. So, tell us *your* truth, sir?"

Sid: "The babies of man are the responsibility of man. You should not create offspring and try to put them off on God. The *true God* is innocent of all procreation, be it by lower beast or by *man*-beast. Please…there are others behind you. You must go to the back, if you have more."

Browser: "Sid, please say that you aren't denying the existence of *Christ!* You just said God is innocent of procreation. I think you know what the Bible says—."

Sid: "If that is your belief, why do you concern yourself with what I say? I speak a truth that is only for those without mental *block*…obstruction of *vision.* You should not talk to me or listen to me, if what I say offends you. You are free to change the 'channel.'"

Browser: "Hey, Sid, my man! What was that you said about them rich people? You don't love 'em?"

Sid: "The *true God* directs me to love the poor more than the rich. But that's me. You may love whom you choose."

Browser: [Continuing] "Nooo—I don't love 'em either. Damn 'em. …I know, I know…I'm gone to the back of the line."

It was in this way that the practice started. At certain times of certain days, Sid now took, and answered, brief questions from lines of ordinary people on the street. For seekers of his "spiritual opinions," there was no predicting when Sid might be inclined to share them. It was in fact dictated by decisions coming from building 225 on Albert.

The Order had no intentions of risking Sid's exhaustion from an oversupply of requests for his attention. Therefore they promoted, through remote communication, Sid's default disposition, when they thought it best. That, of course, was preference for solitude. So, for the most part, Sid's audiences were due for his brand of enlightenment only at the discretion of the ONES.

Just as before, when Sid wasn't handing out "opinions," he either was ambling about, standing solemnly alone, or sitting somewhere socially unresponsive. As far as Order members were concerned, these were

Sid's deserved "downtimes." When it was time for him to "work," they predisposed him to stand near one of the mounted, hidden microphones at a building front, on Albert Street.

Sid had a small collection of similarly penniless associates who hung around him, to varying degrees of conspicuousness. These became particularly sensitive to his moods and patterns over past weeks. Usually, they would be the first to recognize the melting of Sid's cool exterior, subtle though it was. It would be this group, then, who could be counted on to start a "line of inquiry" in front of Sid.

Sometimes, though, no one in the immediate environment acted on Sid's "in the mood" signal fast enough. It was then that the Order sent out "starters" to get Sid's *spiritual opinions* rolling out to lines of the curious, that formed subsequently. As before, *non plants* ran the gamut from the playfully inquisitive, to the seriously interested, to those desperately seeking spiritual guidance.

After months of observing, day and night, areas scanned by cameras, the Order compiled much data on Sid's environment. They identified individuals they suspected would maim or even kill in a spontaneous bid to gain a quick and easy *five* dollars. Virtually all the night walkers took illegal substances of one sort or another or were mentally ill—or both.

Sid was not among the *night people* who stalked about, *beyond* ten p.m., but he was not averse to late evening wanderings. It was at these times, thought the Order members, that he most required special protection. That, on occasion, Sid's *shielding* take on an "otherworldly" aspect fit well with the image of him they sought to sculpt. Thus, by prearrangement, anyone appearing to menace Sid in certain monitored areas of his usual environment could be in for a real *shock*.

According to the Order's schedule, it was time to "step up" Sid's effect another notch. So far, he'd shown that he could draw a crowd when so predisposed. Courtesy of his Order communicants, he had publicly revealed the presence of mysteriously missing articles of note within the city. This, too, added to his enigmatic image.

As ONES planners knew, all the local news stations regarded Sid as a small phenomenon in their midst. Whenever they could work it in, reporters representing their stations would *set up*, to film one of Sid's "lines," in action. But as Order members also knew, over time people become inured to the same old feats of amazement. Thus, they prepared a new deal.

One mildly cool and dusky evening, witnesses clearly impaired by drugs and alcohol saw something. They observed Sid making way, in his roundabout fashion, to the place that gave him shelter at night. In a back alley of Albert, the 200-block, a young man, they reported, knocked Sid to the ground. To dissuade resistance, Sid was punched a few more times, as the assailant rummaged through Sid's pockets. Gaining possession of the sought-after three dollars, he fled down the length of the alley.

Before the mugger reached the alley's end, said witnesses, a "blue streak" of some sort, in the night air, "caught him." Whatever it was knocked the absconding malefactor to the ground, causing him apparent great pain. Mere yards from that passageway's end, the sprawled body, though darkly clothed, was quite visible. In seconds, reportedly, it also was quite still.

People incidentally passing by the alley's intersection with Wine Street called for police. In less than five minutes, the authorities were on the scene declaring the young man dead where he'd fallen. Later, a determination of inexplicable heart failure would be made, as the cause of death.

By two o'clock the following evening, Sid was ready to speak to a street audience. To the police, he had already given his tacit statement of what happened to him. As for the nineteen-year-old mugger, beyond slight recognition of his face, Sid knew nothing of him.

To anyone viewing the corner of Albert and Wine, Sid's gathering had the look of a press conference, albeit a decidedly *informal* one. Around him people stood, and gawked, in a wide arc, careful not to crowd the orator standing on a step. Leading to him was a line that stretched a quarter block's length.

Across the street at 225, the Order's project executers watched the unfolding of Sid's latest street talk. At times they peered through curtains and shades that disallowed a view back into the window. Mostly, though, they watched the event on large screens that caught the action at various zooms. To their delight Sid appeared rested from good sleep, unruffled, and relaxed. They nearly rubbed their hands together in eager anticipation.

Person 1:   "Um, Mr. Sid, can you bless my baby? She's got a bad case of jaundice. The doctors say…."

Sid: "Miss, the *true God* does not give me the ability to *bless* anyone. I'm sorry she is ill, but you must let medical doctors…."

Person 1:   [Continuing] "But, can you say a *prayer* for her…to get well soon?"

Sid: "Miss, you don't understand the *true God*. The *true God* does not *answer* prayers. I think it a fair estimate that, *each and every ten seconds* in the world, a billion or more prayers are thought or uttered.

" Answering half would make impossible answering the other half, as one person's wants conflict with those of others. Answering a quarter would interfere with a course the *true God* has set. The *true God* does not favor one individual over another or allow prayers to interfere with *Design*.

"The *true God* would have you find the truth and live by it. There are many truths. Here's one we all can live by: Don't worship the wealthy and influential and don't' follow their indulgences.

"Find the truth and care for your own. Your child is *your* responsibility—not that of the *true God*. Put all your care into the service of your child's recovery and do not let your focus be distracted by anything else."

Person 2:   "Mr., can you really talk to God?"

Sid: "Young lady, no one can speak *with* God, in a *back and forth* exchange, if that's what you mean. Anyone can say things aloud or in their head, with intent to get their God's attention. But the *true God* has little care for what you *intend* to get across.

"The *true God* already knows you, *through and through*. It is up to us to seek and find truth, not to try to have discourse with the *Creator of Universe*. If you are sincere, the *true God* will help you find the truth."

Person 3:   "How do you know so much, if you don't talk to God? Hold it—I know. God talks to *you*, but why? Why *you*?"

Sid:	"Why *not*, me? Why *not, you?* If you set your mind for truth, you receive truth. Truth is blocked by distractions. Why me? I'll answer that I practiced shutting out distractions. In due course, truth settled in. I 'see' thoughts and pictures that I will tell you are from the *true God*. You are free *not* to believe it, if you chose not to. You are free not to accept anything but what you already know."
Person 4:	"I want the truth, too, Sid. But how—? How do I, as you put it, *block distractions?*"
Sid:	"You may or may not be *ready* for truth. Look at the world around you. Study, examine. If you can't make out the distractions to truth, you probably aren't ready for truth."
Person 4:	[Continuing] "I love it when you talk in circles, Sid. I can't see the truth for the distractions. But I need the truth to be able to *see* the distractions. Pardon me for being blunt, but it sounds like you're sort of playing *word games.*"
Sid:	"The games are yours. I didn't say you need truth in order to identify distraction. You need a certain level of sincerity, of desperation, of bravery and intellect. What you *don't* need is to try to misstate my own words back to me. That will not lead you to truth."
Person 5:	[In initial low tones] "That guy's a jerk, Sid. But, look, is it true that you got robbed last night? There's been a lot of talk, Sid. What happened? You look like you got a couple of bruises there."
Sid:	"It was, and is, of no consequence. I stand, of well health, here before you. A woman was shot to death in her own home last night, on Grosser Street. Direct your care to those that need it most."
Person 5:	[Continuing] "But I just—. I *believe* in you, Sid. I *really* do. But it just seems odd that the 'true God' would let you get punched around, and robbed. I mean, why didn't you get a *vision* or something to warn you?"
Sid:	"I would say the *true God* simply chose not to. I do not put expectations on the *true God*. I believe you are confusing the things you expect from *your* God with qualities of the *true God*. The *true God* wants us to find truth and speak

truth. The *true* God is not anyone's personal *keeper*—not mine, not yours."

Person 5　[Continuing]: "I don't understand. Isn't God supposed to *protect* us, if we're his *servants?* I mean, that's why we pray. We pray for protection, forgiveness, and to be led in the right direction. Your '*true God*' doesn't do any of that, huh?"

Sid:　"You left out a hundred *other* things that the *blind* and the *selfish* pray for. But I will not answer, as you are taking time away from the lady behind you. So unless she has the same question—."

Person 6:　"Uh, yes—I think I'd like to know how you answer the question of whether God looks out for us. I mean... He's God. We are His children. He watches over his children—those of us who believe in him and serve him righteously."

Sid:　"Again you are confusing the God you were taught with the *true* God. If what you believe about *your* God is sufficient, you should not be here talking to me. I will tell you that the *true God* does not do favors, but does things, at times, to make a point.

"People break their necks struggling to get what societies say they should have and then when they get it they say God *willed it.* We create the most deadly weapons possible, to date, and when we win the war we say God *willed it.* When we don't get what we want, we say God *has His reasons.* In other words, God *willed* that, too. No matter what the outcome, we are taught to see God in it. That way we never fall out of *supposed* grace, we never feel alone.

"Whether you realize it or not, the idea of being a *servant of the Lord* comes out the Middle Ages in Europe, where Christianity was formalized. The *true God* has no need for servants. You could not serve the *true God* any more than a speck of dust on earth can serve a thousand galaxies. And do not be misled: We all are but specks, *within specks,* of Earth-dust, in the universe.

"But, if you prefer the view of God you were taught, then please get out of line. My talk is only for those who are interested in knowing the *true* God. The *true* God is not your keeper. Man puts up distractions in front of truth. The *true* God only wants you to see *truth*. Then we will know how to treat one another. We will improve life on earth, dramatically.

"Let me be clear: The *true* God does not improve your life. You improve your life—in real ways—only with truth."

Person 7: "I don't mean any disrespect, Sid, but people are saying your true God *kicked the shit* out of that guy what robbed you last night. Now, Sid, come on. Is that protection—or *what?*"

Sid: "I don't expect protection by the *true* God. None of us should. Does the *true* God bring *misfortune* to those who do bad? I would say, instead, that the *true* God has a system set up whereby, when we behave out of certain accord, we set things into motion—dominoes, like—that go around and come around."

Person 8: "No offense, Sid...I love you, man. You know that. But that was one hell of a *domino* that fell on that Potts boy. People are saying your true God zapped the *true piss* out of his godless ass."

Sid: "People say all sorts of things, for all sorts of reasons. You are free to believe what you choose."

Person 9: "I wasn't gonna' say anything about last night, Sid. But, since everybody's bringin' it up—. They say he got three dollars off you, Sid. I remember you said the true God is against money. So...."

Sid: "I believe I said the *true* God is not a *fan* of money. Now I'll say farther that the *true* God is particularly not a fan of *excess* money or excessive preoccupation with accumulating money. I'm shown also that the *true* God disfavors *unearned* money."

Person 9: [Continuing] "But, Sid...you don't have a job. How...?"

Sid: "I do chores of various sorts where I stay—and other places.

	Members of the household in which I grew up compensate me for my work, also."
Person 9	[Continuing] "Oh, I'm sorry, Sid—. I...."
Sid:	"Don't be sorry. Continue to seek truth.

Here was the opportunity for which the Order members waited. For the present phase of Sid's public showcasing, it was designed that he show—or *appear* to show—an even more awe inspiring connection to the *"true God."* All planned-for conditions were in place. Within six storefronts awaiting renovation on both sides of Albert—Sid's official *hangout* block—researchers stood at the ready.

Four of these were located at the corners of Albert at Wine, and Albert at Tilman Avenue. From second story windows, the researchers awaited a signal to act. The final two, of the six buildings mentioned, were more centrally situated within the expanse of edifices. These latter were chosen as sites for displaying some unusual goings on.

Not only was there a growing line and crowd of bystanders, but police were also starting to monitor the spectacle. "News tips" phone numbers were called anonymously by ONES workers, to alert the local TV stations. Just as before, Order members channeled to Sid ideas, to include in his statements:

Plant:	[Shouting from a sideline] "Sounds like you're borrowing from the old *money is the root of all evil* line, Sid. It's funny that many religions state it, but few *in* the religions practice it."
Sid:	"That is not my 'line.' The truth is that currency serves an important purpose in society. But at a point, it becomes a distraction, away from the light that the *true God* would have you see."
Plant:	"Sid, out here, you're totally alone with that idea. Everybody wants as much money as they can get, any legal way they can get it—free or not! "Am I right people?! Let's hear it! Am I right?!"
Sid:	"Those among you who agree with what is just said should not be here blocking the way of those who want *truth*. You are yourselves a *distraction* to truth. I would bid you to

	move on to your money-worshipping pursuits. Leave this ground for truth seekers."
Skeptic:	"How about a little truth *and* a little money from the true God. What's wrong with both?"
Sid:	"You do not listen. You are here for amusement—not truth"
Plant:	"Yeah, and what are ya' gonna' do about it, Sid? I know— nothin'! You and your 'true God' *talk* a good game, but there is not one 'truth seeker' out here who wouldn't stampede over his mother for free money!

"All of you who would turn down *free money*…raise your hand, so the rest of us can leave you here…seeking truth with ol' Sid."

The stage was set. Behind where Sid orated was a boarded up storefront whose windows showed plywood replacements for glass. At the third floor level a narrow slit had been made in all three of the "wood-window" structures. The same slight modification had been made in various areas within bricks of the building's front. Behind each slot was placed a small and simple machine designed to spit stiff bills straight forward. Narrowness of the ejection slots and speed of the bills "fired" through them were designed to obscure the exit point.

The first three seemed to appear out of "nowhere." When the bills landed within the crowd of people and hit the ground it was clear that they were bills of fifty-dollar denomination.

ONES workers found it fascinating to watch the reaction of those staring down at the paper currency. At first everyone looked back and forth at the sky and the money, keeping a little distance from the tender. Many glanced automatically at Sid, recalling his "sermon" on free money.

Finally, while looking suspiciously at his neighbors, a man closest to one of the alluring green bills bent slowly. With arm and hand outstretched, he touched a corner of the money.

From across the street, through an obscured opening in a third-level window, shot a beam. The instrument from which emitted the straight-line stream of concentrated electric current provided dead-level accuracy. It struck squarely at the man's shoulder as he attempted to grasp the bill. Fortunately, the shooter chose to deliver only a mild shock. But it was enough to get the message across. The "message" was to make people wonder if, perhaps, the "money from heaven" had appeared as a warning.

When the crowd saw the man recoil in apparent pain, the people gasped and formed three respectful circles around the three bills.

As to be expected, maybe, with any mostly random gathering of people, there were the risk-takers. Suddenly, a second man lunged forward and snatched up one of the green, paper rectangles bearing the likeness of President U. S. Grant. As he gave it thorough examination, another invisible laser-like beam made contact with his forearm. Yelping in pain, he released his bounty, the latter floating gently to the pavement.

Now, with the crowd completely flustered, Order members felt it was time to act again. Accordingly, they arranged to have several more bills ejected over the roof's edge, just above the crowd.

Paradoxically, the falling money threw the people below into a near panic of apprehension. From across the street in building 225, the ONES watched with much amusement. The spectacle eliciting their laughter was of people ducking and dodging the paths of falling fifty-dollar bills.

In a nearby building on the same side of the street, their laser-wielding cohorts followed the downward movement of each green-hued rectangle. Each person upon whom a fifty happened to fall was "rewarded" with a mild electrical shock. Although it produced barely a sting, the receiver of the *current* magnified it in his or her mind. Later, each would describe the "feel" of the money as akin to a red hot poker boring through the skin.

After a minute of the excitement, the policemen present had seen enough. Employing formal procedures, they ordered everyone who was present to witness Sid's show to disperse.

As for Sid, himself, he showed his cooperation with the police by helping them gather the $700 in fifty-dollar bills. With staid diligence, he turned each one over to officers, who were quite gracious in acceptance of the currency. To say that they handled the paper gingerly would not be an overstatement. Like everyone else on the scene, the police had witnessed the crowds disquieting experience with the bills.

When the first news-crews arrived, they barely caught the tail end of the extravaganza. All that they actually witnessed was the police detouring traffic from the 200 block of Albert, in both directions.

Only barely did they make discernment that it was to keep the more frantic members of the agitated throng from getting run over. Once the erstwhile "money runners" were safely scattered down the streets and around corners, reporters took statements from police officers. They also got what they could from Sid.

From building 225, Order members watched the next unfolding of events. Reporters set up their filming equipment, as before, right near the corner of Albert and Wine. Sid had taken a seat on a storefront step and seemed to reflect on the recent turn of circumstances.

Human traffic in the block was comparatively sparse now. It was comprised of those who actually had destinations beyond the immediate environment. With the calm of conditions, police allowed automobile traffic to resume through the block.

A reporter from local station WSNP spoke into a microphone as his cameraman filmed.

A. Doane: "This is Adam Doane reporting *live* from the two hundred block of Albert, in downtown Crystal. From what I gather so far, a rather stunning occurrence took place right in this very area, just minutes ago. And as you may guess from the location, at the center of it was our city's own Sid Seine. As I speak, Mr. Seine sits right over there. He looks like he's kind of coming to grips with all that has happened.

"I can tell you that crowds were dispersing as we pulled up in the news truck. So it seems that most of those who witnessed the, reportedly, fantastic display felt compelled to leave the scene.

"However, Sid, police officers and a few pedestrians remain. I'm going to see if I can get Officer Tewkes to reiterate the brief description he gave me a minute ago. And believe me folks, you don't want to miss this.

"Uh, oh, the officer's busy right now. But while Officer Tewkes finishes his radio report, I'm going to walk over here right next to Mr. Sid Seine.

"Sir, I wonder if you'd be so generous as to tell us, on camera, what exactly happened here that got everyone so excited. Pulling up, we saw people running every *which* way. ...Oh, let me help you to your feet.

"Folks it looks like Mr. Seine is going to be kind enough to shed some light on the recent occurrence!"

Sid: "Only those who want connection with the truth should come to hear me speak. People came who were merely curious. They sought *entertainment* over truth."

Doane: "Okay, so there was a crowd here, as sometimes there is, that came to listen and maybe ask questions of you. But it sounds like you're saying some numbers of them weren't genuine *truth* seekers. Were there arguments of any sort?"

Sid: "I would say not. The *true* God simply made a point by sending to the *money wolves* what they desired. The point was that *free* money comes with a hidden price to pay. The *true* God rained down upon them fifty dollar bills—along with a measure of pain that came with their touch."

Doane: "Folks, you heard it straight from Sid, here—*money raining from the sky!* Is this *big*—or what?! ...Oh, it looks like Officer Tewkes—my mistake, Sergeant Tewkes—is free to talk with us.

"Sergeant! Sir...please! Can you—? Thank you, sir. Thank you. A few minutes earlier, you said you actually saw money falling on people and causing—by all appearances—painful sensations, upon contact."

Tewkes: "At this time, it is my intention to be—and I'm *going* to be—non-sensationalist in my account. Yes, a number of bills, denomination fifties, fell upon a crowd of people out here earlier. As yet, we have not determined the source. From what I could tell, the money fell from a distance several yards up, or maybe higher.

"As I described earlier, the crowd began to panic and some number of them did appear to experience aversive reactions to contact with the money. I would describe it as not unlike the *hysteria* of groups who believe that an *unnatural* force of some kind is operant in the environment."

Doane: "And I understand you have the bills in your possession. May we film them briefly? They haven't disappeared or anything, I hope—having returned to whatever was the mysterious source."

Tewkes: "No. We are in possession of the bills. So far, they appear very natural, earthly, and manmade, although a bit stiff. Sid, in fact, helped us gather them. And, no, none of the police officers handling the money, nor Sid, experienced any of the seeming distress shown by the former crowd."

Doane: "Right there, folks...you can see them yourself. There are the mysterious fifty dollar bills that, according to report, fell inexplicably from the sky. They do indeed look quite normal.

"May I touch the bills, Sergeant, just out of journalistic curiosity and the enlightenment of our TV viewers?

"Hmm...no mirage here—just plain money, from all tactile and visual appearance. It would be wildly sensational if one were to disappear at my touch, but no such luck. It just feels like what the Sergeant describes as a fresh, crisp collection of fourteen 'U.S. Grants.'

"In any case, we can rest assured that the money will be taken to police headquarters and given a good examination. If it's *funny money* in any way, we're sure to hear about it.

"Uh-oh...wait. It looks like Sid's of a mind to move on. ...Uh, Sid! ...Sid! One more word, sir? ...I guess not.

"But look here. One door closes and another opens. It appears we got ourselves a real live *eyewitness* member of the crowd that was here earlier!

"Ma'am, your name...and what did you see?"

Watching Sid drift away down Albert, the ONES workers were beset with mixed feelings. On the one hand, they were proud of his flawless performance. He had conveyed perfectly the "spiritual opinions" they wanted to disseminate.

But on the other, they were aware of the new *station* to which the latest drama had catapulted him. Nothing in the recent set of events surrounding him suggested his having performed miracles of any sort.

Yet, as the Order had planned, he was likely to be associated with *otherworldliness*, now, more than ever before. Likely, too, it would come at a price.

Vigorously, reporters sought out witnesses to, and participants in, the "falling money scourge," as the incident was dubbed. Taped narratives of those who had been on the scene were totally startling to viewers. Sometimes, though, the effect of news accounts paled alongside person-to-person enlightenments. Whether delivered in private talks or news report, the story's credibility was enhanced by confirming statements by the police.

Thus the story grew wings, so to speak, and soared over the city like the outline of a great, menacing condor.

Immediately after dispensing the bills, the Order's workers went about the task of covering up their deed. Even though the buildings were privately owned, the Order postulated scenarios wherein city officials might call for intrusive investigations. They were at least partially correct. However, from roofs to ground, back and front, no features of the edifices seemed amenable to currency discharges. Nothing was found anywhere to suggest relationship between buildings at the scene and the falling fifties.

The bills were traced to the banks that initially issued them, two years prior. The conclusion drawn: It was likely that they experienced very few hand exchanges in that period. No finger prints were found on the bills and their stiffness seemed the result of processes of preservation. As the money had not been reported stolen or even missing, there was no apparent criminal connection. To Crystal City's law enforcement people and other municipal officials, appearance of the paper money remained a mystery.

Other than Sid's low-profile *regular* attendants, amblers about Albert Street walked a little distance around him when they passed. But that was the case for only a few days after the "falling money scourge." Gradually, people had time to settle their fears of encountering *otherworldly* events, in association with Sid. When finally they did, curiosity and genuine interest in Sid's message compelled them back to stand around Albert's 200 block.

The reestablishment of his audience came first in a trickle. Eventually, the block became, again, so crowded that police were ordered to keep a presence there.

For city officials a dilemma was brewing. They began grappling with the issue of Sid's right *to be Sid* and his constituting a public nuisance. The need to dispatch and maintain a contingent of law enforcers within a single block of the city brought an added municipal expense. Eventually Sid's celebrity was either going to require overtime worked or the hire of extra officers.

That was unless he was deemed a public menace, somehow, and disallowed his sessions of giving "spiritual opinions." With that idea came "visions" of the ACLU fitfully gearing up for an extensive and prolonged legal battle. No member of the city's council wanted that.

In time, reports spread widely of Sid's growing fame as well as accounts of bizarre events said to follow him. It wasn't long before news networks *across the nation* donated at least a small segment of their broadcasts to Sid's mention. Locally, it added to city officials' dismay that people were beginning to come in from *out of town* to experience Sid, firsthand. In keeping with the times, people filmed Sid with small, handheld devices and presented stories of him on the Web.

The Order had prepared well to respond to conditions developing around Sid at this point. At the edge of dawn one morning, he was *remotely* "summoned" to a back alley of the 200 block of Albert. Beyond observation by any except hidden ONES operatives, he entered into a lightless recess between buildings. Once there, a secret portal admitted him inside the rear of one of the abandoned stores on Albert.

Residents of Crystal City, waking to the new day hadn't a clue, as yet, that Sid was at the center of still another strange event. This time, it was his own disappearance. Days, then weeks, would pass with no one seeing hide or hair of the Albert Street "augur." In time, many of the town's residents began to suspect they may never see Sid Seine *live* in Crystal City, again.

Chimerik Heights Cemetery, within the city of Topal, spans nearly a square mile, all total. Inside the gross non symmetry of its boundaries are mostly flat lands, perfectly suited for burials. Other areas, completely devoid of headstones, encompass rolling hills that provide the tranquility of meadowlands. Within, also, are abrupt depressions and elevations in the topography, displaying wide variations of crust—from clay to rock and shale. As if to tie together the disparate cemetery sections, a stream meanders through, until it converges with county drainage, underground.

Two boundary types are incorporated, for defining the cemetery's limits. For most of its expanse, a wall of huge blocks, called *formed-stone*, was erected to separate cemetery from public sidewalks. Fitted and mortared in place a century and a half past, the craggy, gray-black stacked blocks show heights of between five and eight feet. In less refined areas, a wire fence stands as border between cemetery and city overgrowth.

For nearly a hundred years, appointed groundskeepers and their families actually occupied a dwelling located within the cemetery. Constructed of those huge *formed-stones*, the edifice is dark, austere, and quite forbidding, in appearance. Over time, its use as a family residence became untenable. The house of stone came to be used only for storage of materials, and occupied only during working hours. That arrangement prevailed, to the time the cemetery was bought by the *Order of Neo-Euthenics Strategists*.

Within an economically depressed area of Topal, residents were adjusting to a new construction in their midst. At the start of the cold season, city officials initiated construction of an earth-and-concrete design there, known as a *roundabout*. Now, as fall approached, the traffic circle was complete. But folks passing nearby were in for yet another surprise at the site.

At the roundabout's center was a grassy knoll where a cement block memorial sat. On this day, atop the cement block stood Sid Seine, capturing the attention of passersby with his unique brand of oratory. A number of them paused awhile and then moved on. Others stayed to listen and wait for what they knew was the inevitable arrival of police, to unseat the man from his perch. Sid spoke with both confidence and conviction:

Sid: "All within hearing distance take heed. You need to reexamine what you've been taught. Unfortunately, not all of you seek the truth. Not all of you *want* the truth. Not all of you can even *tolerate* the truth. But, for those who do—and can—I give you this warning:

"The *true* God is not like the God you've been taught. Your religions cannot bring you to an accurate understanding of your life or of the God responsible for your *being*.

"I am here today to try to guide *you who want the truth*. How many of you want truth? For those who do, you need to know this: When the *eagles* land, it is a *sign* for you to clear your minds, clear your hearts, clear your spirits.

"Always, the truth starts with the few. These are the few who are not lost in fear—fear of *change in thinking*. These are the few who are skeptical of convention. These are the few who distrust blind acceptance.

"It is all right that some of you laugh, and others shake your heads in pity. Why *wouldn't* you laugh? Why *wouldn't* you pity me? You have been taught to reject the *real* truth. You have been taught to *believe* in *distractions* to truth. I understand that. For I, too, was taught to believe in *distractions* to truth.

"But when I stopped focusing on distractions, I became able to listen to urgings of the *true* God. And the *true* God has told me to tell you that when the *eagles* land, it is to notify us that the time is *at hand*. It is time to deny the distractions to truth and to get our minds ready to acknowledge the *true* God.

"Oh, look, the police are arriving. This is good. I say this is good because there is a time for all things. Right now it is time for the police to tell me that I cannot speak to you in this forum. That is okay. I am not here to break the law, but only to try to prepare you for truth.

"And I believe I have *done* that, for the few of you who are *ready* for truth. I say so because, look above—the *eagles* are preparing to land."

The police officers alighting from their vehicles had not yet seen the harpies gliding about in the sky. They did, however, notice the upturned heads of Sid's audience, folks from the surrounding poor neighborhoods. Sid spoke to them directly:

Sid: "Officers, I came here only to warn the people of the *eagle's landing*—and of the danger in denying *truth*. As you can see, they do prepare to land and, maybe, right here where I sit.

     "Therefore with your approval, I should like, gladly, to turn this block over *to them*. I no more desire a challenge of *their* 'authority' than I desire a challenge of yours."

In his flannel jacket, threadbare pants, and worn, overturned shoes, Sid still appeared as one of the walking indigent. Nevertheless, the officer standing before him hesitantly asked the question. She did this as she and fellow officers gawked in awe at the three eagles now commandeering Sid's former lecturing spot.

Officer: "Are, uh, those your birds?"

Sid: "Oh, no ma'am. I could not afford to keep such fine birds as they. I am a messenger of the *true* God. I came here to tell people that I foresaw *the landing of eagles*. They are a sign that it is time for those who *want* the truth to set their minds for truth. I meant to break no laws, but only to issue the warning until such time that you and the other officers arrived."

No sooner had Sid spoke the latter than the trio of eagles, one by one, leapt upward flapping their wings in startling display. In seconds, they were hundreds of feet in the air and finally flew off to places not determinable.

The officers glanced quizzically around at one another and scratched their heads under their policeman's caps. Finally, they gently urged the crowd to move on, or at least stand where they did not disrupt traffic, human or vehicular.

Officer Luna was not quite finished with Sid. The odd fellow had appeared quite calm, presenting no threat of any kind. His explanation for being in a publicly non-allowed area was strange, to say the least, she thought. Still he had been quite compliant and seemed only to have been interested in warning people of something bizarre—that actually came to pass! What then, she wondered, was the appropriate response for the occasion?

Once Sid had confirmed for her that he wasn't from around the area, he added that he often walked for miles. By his appearance the officer had no trouble believing that. Clearly he wasn't one of the regulars she encountered in her patrol of the city's Meezley section. Yet, something about him seemed a tad familiar.

Finally, before letting him go on his way, with a warning, the officer asked for Sid's I.D. He showed a dilapidated social security card and another indicating his occasional employment cleaning grounds around Chimerik Heights Cemetery. At that point Luna was mulling over two points: One was that Chimerik Heights was two miles eastward; the other was the seeming familiarity of the name, James Sidney Seine.

Free to go as he pleased, Sid ambled two city blocks in the comfortable outside cool. He could "feel" the stares of those who had heard his speech, as he leisurely put distance between them and him. When he was sure no one was watching, he stepped into an unmarked van parked at a corner. Through tinted windows he watched the inner city scenery pass by until the vehicle reached the cemetery.

When the van rode through the open gates of Chimerik Heights Cemetery, it moved slowly to an area not visible from outside. There, Sid disembarked; and as he was "programmed" to do, he walked to the entrance of a large mausoleum. The palm of his right hand he pressed against a black porcelain plate. With the lock mechanism disengaged, Sid pushed open the door and walked nonchalantly inside. This heated and lighted abode was where Sid now lived and received guidance and programming from the Order.

As ONES mission-planners admitted at meetings, the *Created Faith Project* was expensive. They tallied the cost to date. At the top was acquisition of state of the art laboratory equipment, required from the outset. After recruitment of scientists, engineers and technicians, salaries had to be disbursed. Then, there were the other required workers: monitors, observers, engagers, sympathizers, eagle trainers, and collaborating bit-players. All, of course, required reward. The process of ensuring dedication and loyalty was long and costly.

The *Order of Neo-Euthenics Strategists* aspired to a very lofty goal. What they sought was no less than a *turning point* in social evolution. An *epoch*, one might call it, a *major leap forward* in the *spiritual* thinking of mankind. Given a successful mission, poverty over the world could be virtually eliminated. And if not overcome, it might be reduced to tiny, stubborn pockets, situated here and there, over the planet. These, in turn, could be expected to disintegrate within the throes of their own social upheavals. In short, the ONES foresaw and planned for a new *world order.*

Through the Order's brand of mind control, when, and whether or not, Sid left the cemetery was under facile control. Outside its boundaries, it was arranged that he should never be left unmonitored. Within, much care had been taken to provide Sid a comfortable, if modest, existence. Indeed, he found complete serenity in his day and evening wanderings through the cemetery.

Sid had been advised that the "true God" provided him followers, now, in the literal sense. These were individuals, men and women, who understood his mission of preparing people for truth. Outside the cemetery, they were always somewhere nearby. By means of the Order's special communication, it was arranged that he would know them, on sight.

Regarding the Order's *thought transfer* process, the technology involved, now, was the same as that employed at 225 Albert Street. Here, however, the transmission *source* was not a renovated downtown store, but an unimposing building that stood just outside a section of the cemetery. Rather than transmitting, remotely, across a busy downtown street, signals wafted over a quiet and narrow lane running alongside an area of the cemetery wall. From the two-story office building on Olive Lane, they spread into and throughout the still and quiet graveyard.

The *landing-eagles* event triggered recall in some of the observers. That which followed was a kind of chain reaction wherein the memories of successive individuals and groups were jogged. As mentioned, Sid's exploits in Crystal City had achieved notoriety nationwide. News organizations about the world had felt compelled to give Sid's activities at least *some* press.

In wide-eyed wonderment, people concluded that the central figure in the "falling fifties phenomenon" had resurfaced. Even though four states lie between the former and newer site of strange occurrences, there seemed an undeniable link. Would there be more sightings of the enigmatic man in their city, Topal residents asked. Or had theirs been just one stop along some mysterious itinerary that Sid followed?

ONES workers meant to answer those questions as soon as was strategically possible.

Sid was made to believe that his "true God" had mysteriously arranged a sort of freelance employ of him at Chimerik Heights Cemetery. During the cold days of winter past, he stayed mostly in his warm mausoleum "flat" writing on, and trying to organize his insights from, the *true God*. On clement days, he had helped keep the inside grounds clean, but it was clandestine and beyond work hours of regular cemetery employees.

On a blustery Saturday evening, Sid intercepted a "spiritual impression," wafting from the building at 111 Olive Lane. It concerned a two-hour stretch leading to 1:30 p.m. the next day, Sunday. The message advised Sid that it was time, again, to tidy the *outside* boundaries of his "Eden." The impression Sid got was that the act was to be more token than trial, more ritual than rigor. Presented to him, too, was this idea: Somewhere in the strict confines of two hours duration, he should watch for the "right" occasion for sharing his understanding of the *true God*.

It was now Sunday, approaching 12:40 p.m. Sid had started at a far western end of the cemetery picking up debris and moving back eastward. Having worked his way down a half mile, Sid added moderately to the city's wire-bodied trash receptacles. With broom and long-handled pan, he scooped up paper and cans and bottles and like items. Right at the intersection of Wicker and Olive, Sid had raised the contents of a can to near full. Among the discarded items he dutifully pitched into the receptacle was a large, broken picture frame.

At 12:45 this day, the double doors of a church facing Wicker Road opened, and the faithful began a tranquil flow down the long stairs. Chimerick Heights Cemetery, just across the wide street, might well have been blocks away, rather than several yards. It was due to the congregation's predominant focus at this time on church matters.

The cemetery expanse would have garnered no more of the members' attention this day than any other, had it not been for the odd occurrence across the road. A few of the church members noticed the poorly dressed man with broom and pan and trash bag standing before the gray-black cemetery wall. That something perplexed him was evident.

Some watched as the man leaned slightly, apparently staring at a section of the great stones. They saw him step back to appraise it from a more distant perspective. Placing his cleanup articles down, he paced a little and returned to stare anew. He scratched his head appearing to be in total bewilderment. Finally, watching for any approaching cars, he carefully backed to the middle of Wicker Road to view the wall from an even farther distance.

By now, most of the church folk standing about the base of their *House of God* had become intrigued by Sid's activity. One of them took the initiative to venture dialogue with Sid from the street curb. In time, others followed:

Mr. Noten: "Excuse me, sir. You seem to be having a heck of a time trying to figure something out across the street, there. After watching you the past minute, I have to say, you've got me curious. You mind saying what is at that wall that's so...befuddling?"

Sid: "One of the stones appears to show an image. It looks rather *definite*, as a matter of fact. But I just don't understand it. I've walked and swept up and picked up along this pavement before. And this is the first time I've noticed this...oddity."

Mr. Tithy: "Well, big ol' stones like that, with all the bumps and crevices, are bound to show configurations that remind us of one thing or another. What kind of picture are you seeing?"

Sid: "I...don't even think I want to say. A thing like this causes people to...."

Mr. Noten: "How about a few of us going over and taking a look at it with you. It's probably one of those cases where, if you look at it a different way, you see a whole new pattern.

    "Oh, by the way, I'm Noten...Louis Noten. That's Mr. Tithy. This is Mr. and Mrs. Vaner. Over there is Mr. Probeson. ...And, your name, sir?"

Sid: "Sid...James Sid Seine. Everyone calls me Sid."

Mr. Vaner: "Well, Sid, let's have a look at your 'picture.' Where exactly...? Oh...oh, my—."

Mrs. Vaner: "You see something, Frank? I must not be looking in the right place. ...Oh, I do see a sort of.... What is—?"

The idea had struck Sid to retrieve the broken wood picture frame from the nearby trash can. Having acted on the whim, he was now back among the growing number of the faithful-curious, approaching the cemetery wall. He positioned the frame to focus attention solely on the image he saw, in the stone.

Mr. Tithy: "Jesus, Lord...I see it clearly, now!"

Mrs. Vaner: [gasping] "Oh, my God. I'm starting to feel faint, Frank. This is beyond astounding. But... all this time...right across the street—. How long? How long has it been here? How long have we been unaware—?"

Mr. Noten: "Mr....*Seine*—am I calling it right, your name, I mean?

Sid: "Sid."

Mr. Noten: "Sid, you have made a tremendous *discovery* here. An image, although faint, uncannily resembling the face in the famous *Shroud of Turin*—this is wondrous, perhaps a miracle!"

Mr. Tithy: "I'm taking a picture of this. Sid, good buddy, could you hold that frame there once more, while I capture this with my cell-phone camera?"

Sid: "I do it with some reservation, considering I think you-all are moving too hastily to conclusions. I only wanted you to see a *curiosity*—not to promote your belief in miracles or the supernatural."

Mrs. Fleating: "Mr. ...Sid, you almost sound apologetic. Do you realize what you have discovered here? Right across the street from Gospel Holy Savior Church, you have found the image of...*the Savior!* Do you see the near ecstasy in the people here? Some tremble. Some appear to be in shock. A number of us are in tears!

"You warn us not to leap to conclusions? The conclusion is before us! The image of *the Christ* has appeared to show us that our faith is justified!"

Sid: "I suspect that something has occurred as a fluke, as a thing happening purely by chance. That is the case under

	the best circumstance. At worse, it may be nothing more than deliberate trickery. I would not allow myself to get fat with delusion and unfounded hope."
Mr. Beltol:	"What are you, some kind of present-day *Doubting Thomas?* The image is unmistakable—right there before you! …Oh, it's faint—sure, it's faint. But, it's *there*, and it's true! And, you're the one who saw it first! And yet you stand there and deny that which is as plain as the nose on your face!"
Sid:	"The nose on my face has not been altered to look like that which it is not."
Ms. Cross:	"We shouldn't be listening to him. He cleans streets on the Sabbath at a time when he should be worshipping the Lord in the House of the Lord. What does he know of the power of Christ, for giving spiritual signs to the faithful?
	"I say we call the news stations. This miracle needs to be broadcast all over—as far as possible. Everyone must be made aware that *Christ is Lord*—and is *here!* The only begotten *Son of God* is here, among us!"
Sid:	"But, the *true God* has no *begotten* son. All who have left the womb are equal in the eyes of the *true God.*"
Mr. Noten:	"Whoa, there, Sid, my friend. You don't want to be saying that—not after the great thing you've done for us out here."
Sid:	"Mr. Noten, I *do* want to be saying it. I *must* say it. And I *will* say it. The *true God* has never impregnated a virgin with the seed of a child. The *true God* has set rules for us to learn and live by. And they start with learning to recognize distractions to the truth.
	"The two-thousand year old story of the *virgin birth* is a distraction. The idea of resurrection is a distraction. This wall image seemingly related thereto is a distraction."
Mr. Beltol:	"And you are *worse* than a distraction! You are a fool—a blithering, babbling fool who sees and still believes *not*."
Sid:	"Will one among you who believes me to be a fool allow me the opportunity to justify my skepticism? Is a Sabbath day street-cleaner worth that much?"
Mr. Noten:	"Ms. Cross didn't mean it as a *put down* when she referenced

	your work. Any and all honest work is good. I'll even say blessed. Don't you agree, Esther?"
Ms. Cross:	"You're right. I wasn't trying to demean cleaning the streets, but when someone appears to be denying *Christ*, that gets me *hot*."
Sid:	"Why should you care if someone denies Christ?"
Ms. Cross:	"Why should I care?! ...*I'm a soldier of Christ*, that's why!"
Sid:	"And what does that make your Christ: The supreme *medieval* knight...king...*commander of warriors*? Is he, for that reason, weakened by denials of his supremacy?"
Ms. Cross:	"I'm beginning to think that you are a very sick man, *Mr. ...Sid*—or worse, maybe an *evil* one. You'd better take heed of the discovery you just made. *Jesus* is trying to reach you, probably you, first, before the rest of us. You'd better take heed. Hell awaits *ye of little faith*."
Sid:	"Hell is a *myth*...just like the image here on the wall. A bottle of turpentine, perhaps even plain rubbing alcohol, can expose the wall. ...Only reason and intellect can expose the *entire* myth of the Satan's *Fall from Grace* ."
Mr. Tithy:	"Don't go there, Sid. Let's just stick with the wall. I'm sensing foul moods out here. So...now, you're saying the image has been, somehow, painted on? Uh...I'm just not seeing it."
Sid:	"*I* did not see it at first. But as I examine it more and more closely, I see a clever ruse. It is the work of very skillful hands, perhaps more than just two, over who knows how much time. I think I see the fine chiseling strokes of a sculptor beneath the deceptive handiwork of, perhaps, a portrait painter."

At just this time, a news van from a local TV station pulled to the traffic light at Wicker and Sinnert. From where they awaited a green light, the crew could see the clusters of finely dressed church-goers milling along the pavement bordering the cemetery.

Some of the crowd stood partly in the street near the curb. Other bands of the faithful had returned to the church side of the street after getting their pictures of the wall "phenomenon." Most of them seemed to grapple with feelings of uncertainty. Their quandary was similar to one inherent in an age-old question: Should the *Second Coming* be awaited with a sense of immediate expectation or with relaxed conviction that it was far in the future?

The news-van driver coasted slowly across Wicker Road. As the van approached its destination, it gently prompted the movement of people standing in its path. With the length of the vehicles' passenger-side resting on the sidewalk, the reporter and photographer emerged.

Someone among the church members had called in the news tip that a *Christ-image* was mysteriously on display, on a cemetery wall. Via cell phone internet capability, pictures taken of the anomaly were *e-sent* by that same tipster. Coincidentally, an anonymous call made from 111 Olive was made to the same TV station, regarding the wall phenomenon. As was evident, those calls were compelling enough to result in the dispatch of a small investigative team.

The news crew worked with practiced diligence. Amid excited onlookers, a tripod camera was duly erected. As he had done a score of times before, the reporter prepared microphones into which to speak and by which to take statements. Although they weren't, as yet, certain they had a story worth airing on television, the team forged ahead.

Minutes earlier, church members stood before the wall image in an arc of ever changing wall-watchers. Now, they slowly relinquished the area. For them, Sid's words had sprinkled unholy water on the fire of their spiritual excitement. Nevertheless, they mustered hopes of being recorded as *first-on-the-scene* eyewitnesses to that which would prove to be a miracle.

Up to now, only a handful of the faithful found Sid oddly familiar. They were hard-pressed, however, to come up with a significant link, at just this point. For them, like most everyone else, news stories originating *out-of-state* had a limited recall-life.

However, news reporters often show a longer retention of quirky, weird incidents, broadcasted from far away places. Likewise, memory of faces associated with those happenings may stay with them longer. As Sam Minski of channel 15 took in the scene of the crowd and the seedily dressed man standing out among it, something clicked, so to speak. Minski spoke into his handheld mike but gazed intently as Sid:

Minski: "Excuse me, sir. Am I hallucinating or are you the man once dubbed the *Crystal City Seer?*" .

Sid: "I am known best as Sid Seine."

Minski: "Oh, my God! You *have* reappeared! And here you are, just like in the news footage I remember from months ago, once again in the middle of an excited throng of local folks!

"Bernie, get a good close-up of Mr. Sid Seine, here. We got ourselves the man who was at the center of that *falling money* mystery a while back. This is astounding!

"You folks watching this at home—standing inexplicably before us is *Crystal City Sid.* It was some months ago, but doubtless a number of our viewers will recall the unbridled excitement Mr. Seine here generated, back where he comes from.

"His hair-raising feats and messages started there. But news of them spread across the nation, rather like a meteor lighting up the skies from Washington, D.C. to Seattle. And then, suddenly—and, of course, mysteriously, this being Sid Seine—he disappeared. The light just went out with the same flash with which it appeared—poof.

"After several weeks passed, everyone thought it was over."

Now, clusters of the faithful, recently sedate, began to show agitated movement and apprehension. Recall of the Sid Seine *mystery* began to flood into awareness. Their blessed event was now a coin with two sides—the face of *Christ* on one, that of *Sid* on the other. For many, the mixed emotion was excruciating. They didn't know now whether to expect blessings or a curse—or some combination of the two, bound to thrust one into an intolerable purgatorial state, spiritually.

Sam Minski continued his talk to future TV viewers, at such time that the segment aired.

Minski: "Before delving headlong into this current case, I'd like to remind viewers of something else that happened a couple of weeks ago. It was here, in Topal, in the Meezley section. There was this guy standing on a monument, in a *roundabout*, predicting the arrival of...of all things...a bunch of eagles! And according to police report—it happened!

"Now Mr. Seine, something tells me that the one thing *that* incident and *this* one have, *in common*, is *you*. I'm right, aren't I?"

Sid: "Everywhere I've been, everywhere I go, I have the same mission. It is to speak of the *true God* to those who want truth. It was the case at the sight where the eagles landed. It is true here."

Minski: "I don't mind telling you, Sid, sir—this is a thrill! You are just like in the footage I remember from the Crystal City interviews. Look at my hands! I'm actually starting to tremble a little. But, hey, let's not let that get in the way of progress.

"Now, folks, we get to the matter at hand. Bernie, my cameraman, has been periodically turning the camera at the wall behind me.

"Uh, this lady looks like someone *in the know*. Ma'am, I wonder if you'd like to speak into the mike to tell what all the excitement has been about, here?"

Ms. Vokall: "Well, it's one of the stones in that wall—one right near the top. It has the image of...it appears to have the *facial* image of *Christ*, as depicted on the Shroud of Turin. That man there, Sid, he was the one that first saw it."

Minski: "Holy Moses, you've got to be kidding. Let's get a close-up of the stone this nice lady is talking about, Bernie. Which one ma'am? Can someone point it out?

"Okay, what is this? Mr. Seine's got something in his hand there. He's attaching the sides of some kind of broken frame. Oh, okay, he's going to literally *frame* the place on the stone that shows the image. Alright, alright...let's see.

"Holy sh...! Yikes! This is...this, folks, is positively breathtaking! *You see it for yourselves*—well, I hope you do. It's faint, but I can make it out. A *relief* design, in stone, of the image burned into the Shroud of Turin!

"Oh my God! Sid...you have outdone yourself, this

time. You are *the news figure of the decade,* as far as I'm concerned."

Sid: "But, sir, you don't really have news here. You have a hoax. I've been cautioning the people standing around not to indulge their penchant for delusion. I offer you the same caveat."

Earlier, a teenaged member of the church had heard Sid say that a proper cleaning solution might help prove his disclaiming statements. It wasn't long before the boy had recall of paint and related items stored in the church basement. Unlike the adults, who were caught up in believing a sign of God was present, the youngster became more curious than captivated. Accordingly, he repaired to the church basement and retrieved a canister of paint thinner.

In a gesture whose timing couldn't have been better if preplanned, the teen appeared before Sid with his elixir.

Sid: "Paint thinner? This, for me, is as astounding as the view of the stone is, for you. How fitting it is that the means to expose the fraud is provided by a youth. It is perhaps a sign that it shall take *future generations* to reform the lies and erroneous beliefs of the past."

Minski: "Incredible, folks! This event just...*generates its own continuing suspense.* So, let's look again at the backdrop: a church of God, recently exiting church members, *Chimerik Heights Cemetery,* an apparent image of *Christ,* in *stone—* and Sid Seine! Can it get better?!

"But now we have a twist. Sid Seine, here, believes that the image is not a miraculous manifestation at all. By all appearance he is positioning himself to prove that the *Christ*-image has been, well, *manufactured!*

"As you can see, Mr. Seine has taken a cleaning cloth from his pocket and dowsed it with paint thinner. And let me not fail to mention that the liquid comes from no other place than the church across the street, delivered by a young member of the church.

"Get a shot of this young fellow, Bernie. ....Good, good.

Folks, this youngster cared enough to go out of his way to help shed light on this mystery.

"What is your name, young man? ...Matt? ...Matthew Peter? Okay, this is getting down right spooky, now. ...But, let's look back at Sid. He's daubing the cloth with thinner...rubbing parts of the stones that *surround* the one with the mysterious image. ...Nothing shows on the cloth. ...He daubs again, now an area of the Christ image.

"Oh...my...God! He's showing us the cloth. It's smudged with what looks like gray-black paint...just as Sid predicted!

"Now he points out where it looks as though some scraping of the stone has been performed. From what I'm seeing, the conclusion to be drawn here is the one of which Sid forewarned.

"The stone was doctored to give the effect witnessed earlier. ...But who? ...And why? And how marvelous it is that all this happens in conjunction with the reemergence of the *mystery man of the decade!*

"Give us your thoughts, Sid. I hope you don't mind my addressing you so informally. Right now you just seem so much a *man of the people*...of the *common* man. Will you grace us with your idea of what to make of all this?"

Sid: "As always, I say this: the world's societies have set up countless distractions to truth—many unintentional and many intentional. Those who really want truth—truth that is free from taint—must forsake distractions. Only then can we come to understand better the *true God* and how we should act in the world."

Minski: "Whew! There you have it, folks. The man that speaks like a real *prophet*—and speaks to us right here in Chimerik Heights. He's moved on from the interview, though. Seems to be searching for something. Oh, okay...a broom...a trash collection pan....

"Well, I'll be a bug in a mug if Sid's not out here working! He's tidying up the sidewalk. He's employed! Honest work for honest pay, I'd wager. And he took the time to find, and solve, a *mystery* right in the middle of it. Call me crazy, but I think I've found my hero.

"I'm going to respect his apparent wish to disengage from the interview. But for better or worse, whether right or wrong, I doubt this is a man likely to be ignored, while he's in town.

"I'm Sam Minski—*Channel 15 News*, reporting at the site of the Chimerik Heights Cemetery."

As the reporting reached conclusion, various groups of church members scattered in silence. Having made their own examinations of the erstwhile "miracle stone," they drifted in various directions, some back across Wicker Road. Generally, their mood was solemn. The supposed reason for their former excitement was dashed. A new and important justification in the physical world for their religious faith was denied. The feeling was akin to symptoms of withdrawal from effects of a powerful drug.

While the news crew collected equipment, some of the faithful climbed the long ascension of church steps. From there, they decided collectively to watch Sid for awhile and ponder his having turned up in their city.

Some noted the time, 1:17, on this mildly cool Sunday. It didn't register in their conscious thoughts that the cemetery's typical weekend gate opening was thirteen minutes away. Even if it had registered, they couldn't have known there would be a link between that time and Sid's upcoming disappearance. In their subtle surveillance, they made only the assumption that he was employed by the cemetery.

Ignoring the slow and idling pace of people newly arriving on the scene, Sid resumed his work. Periodically, he glanced at his watch to keep abreast of the time. At 1:25 Sid headed for the office building on Olive Lane, just off Wicker. Very nonchalantly he entered a gate that was part of a tall wooden fence surrounding the building. By all appearances, Sid was returning to the place from which he had launched his clean-up efforts. After a few yards distance, he was at a back area of the edifice and out of sight of all onlookers.

At this ground level of the building was an indented space, a recessed area, in the back wall. With dimensions of a typical doorway, its depth was thirty inches. Once inside, to the right was a similar space. Sid now stood within this second recess. Before him was an obscure door without a knob or even hinges. He placed his hand against a porcelain panel, and a portal slid open leaving a space so narrow, it could only be entered in a sidewise posture.

Once inside, with the portal closed, Sid followed a path that descended gradually. Under the office building it ran, as well as beneath the width of Olive Lane and a section of the cemetery wall. After ascension of the tunnel back to ground level, it terminated inside a mid-sized mausoleum. The latter itself had three places of entrance and exit. These were all elements of a set-up affording Sid the luxury of secrecy, in entering and exiting the graveyard as he so desired, beyond prying eyes.

Although ONES project managers planned for Sid to stir much attention within his newly adopted town, keeping him a phantom was top priority. They had reasons for not wanting people to know that he lived *inside* the cemetery. Many people, they assumed, would postulate a connection between Sid and the facility. Nevertheless, just as the Order desired, they could never be sure exactly what it was. As before, in Crystal City, people would know his "haunts," so to speak. But unlike before, no one outside of the Order could now be certain where he studied, meditated and slept.

Quite to the satisfaction of the Order, Sid was learning well the content-ideology of the "revelations" he received. The ONES had by now been transmitting to him the tenets of a new philosophical faith for over a year. As planned, and hoped, he was voicing particulars of the doctrine to which he had been wed, with increasing *independence*. That is, he no longer required line by line prompts. More and more his mind was saturated in an understanding of a new *reality*, imported through thoughts and suggestions from ONES workers.

But as the Order determined, practice made perfect. Sid would have to engage in more "teaching" events before being judged ready to enter the next phase of his planned-for odyssey.

When the segment aired on Sid's involvement in the *Christ image* incident, it almost immediately went national. The *pauper prophet* was back and as controversial as ever. Word traveled fast also of the last place Sid was seen, on the day of the taping.

Onlookers had watched him enter a side gate of grounds surrounding the office building at 111 Olive Lane. From there, they determined, he must have found another exit point and faded into the general community. A consensus was reached that Sid must be employed in some capacity by those running the business offices for the cemetery. If so, a number of the curious wanted to know more about it.

Soon, employees at the Chimerik Heights Cemetery office began to get a lot of attention. Unfortunately, in terms of business, these weren't potential customers, but people asking about Sid. In response, answers were given as routinely as the questions were issued:

"Is he a salaried employee at the cemetery?"

"No, he is given a few dollars for sweeping up outside the cemetery on weekends and some Mondays."

"Does he do any work *inside* the cemetery?"

"No, the groundskeeper hires salaried people to maintain the grounds inside."

"When did Sid first appear at Chimerik Heights Cemetery?"

"It was sometime during last winter. No one made specific note of it."

"Does Chimerik Heights Cemetery provide Sid shelter?"

"No."

"Do any of you know where he lives, where he stays?"

"No."

"Are there specific conditions of his work that he understands and follows?"

"There are no specific conditions. He sweeps the sidewalks and picks up litter from other areas around the cemetery. Someone who works here is almost always coming or going and sees him working. Or sometimes we just see the result of what we assume as his cleaning up.

"You must realize that the few dollars he receives from us may be seen, somewhat, as a charitable donation."

"So, the whole thing is very informal, you're saying."

"Mr. Seine just...visits at the office some mornings and Mr. Seeds gives him a few dollars. Mr. Seeds is the pay disbursements officer for CHC."

"And this arrangement has been in effect for how long now?"

"If Mr. Seeds were here, I think he'd estimate: since some time the past winter."

"When did you-all realize that your…employee was the famed James Sid Seine of Crystal City?"

"Until the TV report some days ago, we had no knowledge of Mr. Seine's identity. We just took him to be someone down on his luck, willing to do a service for a few dollars each week—no more, no less."

"Well, now that you know who your employee is, how might it affect your arrangement with him?"

"We don't anticipate any changes. It has always been up to Sid whether or not he wants to provide the cleaning up service. If he wants to continue, I don't see Mr. Seeds having any problem with it."

"You do realize that Sid Seine is something of a celebrity—albeit of the most unconventional sort."

"That's Mr. Seine's issue, not ours. We simply wish him the best…in whatever *legal* endeavors he undertakes."

To throw off individuals scouting about the cemetery for signs of Sid, the Order secretly transported him by van to various surrounding areas. There, they found inconspicuous places to which to deposit him, unseen by anyone nearby. As usual a group of ONES workers was also dispatched to keep watch over him.

By now, these periodic excursions had become routine to him. Sid knew his mission to be that of enlightening anyone desiring truth, as it pertained to revelations from the *"true God."* It had, for him, become his only reason for being.

In its *Brunswick* section, the city of Topal could boast a popular attraction. It was a small, natural lake visited by Topal residents from all over. Although originally formed by geography, it had manmade appurtenances that addressed issues of maintenance and appearance.

Above ground, a fountain rose from Clary Lake's center, upon which shone lights of various colors. Viewed amid surrounding trees and acres of grass "carpet," the lake was a pleasure to behold. Underground, a series of pipes kept the lake at a constant level, employing a filtering system that maintained the lake's touted sky-blue near-transparency.

Significantly, as will be seen, the central facility for operating the lake's system of pipes and water treatment was a typical concrete "pump house." Cleverly hidden by brush, the blandness of its construction subtracted neither from the lake's attractiveness nor its surrounding beauty.

The Order arranged the venue of Sid's next wonder to be Clary Lake. Methodically, they scheduled it for a Thursday afternoon in May, for purposes related both to weather and lake maintenance. Early the next morning, Friday, city crews would begin making sure Clary Lake was ready for weekend festivities. In contrast, from Tuesday to Thursday, only minimal and cursory municipal attention was paid to the lake and surrounding park. Armed with this knowledge, the ONES planned painstakingly over several months, for Sid's "event."

At about 2:00 p.m. Sid exited an unmarked van of the cemetery, on a street leading to Clary Park. He went immediately into the front door of an apartment building, one within a row that stretched a block. Through a dimly lit hallway he moved and descended a stairwell. From there, he exited a back door, just as it was planned for him to do. Unhurriedly, he walked toward the nearby park and its locally famous lake.

Activity within Clary Park was the same this day as any other weekday showing clement weather. That is, people sat, sauntered and jogged within and around its borders. It wasn't long before Sid, in his conspicuously shabby attire, attracted attention.

By now, most everyone who watched a TV set from time to time had heard of Sid. He was the wanderer who toted messages like a businessman totes a brief. To many, these bordered on weird, were decidedly nonconventional, and seemed mocking of religious beliefs. Still, some number the *hoi polloi* was attracted to the rhetoric, despite the offended feelings they may have harbored.

Without fail, when Sid walked about the city, he came upon an amiable and enterprising soul who'd ask the inevitable question: "You're *Sid*, aren't you?" Before long, others would join the ambling pair until Sid had an audience with whom to stop and conduct discourse. More often than not, this continued until Sid had presented all that he would. At that point he remarked something like:

"I must be getting on, now. My present mood leaves me with no more to say at this time."

This day was no exception, regarding Sid's tendency to attract attention. A woman taking her child for a walk initiated conversation with Sid. Her demeanor, at first, was tentative, wary, but soon apprehension gave way to eager willingness. She could see that Sid had no interest in her other than to respond to her musings. Slowly they walked toward Sid's destination, exchanging comments with ease. Others recognizing Sid joined in the procession, captives of their own curiosity.

All around, timepieces read 2:11 but walking and talking with Sid seemed to have a timeless quality for his entourage. Presently, Sid's initial stroll-mate made this comment:

Audrey T.:   "I just don't understand how, if you know so much about the *spirit*, you can put down people's religion."

Sid: "Religions are *manmade* constructs. And like any other manmade construction, it has faults. Why would you think your religion is perfect?"

Audrey T.:   "I.... Well, I...."

Sid: "No need to answer. You think your religion is perfect simply because it makes you feel *better* about it and *more certain* about it. Typically, we believe and *believe in* what makes us feel good."

Devin Y.:   "And what makes what you offer any different? Yours is probably a *feel good* set of beliefs, too."

Sid: "Actually, it's not, if you really understand it."

Jennifer D.:   "So, your message about the 'true God' is, what, a feel *bad* construction?"

Sid: "It's the *truth*. The truth is not always an occasion for happiness."

Audrey T.:   "How do you...conclude that a faith that's been around for one...two or more thousand years has less *truth* than something you've been studying for, what, just a *few years?*"

Sid: "Old religions come out of old times. And they come out of the old, stagnant minds of, often, old men who helped shape them. Now when *old* comes with selfless wisdom, *old* is a good thing. But here is what we need to understand:

    "Selfless wisdom follows from having no self*ish* agenda. It follows from being able to *see through* the distractions *caused* by selfish agendas. Religions were, and are, created by people with selfish agendas."

Audrey T.:   "How can you say that? What gives you the authority to say what was selfishly derived?"

Sid: "Knowledge. Reason. *Common sense.* Religions were, and are, developed to control. Wherever there is control of people based on faith, the opportunity to advance selfish aims abounds. Religious leaders are typically self-serving, first and foremost. They have great stake in perpetuation of the religion—*to preserve their status.*"

Jonathan W.: "Sid, without religion, this world would explode into a barrage of immoral acts, one after another, the next worse than the last. Now, I *know* that's the truth. *Reason* and *common sense* tell me that."

Sid: "People need a source of firm control. Religions can provide it, whenever and wherever there is no properly enforced law, and no *rule of law.* But once *just* laws are in effect, it is not religions that make people behave, it is law and enforcement.

"Perhaps you've gotten the notion that most immoral acts are committed by people who profess no religion. If you revisit that position, you may find errors."

Jonathan W.: "Immoral acts are committed by people who don't *truly* have religion or faith."

Sid: "I'll line a million people up all over the world one day, and I'll ask you to accurately point out those who *truly have religion and faith.* You won't be able—not accurately—to do it until you research their deeds. That's according to your last statement.

"I don't know if your *reasoning* tells you what I'm getting at. But if faith is defined by deeds, then religions should be replaced by the recorded histories of everyone's acts. Because those histories would define what they truly believe."

Arthur B.:   "Let's hear your message again, Sid. What should we believe, according to you?"

Sid: "According to what I perceive from the *true God,* we should suspend beliefs, or at least set them down in a corner, in *quiet time,* like an unruly child. The mind of man is not currently fit to devise and truly follow an elaborate system of theology. He is especially ill-equipped to adhere faithfully and intelligently to one *man*-made eons ago."

Devin Y.: "Somebody's going to wind up putting *you* in *quiet time*— for keeps. Don't you realize that people are as invested in their religion as someone with a billion dollars tied up in the stock market? Nobody's trying to hear your crazy talk."

Sid: "Then they shouldn't listen to it. Everyone's 'billion' is safe from me. If people want to hear the truth, they should hear me. If they are satisfied with the 'truth' they've been taught since birth, they should ignore me.

"My guess is that you *like* to get angry. Why else would you place yourself among these listeners?"

Jennifer D.: [after some seconds] "I guess that guy could tell by the looks on everyone's faces that he was on the wrong 'bus.' Now, Sid, can we get back to my snide comment about the *feel bad* message from your 'true God'? Is it basically that *reality bites*?"

Sid: "Well, that and more. Human beings, like *other* animals, are *pleasure seekers*. Or, perhaps more specifically, the *brain and mind* are pleasure seekers. Our desire for pleasurable experiences drives us in two ways that are important to keep focus on.

"One, it has the power to override our sense of morality, ethics, decency and common sense. Two, we build structures—or institutions—in our societies that allow us to indulge desires in socially acceptable ways.

"Now in the course of building those 'structures,' our attention from certain *truths* have to be diverted. That condition brings what the *true God* reveals to me as distractions to truth."

Wendy K.: "Examples, Mr. Sid? Can you give examples of the 'structures' in society that allow indulgence of our deep, dark, delicious desires?"

Sid: "Let's start with sexual desire.

Wendy K.: "Yes. ...By all means.

Sid: "Well—just briefly—it is made permissible through the institution of committed, legally binding unions. Another *societal structure* is professional sports. These satisfy desires for alignment with power, although it is mainly symbolic. Through professional sports, aggressive impulses are made acceptable, both actually and vicariously.

     "Extreme interest and engagement in politics satisfies the need to feel powerful as well as align with powerful others. You've heard the term, 'dog eat dog world,' in reference to getting ahead professionally. It speaks to a sort of civil depravity that is socially acceptable.

     "A few individuals, relatively speaking, *love* war, as it justifies the desire and urge to kill those who disagree with and oppose values held by their own group.

     "The great multitude of restaurants in evidence the world over is a testament to our animal-like desire to *feed* constantly."

Charles A: "*Damn*, Sid...I mean...wow! Sooo...if I'm following correctly, your point is that, as you see it, all these social institutions come with distractions to the truth."

Sid: "They come with distractions to truth, as it is revealed to me by the *true God*."

Audrey T.: "Okay, you know something, Sid? Right now, we need to talk about the 'true God.' What is the difference between your *true God* and the God that everybody over the world acknowledges?"

  By this time, Sid and his collection of inquirers-on-truth were standing at a border of Clary Lake. Absent, however, was the water's usual clarity and allowance of light penetration to several feet. No one in Sid's talk-exchange entourage of thirteen noticed it, as yet. Everyone, including the fringe of onlookers straining to listen to Sid from a distance was focused on him.

  Sid's arrival at the lake accorded, in timely fashion, with instructions received earlier. Now, he had but to wait with the others to find out what, if any, significance it had with his spoken messages. Without hesitation, Sid began addressing the last question put to him:

Sid: "What is the difference between light and shadow?"

Audrey T.: "Come on, Sid, don't do this. You were being so straightforward, up 'til now."

Sid: "Religions *create* God out of absence...out of need...out of a perceived void. Manifestations of the *true God* are everywhere—under your feet, in the air, that which you see, and hear and smell.

"With the *true God*, there is nothing that you must *believe* in. The *true God* is always with you and around you. If you want the *true God*, stop believing and start seeing and feeling and hearing and smelling and tasting and touching and—yes—*thinking rationally.*

"Now what is rational thinking but acceptance of *natural* reality? Look to the *natural* world for the *real God* and utilize rational thinking. Don't waste your focus on ghosts and spirits and things that can't be studied naturally.

"Clear your mind of distractions and you will find your thoughts to be in tune with the *God* of the natural world and universe—the *true God.*"

Clarence F.: "Okay, now you're against the God of *religions*, because, to you, it's like chasing a ghost. But isn't your 'true God' also just *in your head?* Isn't it, in the final analysis...a belief? You believe in your *true God* just as we believe in the God of our religion.

"It's *in your head,* Sid. You *hear* things in your head, according to you. And these have no source that you can see or feel or hear or taste or touch. So, you got a 'ghost,' too, Sid. Your 'true God' is as much a 'ghost' as what you say the God of *religion* is."

Sid: "I'll answer you like this: Suppose I say the *true God* speaks to me from the *physical world,* the physical *universe.* Suppose I say that when you clear your mind of distractions, the *true God* may speak to you from the wind, the sea, a sudden inexplicable fragrance."

Clarence F.: "Suppose I say—with all due respect, Sid—that I threw to

159

	you a question that you're having to reach far, far, far out in the *field*, to answer."
Sid:	"Actually, I'm presenting you a challenge—one that you can test. I'm not asking any of you to believe anything on my say-so. I'm saying: suppose that you can find the voice of the *true God* speaking from sources in the *natural world*. Suppose you can *hear* that voice, if you clear your mind of distractions.
	"Test it—that's all I'm saying. I can't give you *my* experiences, but I can tell you how to find your own equal ones."
Bernice Z.:	"But Sid, can't you see? It sounds like a riddle and a turning wheel, sort of. You say, clear our minds of distractions. But then, if we don't hear the voice of the 'true God' in the wind, then you'll can say, '*You haven't cleared your minds enough of distractions.*'"
Sid:	"You're giving up on the process before you even try. I'm presenting you a challenge. If you care to—just take the challenge. If you're satisfied where you are now, let it be. I'm telling you that the *true God* is not in a book or in your faith or a spirit you see after you're dead. The *true God* is, and *is in*, all the natural things around you."

For some seconds, a few members of Sid's attendants had noticed a slight agitation in surface water of the lake. As Sid completed his last statement, other members of his group noticed the focus of those staring at the large pond. Suddenly, the lake's center began a violent emission of bubbles as though it were boiling. All eyes fixated with apprehension and wonder at the sight of great ebullience and froth in the water.

Soon, a pungent smell was in the ambient air, a fragrant odor combining lilac and seaweed. Coupled with the apparent explosion within the lake, an *eerie sensation* was also promoted: The "feel" was that part of the *natural world* was going slightly berserk.

Then, seemingly, out of nowhere, pellets began to rain down. For the seconds that they could be seen airborne, the little orbs followed an upward trajectory before succumbing to gravity. Some among the observers would aver later that they were thrust upward out of the lake, along with the splashes of water.

Although the time-span seemed longer, the whole display lasted only about ten seconds. In that period, people near the lake moved about to flee the falling white pellets. When most of the excitement seemed over, some edged over to examine the little balls that lie about the grounds surrounding the lake. With shocked amazement they saw that the orbs behaved quite peculiarly. Each slowly dissolved right before everyone's eyes, giving off a clear mist until it had completely disappeared.

A return view of the lake revealed that its surface had become completely calm again. Also, the seaweed and lilac odor was dissipating in the area's gentle breeze. Now, all attention turned to Sid, who wore an expression of perplexed thoughtfulness, as he gazed at the lake. To some, he seemed almost to be communicating with it. Most everyone became silent for some seconds, waiting for Sid to give commentary. At length, he complied:

Sid: "A most curious occurrence. If any of you think I have a better understanding of it than you, at this point, you're mistaken. I would say only that I think we should all give tranquil thought to it, in *private* moments. If your mind and your thinking are clear, you may find a meaning that is close to whatever is the true one.

"In fact, I think that I shall want to engage in that meditation right now. And so, I will be on my way."

With no further explanation or verbal niceties of departure, Sid turned and ambled, alone, along a perimeter of the lake. After some distance, he turned onto the first street leading away from the park, maintaining his leisurely pace.

Watching him depart, his former attendants glanced, in turn, around at one another and at the lake. They shook their heads in a state of dazed enthrallment. Besides the murkiness of lake water, caused by a stirring of sediments, the environment was as normal as when they'd all arrived. If not for collective witnessing of the spectacular turbulence, each might have wondered if it happened at all.

One thing was sure: No one felt inclined to follow Sid in his walk away from Clary Park. As he now was quite practiced in doing, Sid walked a sauntering, unpredictable, zigzagging route. At a point, he saw the small, unmarked white cemetery van pass him slowly then turn a corner. In one of the secretive maneuvers known to him and his drivers, he caught up with the vehicle. Thereupon, he entered it without detection.

While Sid was making his elusive exit from the park, unseen ONES workers and collaborators remained on the scene. Their task was to cover, or remove altogether, evidence of their recent work inside the Clary Lake pump house.

Members of the Order had not only activated a flow-rerouting capacity built into the station. They also made use of a powerful air compressor that was present. After isolating pipes for water flow, they engaged another for the flow of air. With great thrust and volume, air jetted through a lateral pipe that upturned near the lake's center. Its top reached just feet from the lake's surface. A hinged flap-valve kept water from entering into the pipe in great amounts but flew open from pressure in the opposite direction. ONES engineers even arranged for the flowing air to be heavily scented.

Finally, from the pump station's roof, obscured by tall brush, they had employed a pellet slinging device. The little missiles were in fact balls of frozen-solid carbon dioxide, otherwise known as "hot ice." In open air, of course, *hot ice* quickly vaporizes and disappears completely. As ONES members designed, the violently bubbling and splashing water appeared to give rise to the vaporizing orbs. The more dimensions of sensory perception, the greater the impact on the viewers, it was thought.

New eye-witness accounts of strange occurrences surrounding Sid brought public interest, curiosity, and wonder to new heights. More and more, people of Topal were convinced that Sid possessed extraordinary attributes. They believed it even though they were hard-pressed to name, much less define, what those attributes were. And *many* were afraid. Sid's message was strange, audacious, and not of a kind they liked or wanted to hear. But *just as many others* were fascinated, and experienced a sort of nervous titillation by reports and broadcasts of his talks.

Sweeping and picking up litter on weekend mornings outside the cemetery, Sid was nearly mobbed with questions. After he'd said his fill, Sid would ask to be left alone. For all the good it did, however, he may as well have been talking to one of Chimerik Cemetery's wall blocks. On these occasions, Sid did his best to continue working, without speaking further.

Later, just barely was he able to make it to the gateway whose fence surrounded the sides and back of 111 Olive Lane. All along it were warnings to trespassers of possible prosecution. The inquisitive groups, then, could only stand by and watch Sid enter, to return the implements of his clean-up activity.

At least, so far, the throngs respected private property. They did not try to pursue him inside, but instead found ways to try to peer through the fence. At such times, someone working within the office building would let Sid into a back door. It was planned that he should, then, watch the crowd from the door window until the pursuers tired and moved on.

After the Minski interview, all the local news stations desired interview with Sid. Just a few times more, they met good fortune, catching Sid in an accommodating mood. At these times, more of Sid's elucidations on the *true* God were taped, with reporters and viewers, alike, always astounded and intrigued by his conviction.

As before, the "Sid Interviews" were locally aired as a news segment of odd and interesting events within the city. But with each broadcast, many Topal citizens experienced more than just momentary amusement. Sid was attaining the look of the "bad prophet," whom they might be more content and at peace—without. A contingent of them would just as soon have him vanish as mysteriously as he'd come. To them, the true *"god-spel"* [Old Eng. for "good news" and from which "gospel" is derived] would be that of his turning up in another place, far away—to disquiet new hosts with his "spiritual understanding."

National networks contented themselves with airing tidbit reports and footage of Sid, originating in their smaller, affiliate stations. But *World News* organizations also began to follow Sid's growing status—as a figure of *international* interest. News enthusiasts therein came to follow closely stories of Sid's escapades. It was one such "world news" entity that sent a reporter to Topal, for determining prospects of getting interviews with Sid.

Just as before in Crystal City, police officials in Topal were becoming concerned about possible consequences of Sid's fame. Specifically, they were wary of the crowds that formed when he resurfaced on occasion, in certain city locales. The potential for *spontaneous social combustion* when masses congregate made Topal police apprehensive. Municipal leaders met to discuss ways of dealing with the "Sid phenomenon" in their city.

Meanwhile, the Order, thoroughly pleased with the evolution of their *pauper prophet*, planned Sid's next course. One aspect of it involved expanding his live audience. Given the carefully planned publicity arranged for Sid to this point, they had no doubt his fame would go *fully* global, sooner or later. It was time, then, to promote Sid's travel—worldwide.

Another plan for Sid concerned his brain physiology. Project organizers knew the time was fast approaching when he would have to undergo *de-implantation*. Sid's travel outside the perimeter of the Order's influence could bring unwanted consequences. For one reason or another, Sid might require medical examination, beyond the Order's oversight. Treatment of him could possibly involve a degree of surgical invasiveness. Thereupon, a certain uncomfortable truth might be discovered—namely, that Sid was a "product" of technology. It was planned, therefore, that he should undergo total removal of remote-communication devices placed in his brain.

But, first things first. At the time, the international agency, "World-24/7," was recently formed and ravenous for global-impact stories. Accordingly, it flew two representatives six thousand miles from Europe to America—destination: Topal City. The address they would ultimately visit was: 111 Olive Lane. It had been well reported that the man of their interest had some connection with that location.

From the point of view of that conglomerate news agency, a lot was at stake. The kind of interest Sid was attracting was sure to lead to a marketable enterprise. First and foremost, at this time, they saw potential for lucrative sponsoring of TV time showing interviews with Sid. Therefore, telephone inquiries over thousands of miles wouldn't do, as it might in another case. The two representatives were given license to do whatever was necessary to gain audience with Sid.

Exposure of the *pauper prophet* to reporters in the *global* news arena had been one the Order's long-range goals. Therefore, when Sarah Leede and Niels Lenoux of "W-24/7" came calling, workers at Olive Lane promised to do their best to get word to Sid of their interest in him. It could take a week or so, they advised. The desired meeting took place the week following the inquiry at Olive Lane. In spite of their experience, the veteran news team of "Leede & Lenoux" felt an eager excitement.

At the cemetery business office, managers negotiating the three-person gathering expressed their one concern to the reporters. It had to do with the possible increase in public perception that Sid could reliably be found at the Olive Lane address. What prompted the concern was Leede's and Lenoux's request to hold the interview between the office building and cemetery, for effect. In the end, a compromise was reached. Sid could be filmed at a section of the cemetery at a far northeast corner of its expanse, well removed from Olive Lane.

At last, the interview date Sid agreed to, was set. A few weeks later, Sid stood before the *World-24/7* filming crew. He outlined the design of his "insights," as he fielded the reporter's questions.

Leede:	"I don't know if you realize it, Sid, but people the world over are starting to pay quite a bit of attention to your talks. So, just for clarity's sake, what do you say it is that the 'true God' *wants* from us, as you see it?"
Sid:	"To live up to our intellectual, moral and spiritual potential."
Leede:	"Well, *what-say* we take those *potentials* one at a time? From the point of view of the 'true God,' just what is our *intellectual* potential?
Sid:	"We have the ability to use our minds to think analytically, all the time, not just in specific situations. Why, for example, respect *forensic science* one hour and the very next, profess belief in *supernatural occurrences* you didn't witness for yourself, like those presented in religions? We have the ability to trust, intellectually, claims *that can be tested*, and be leery of those *which cannot.*

"In another vein, we have the intellectual capacity to *override* compulsions to act in ways that are injurious to society. In every social group, all over the world, we have individuals who intellectually *choose* to fulfill individual desires, at the expense of society. Our intellectual potential is the potential to opt for behavior that is socially positive and good for society."

Leede: "Interesting point. Perhaps we'll return to it. But for now, what does the *true God* say to you is our *moral* potential? …You know, as I think on it, your 'overriding compulsions' statement might be relevant here also."

Sid: "Intellect and morality are linked, for you cannot have the latter without the former. It is essential to understand that we are always under the pull of *animal instincts* and *drives*. But sane people have the ability to override them with *thought, rethought, caution,* and sometimes something as simple as *hesitation*."

Leede: "You're saying we can select the *moral road* through…a lot of thought and caution?"

Sid: "Yes—clear thinking…and wise hesitation."

Leede: "I admit, I'm most curious about what you would say is man's *spiritual* potential."

Sid: "The *true God* leads me to see that man's mind has a spiritual dimension that we often neglect. Those with healthy minds 'stand' in two planes simultaneously. In the one, we are postured to understand *alignment-with-God*. The other reveals our firm stance in the *physical* world. The point to take away from this is that increasing *alignment* with the *true God* is man's spiritual potential."

Leede: "Fair enough, for now. I'll ask how we increase that alignment later. …So, the *true God* is, to you, not the God mentioned in any book or focused upon in any of the established religions?"

Sid: "That is correct. The *true God* is 'That' which gives rise to all *processes* in the universe. The *true God* can therefore not be quantified, qualified, pictorially described, not be attributed characteristics anything remotely humanlike, and not be attributed motives and methods remotely suggestive of an earthly intellect."

Leede: "Wow. That was a mouthful, Sid. Quite well said, I will concede. You sound rather like an established intellectual today—I dare say, more-so than in the early interviews that are broadcast."

Sid: "It is your opinion. I only speak that which the *true God* gives to me to express."

Leede: "Something just *put upon* me, Sid, which seems unclear. If the *true God* is so remote, so unlike what we understand in terms of emotions and even higher level pursuits, how do we meet the *spiritual potential* you spoke of?

"In other words, how can there be alignment with a being who is not even *remotely* comparable to humans, in terms of motives and understanding? It sounds as though you say there is no point of congruence between your *true God* and man."

Sid: "The *true God* is a part of, and is related to, and relates to, all things in the cosmos. But understand: The *true God* relates to a spider in a different way than, say, to a tree. Yet the *true God* relates to both and is a part of both.

"The *true God* relates to man differently than to any other species or to inanimate things. Therefore the relationship between the *true God* and man is different. That which makes the difference is different levels of potential.

"Different species have different potentials. Man has a different potential than, say, a giraffe. But, this does not mean that the *true God's* relation to man is qualitatively better than to the giraffe. Neither is it qualitatively better than the *true God's* relation to, say, a blade of grass. Perhaps a blade of grass, as well as a giraffe, has potential to live up to, in relation to the *true God*. But if so, it is obviously different from the potential of man."

Leede: "Hmm…I actually think I grasp it. That's pretty good, Sid. It's no wonder people are fascinated with your *insights*. You've got them down, proverbially, to a science. Essentially, you've put the relation between man and God in a whole new context. Man is not God's favored, or favorite, creature."

Sid: "That is correct. The *true God* has no favorites, but has set up *a system* that rewards animal, mineral and vegetable for living up to potential. The *system* rewards, or denies reward, according to how some *thing* meets its potential—not the *true God*."

Leede: "I'm tempted to have you say, definitively, what man's *reward* is for living up to his potential, as you described it. But perhaps it's obvious."

Sid: "Consider this: There are people who have no care whatsoever about improving human societies. For them, *man's* spiritual potential is indistinguishable from that of a *creature of lesser intellect*. For them, the only real reward is one that is self-serving and immediate. Each person has to decide the *reward* she or he prefers."

Leede: "Clear. Now, one of your most controversial topics has focused on *human reproduction*. I wonder if it can be tied in with your talk of *man's potential*."

Sid: "The *true God* has enlightened me and indicated that careless reproduction in human societies is an error. We are living the potential of a different species when we reproduce carelessly."

Leede: "And 'carelessly' meaning…?"

Sid: "It means having babies we cannot afford to take care of in the absence of public or other outside support. It means having babies we cannot give the best chance for success to, in meeting the demands of society."

Leede: "In a past broadcast, you attribute poverty all over the world—in the absence of economic recession and depression—to what you call 'careless reproduction.' Do you really think that's fair?"

Sid: "Is speaking the truth fair? Anyone who is not in some sort of denial knows that there is a direct link between poverty and the number of children one has, in most cases.

"If an individual is poor upon reaching sexual maturity, it is probably because he or she comes from a poor family. If two such individuals bring a child into the world, they are likely, then, to be poorer than they were at the start of the reproduction. The more children they have, in all likelihood, the poorer they will become.

"There are always exceptions but I refer to 'the rule.'"

Leede: "Sid, what about the fact that human reproduction is so very…natural?"

Sid: "It is *quite* natural and also quite *selfish*. Stealing is natural, one could argue. I think most people would steal at some point, if there were no consequences. But stealing is very selfish. And it's *socially destructive* behavior, which we call *antisocial*.

"The *true* God leads me to see that careless human reproduction is selfish. And my observations and experience tell me it's bad for society, bad for parents who produce offspring carelessly, and, worst of all, bad for the resultant child."

Leede: "Surely, you acknowledge contributors to poverty other than what you see as careless reproduction.

Sid: "Well, there's lack of, or worse, snubbing of, free basic education. But the latter is, more often than not, another negative result of individuals having babies for which they are not prepared. Often the parent or parents know from the start that they are unable to give a home environment that promotes the value of education. Sometimes, it is not even a major concern."

Leede: "Sid: *the cynical social scientist*."

Sid: "The *true* God has revealed it. You may disparage the messenger, but the message is on-point."

Leede: "I have to say—your ideas about poor people having children are among the more disturbing, or most disquieting, of your 'insights.' My sense, Sid, is that many people who follow your broadcasts are put off by them. Having children is a God-given right of married couples, regardless of their *means*. Any ideology that argues against that right is seen as…well…potentially genocidal. …Your response?"

Sid: "There are certain species that limit reproduction of their group by tolerating copulation only by *alpha* members. Yet, one might argue that it is the God-given right of each member of the group to do so. Now, you're thinking: '*We're not animals. What has that got to do with us?*' Well, the *true*

God informs me you're wrong there. We *are* animals, but with a different *potential* than other species.

"I make the point to emphasize this: Reproduction, though quite natural and quite predominant as a characteristic of all living things, constitutes an 'issue' for many non human species. Over-reproduction and indiscriminant reproduction jeopardizes survival of the species, in many cases.

"For humans, the repercussions are mostly about *quality of life*. The *true God* promotes in me the opinion that we should be concerned about the *quality of life* we hand our offspring. The *true God* promotes in me the opinion that only an egregiously selfish person bequeaths to his offspring the ingredients of his failure in society, when it was totally preventable to do so."

Leede: "So it sounds like you would say that the issue of having children relates both to man's intellectual *and* moral potential, as you described them earlier."

Sid: "The *true God* tells me that it relates also to man's *spiritual* potential."

Leede: "We spoke briefly about man's *spiritual* potential earlier. You said it had something to do with being God-*aligned*. How exactly does one *align* with...your *true God?*"

Sid: "First off, there is no ritual. One does not *pray* to increase alignment with the *true God*. One does not profess faith in any matters supernatural. One is not required to put upon others with any beliefs and ways of thinking. What is essential is that we want truth and be willing to learn how to see through distractions built into our societies.

"When you see through the distractions in society, you improve your vision, your thinking, your decision-making, and the quality of your goals. In so doing, we approach our spiritual potential, we increase alignment with God. We set a better *balance* in our occupying both the *physical* and *spiritual* worlds, which I referenced earlier."

Leede: "Hmm. I note an interesting *standout* in your statement: No one is required to evangelize, to spread the gospel, as it were, of the *true God*. But you seem to consider yourself appointed to evangel...."

Sid: "I believe I said one is not required to *put upon* others. I do not *put upon* anyone. I have not approached a single individual, disturbing his course, in speaking of the *true God*. I do not convene people for the purpose of preaching or proselytizing.

"Once, I stood on a monument and spoke, but only to those passing by, who wanted to listen. On all other occasions, I am approached and asked to respond. It is I who am *put upon* to answer questions. The *true God* directs me to give, to others, the same enlightenment bestowed upon me, when asked to do so. When it is advisable, I honor the request."

Leede: "Is there another directive or advisory from the *true* God that we might expound upon at this time?"

Sid: "Most of what the *true God* would have us understand about how to behave and think relates to the three areas of human potential I addressed. Much thought should be given to them."

Leede: "By all means, elucidate."

Sid: "I spoke of having one 'foot' in a spiritual plane. In everything we do we should be mindful of it. It helps us to stay balanced. The *true God* knows it is not easy—for, the *animal pull* and *influence* on our motivations is strong. Still, it is a potential we should try to meet.

"Note that individuals within other species can be trained to resist natural impulses. But it is not within their potential to override impulses, independent of training.

Leede: "Man's intellectual potential—it sounded earlier as though your 'true' God is in favor of man thinking scientifically. Is it so?"

Sid: "It is so. The more we learn about the natural world, the more we understand the *true God*. I believe I said it before: the *true God* gives rise to all processes in the universe. When we learn the laws by which the natural cosmos operates, we increase understanding of God."

171

Leede: "Alright, I got one for you, Sid: If the 'true' God wants us to increase our understanding of Him…Her…or It—and I'm not being disrespectful, I just don't know the best pronoun to use—then, why not give all of us a complete understanding of the cosmos from birth?"

Sid: "I would not describe the *true God* as 'wanting' anything. I said earlier, we make a mistake in attributing humanlike motives to the *true God*. The *true God* adorns all species with a set of potentials for achieving maximum quality of life or existence—man included. It is always better for species to meet their potentials.

"I would not say the *true God* wants, or asks, anything of, or from, any creature, including man. To emphasize, I would not say that the *true God* wants, or asks, anything from, or of, a giraffe or a blade of grass."

Leede: "Let's see if I can trip you up with this: Does the *true God* want you to talk with me? And if not, why are you doing it?"

Sid: "The *true God advises* me to talk with you. It is not the same as *wanting*. If I point to a particular bird in the shrubbery there, would you say you *want* that bird to build a particularly strong nest? Yet, from a standpoint of giving counsel, you might advise it to do its best."

Leede: "I'll allow this, Sid: You have an interesting turn of mind. Well, here's one more for you. Why *you*, Sid? Why do you think the 'true God' chose *you* as the one to whom to impart all this wonderful council and advice?"

Sid: "I don't have the sense of having been *chosen*. I have the sense of *having* chosen…chosen to see the truth. I found it through a practice of seeing beyond distractions."

Leede: "Well, I can't end this interview without getting your comment on reports of bizarre occurrences, featuring you at the center. I'll just run down the list I have with me here.

"There were early accounts of electrified paper currency falling from the sky. I've been told that you've demonstrated the ability to predict events, even. For example, you foresaw the solving of a thirty year old missing-millionaire mystery. And you've given locations of missing items whose earlier misplacement baffled authorities and regular citizens, alike.

"But those were all Crystal City feats, if you will. Right here in Topal, according to report, you summoned a flock of ill-tempered eagles out of sky, stating that they were an omen.

"You discovered an *image of Christ* etched in stone by weather and erosion, within a wall of this very cemetery. Embellishing detail was actually added to the image by splashes of oily compounds from the road. Many took the set of events necessary to produce the image as miraculous.

"But it was only until, according to report, you showed, in a sudden burst of enlightenment, that it could be washed away with rain water. Oils and etchings, alike, disappeared.

"And just recently near-panic was stirred in observers when a great turbulence occurred in a lake, at which you merely gave a nod. At that point, it is said, the waters nearly parted and belched up golf ball sized hale that evaporated in front of everyone's eyes, instead of melting in typically due course. It is said, that *you* said, it was all courtesy of your 'true God.'

"Pretty fantastic stuff, Sid. Are you, in fact, bestowed with powers like that, or all those reports mere tales from over-imaginative minds?"

Sid: "I have no power other than the ability to see and receive the truth. I speak of what I see and of that which is communicated to me by the *true* God. Beyond that, I am essentially no different than you and any of your attendants here."

Leede: "Did those things I cited happen...at all?"

Sid: "There were some very unusual occurrences. Work of the *true* God—perhaps. I cannot be sure of the source. Without a doubt, everyone will have his and her idea as to the cause. Moderate distortions of events—and you seem to have been provided a number of them—will only promote wild speculation.

"Let me say this: One should be skeptical of tales of the fantastic not witnessed personally. One should distrust accounts of non-natural events that cannot be duplicated under the same conditions as in the original report."

ONES project organizers had been right to expect interest in Sid to increase, exponentially, following the *World-24/7* broadcast. Now, people near and far wanted to see more of Sid and hear more of his insights. Clamor all over the world was loud from those desiring whatever information bits were available, concerning him.

Drawn by curiosity, people with all manner of agendas visited the Chimerik Heights Cemetery office. There, they asked for leads of whatever sort available, as to where Sid might be found. For a solid week this went on, from office opening to office closing. News seekers staked out at places around the cemetery, hoping to catch Sid wandering about.

As did people worldwide, Sid's family, too, heard the reports, back in Crystal City, of his sensational notoriety. Naturally, they were among the first to call the cemetery office they'd heard employed him. But, like everyone else who rang "off the hook" the office phones, they were told the office had no knowledge of his residence.

To console Sid's relatives, office workers made an offering that sounded generous, at the surface. Upon his next appearance at their establishment, Sid would be made aware of a new facet of his relation with the office. He would, they assured, be allowed to call his former home, for free, if he were so inclined. As it turned out, he was not.

For his part, Sid stayed holed up, as the saying goes, in his sanctuary inside the cemetery. He had been advised to venture out only at night and to keep a path not viewable from outside the walls. The Order knew it was time to arrange his transfer to another site, from which to launch the next phase of his odyssey. But before that, Sid would have to undergo "the operation." It was the one that would remove implanted apparatuses by which he received remote communication.

Always, Sid's reception of the Order's messages made him feel like a student, of sorts. To him, the sense was that he studied under instruction of the *true God*. It was with a sort of obedient stalwartness that Sid processed the final directive sent remotely from the Order. It requested that he report to 111 Olive Lane to meet with secret collaborators. There was an important, final, direct-learning (as opposed to remote-learning) process to undertake.

The Order both looked forward to and dreaded carrying out Sid's operation. If something did not go as planned, the whole enormously expensive project would be jeopardized. But if the operation left no unwanted effects, there would be two definite benefits. The first, most obvious, one was that Sid would continue to the next phase of the Order's planned role for him. The second had everything to do with finances.

The *manmade prophet's* mission was to usher in *the start* of a new way of analyzing human existence. People targeted to embrace this revolutionary change in perception were not the usual establishers of social standards. Neither theologian nor theorist, neither philosopher nor politician nor jurist would be counted on to espouse Sid's message. Instead it was calculated that common folk holding the least stake in prosperity gradually would take up a new "vision."

There would be a change in the way they view themselves, view their relation to others and to God. Instead of looking to the rich, privileged, and powerful as models to be adored, they would seek truth in *simplicity*. While social values and *constructions of reality* are often set and mandated from top down, Sid's insights would be in counter-flow.

The underlying aim, of course, was improvement of the human species by inspiring people to modify both thought and behavior, all over the world. The change in behavior, it was calculated, would improve the social environment and, in time, the entire human race would benefit. It was the Order's version of 21st century euthenics.

As earlier mentioned, the project was very expensive. Monetary investment had sources in personal fortunes, corporate donations, and various charitable organizations. But the Order did not intend to go broke and find itself in debt, in the process of achieving its goal. Plans were thusly put in place to make possible the second benefit, alluded to earlier, accruing from the Sid Seine "phenomenon." The benefit intended was cash reward.

Of course, the success of all subsequent plans hinged on Sid's successful recovery from brain surgery. In due course, it was undertaken and completed. To the Order's delight, the best outcome was realized, at least in the immediate. Several weeks of testing were required, with acceptable results, before total success be declared.

While Sid was recovering from the operation, ONES project organizers were busy setting up the next phase of their plan. By now, Sid's messages were being played and replayed over and over in various nations around the world. Filmed images of his talks were becoming as familiar to people living thousands of miles away, across oceans, as were the images of prominent national figures. It was time to cash in on Sid's notoriety. Accordingly, a group of select ONES workers began making contact with officials in various countries. They claimed to be in negotiation with Sid to act as his chosen managers and agents.

Their mentor, this group of seven informed, was presently in quiet communication with the *true* God. Newly aware of the place Sid resided, explained the cadre, contact with him was ongoing. In some of their latest exchanges with him, they said, Sid had expressed a willingness to make appearances. And it could be anywhere in the world where people desired to see him.

But, from what they understood to date, he would not be of a mind to give speeches. Instead, wherever appropriate, he would make visits, participating in filmed interviews with a group of inquirers of any makeup. In addition, announced the self-appointed agents, wherever appropriate, use could be made of vocal recordings of the interviews. An example they gave was that of having them played while Sid rode along routes, in view of throngs desiring to see him. According to present estimates, these numbered to tens of millions, perhaps hundreds of millions, around the world.

It was at this point that the "agents" brought the matter of money to the fore. First, they stated the obvious—namely, that all matters to be presented for consideration had to be legally approved by Sid. Next, they outlined their mentor's alleged wishes. Listed below, they were said to reflect Sid's vision, given the desire by nations and international organizations to host his interview sessions:

All subsequent filming of Sid's talks were to devolve to his ownership, solely. Crowds of people who wished to see Sid in person, riding slowly along a security-provided route, would pay. Fees would accord with financial *means* of the populations in attendance.

Most, if not all, of Sid's converts, admirers and those captivated by interest knew of Sid's stance on money. He often stated that he had small interest in it. Monies accruing from payments to see and hear him were to be channeled to philanthropic organizations with transparent interests and endeavors. A modicum would go toward the modest salaries of Sid's agents. All exchanges, and destinations, of money would be completely overseen by unbiased officials within Sid's *host* nation.

Nations receiving Sid as a visitor could be expected to benefit in the following ways: First and foremost, Sid's messages were starting to usher in a new serenity within societies all over the world. Globally, reports confirmed it. There seemed very gradually to be declines in all kinds of criminal acts and in childbirths for people of the least means. These phenomena alone, if real and continued, promised to reduce the cost of governmental expenses significantly.

Second, when Sid's planned appearance was announced, the host nation could expect multitudes of visitors from beyond its borders. As everyone knew, groups of the kind add significantly to the host nation's economy.

Third, all fees paid by people to see and hear Sid was taxable by the government sanctioning Sid's appearance. According to tentatively discussed plans, Sid would make his charitable donations, only *after* *taxation* of the gross amount collected. The practice stood in sharp contrast to the *model* of claiming religious tax-exemption.

In terms of a host nation's expense, Sid's agents would require provision of effective security for his "events." Beyond that, the host would bear the complete expense of travel and lodging for Sid and his small entourage. When the final analyses and estimates were done, it was expected that the benefit to each host nation would far exceed the cost of Sid's accommodation.

Such were the conditions discussed by Sid's prospective agents, with proper officials of the various nations targeted. As everyone was aware, the plans presented a sketch only. It was an idealized model that attempted to put all parties involved "on the same page." The actual step by step process was to be guided by the model, even while important factors like *global mood* were being assessed constantly.

In spite of all the due caution and tentative drafting of plans, one thing was clear. Sid had achieved worldwide appeal, and proper handling of his fame had the potential for much profit. Reports local, national, and worldwide of Sid's messages were not only causing a widely reverberating buzz. They appeared, in addition, to be causing something *seismic* with regard to societal change.

In the first trials of post-operation testing, Sid showed the physiological results hoped for. To everyone's great relief, physicians could find no difference in the motor skills shown before and after surgery. But the Order was far from out of the woods with that success. Next, Sid's *psychological* state had to be assessed.

Following the operation, Sid emerged bereft of his former *extra sensory* capability. The implanted mechanisms were now removed. In short, his mind would no longer hear the voice of, or receive images from, his "true God." The big question was what his reaction would be to that change. Prudently, he had been briefed, pre-surgery, of the difference to expect. Sid's pre-operation communiqué had been as follows:

He was to enter into a long sleep. Upon awakening, he would find that his direct reception of messages was decreased in intensity. It was a natural course of events, Sid's "true God" made clear. Because he had reached such a high level of clarity in his thinking those months prior, it brought a flood. He had achieved an ability to see through societal *distractions* that resulted in a sort of bombardment by direct truth. Over a period of months, his senses had been sharpened by perception of the *true God*, in stark doses. But the experience could only have limited duration.

As his mind acclimated to the intense volley of relayed messages, change was immanent, foretold the "briefing." It was time for the severity of his reception to wane. Sid would, at that point, be sufficiently fortified by his experiences, to continue with diminished reception of voices and visions. At the end of his "big sleep," he could expect them to be of lesser verve, lesser mental volume, lesser visual clarity.

Characteristically, Sid took the whole revelation in stride.

Also just before surgery, Sid was informed about a set of collaborators chosen to aid him in his mission, upon his awakening. Of these, seven were to be his closest allies. He would know them both by face and name.

While Sid was no longer subject to actual mind control through *thought transmission*, he might yet be considered brainwashed. That was the determination of ONES members. As the Order had hoped, tests showed that he retained the extent of his memory over the past months. Sid, after surgery, evinced the same belief system as before the operation. So even without the apparatuses, he was still a captive of ideas and "insights" that had been promoted.

In a few subsequent months, Sid was back in the news—in person. The worldwide clamor for his reappearance hadn't ebbed much at all. People seemed to know, somehow, that their patience would be rewarded.

As negotiated, Sid's net earnings went to specific organizations. As stipulated, each was reputable and with a history sound practices. What was not known was that most were in some way influenced by the *Order of Neo-Euthenics Strategists*. But even with a public awareness of the connection, there was no reason it should have made any difference at that point. No one outside the ONES knew of any affiliation between Sid and the Order.

What was certain was this: Sid's refusal to accept monetary gain for himself had a major impact on those whose interest he excited. As observers could see, Sid still dressed in the least expensive clothes to be found in stores. His simple appearance coupled with stark messages he imparted had a moving effect on those who came to see him.

Project planners and organizers within the Order basked in the reality of *mission on track*. From his earliest participation, their chief subject, Sid, had performed with a focus that did not avert. Now, even the monies spent on the massive project were returning, as planned and hoped.

Most important of all, though, from the Order's perspective, evidence was mounting that ever-increasing numbers were taking Sid's messages seriously. It was more than just fleeting interest in novelty. Those involved in systematic observation detected change in patterns of people's behavior.

The environments of note ranged from small communities, to towns, to nations. It would, of course, take the passing of years before compilation of statistical data definitively illustrated Sid's effect. But for now, and for most people, the "sense" and perception that the world was entering a new phase, of some sort, was unmistakable.

But there were those who did not like, or were alarmed by, what they were seeing. Changes in society tend to disadvantage some groups while advantaging others. The former, composed of disparate elements, comprised a significant number, when taken altogether.

In his talks, Sid expressed that religions were for people too steeped in fear and indoctrination to analyze with a clear mind. Often, he added that being on the planet with people constantly making references to their religion was like having receded hundreds of years into the past. Clerics and their most faithful flock didn't like that.

Sid said that the penchant for watching adults play ball-related or other games, for exorbitant salaries, was beyond his comprehension. In turn, common people within societies over the world began taking a second look at public adoration of sports and professional athletes. Prominent figures of national, and international, sports enterprises found that development troubling.

Sid also challenged the public's fascination with wealth and the wealthy. As global economies showed the usual intermittent signs of recession, people focused anew on one of Sid's more fervent denunciations. Common people, he said, "are often so adoring of the rich" that they will enter into a host of unrealistic financial schemes. Their purpose is to imitate a more opulent lifestyle than they truly can afford. Over time, Sid pointed out, this practice has a deleterious effect on a nation's economic health.

Sid gave the example of how people succumb to lures that promote unwise risk-taking. Here, people are baited by a "deal" that will allow them to live, successfully, beyond their means. The worldwide economic impact from the default of millions of mortgage-related bank loans bore out Sid's claim.

The real fault, Sid contended, lay with the common people's failure to be suspicious of the practice of profit-worship. He said it was the pastime of those most financially influential in society. Corporate money lenders, corporate investors, and corporate managers of stock stand as devotees to the glorification of unbridled profit.

The list of groups put off by Sid's effect on social thinking continued gradually to rise in number. Those who fueled and promoted public obsession with ritzy style and glamour grew among the disaffected. As a consequence of Sid's talks, interest in garish pomp and circumstance waned worldwide. Institutions affected by this change in attitude included the various pageantries that exalt the rich and famous. Promoters of glitz and spectacular fashion chafed under the new turn of events.

When asked, Sid often spoke of members of societies who chronically engage in behaviors that lead to bad health or unnecessary injuries. The high cost of health insurance and hospital visits, he said, are largely attributable to such people. Those offended, now, were people who thrive on extreme physical challenges, smokers, over-eaters and drinkers, and the slovenly. But, in addition, pharmaceutical companies and some health insurance organizations began to feel that such talk could negatively impact their interests.

So, just as Sid gained converts the world over, his messages rankled those who stood to lose the most. But all those becoming disadvantaged by Sid's upheaval found little recourse—except, that is, to bide their time and wait for new opportunities for gain, to exploit. The fact was: social value systems all over the world were changing. The new "tide" and associated "wave" were sweeping away old money-centered schemes and devises for acquiring unchecked wealth. A new focus gaining strength was that of creating conditions wherein all peoples of the world could live productive and poverty-free lives.

Sid's simplicity, clarity of message, and past legend of having been at the center of few miracles, helped usher in the changes the ONES desired. The Order felt justified in the optimism it felt. There was every appearance that the half century of planning, decade of preparation, and fifty months of execution had accomplished the desired outcome.

But, then, something unforeseen began to appear among societies of the world. Anyone inclined toward analytic observation could take note of a curious phenomenon in the making. As Order members became aware of the development, they started to assess the implications for the new world "order" being created.

Within every nation, two distinct groups emerged within the population. They weren't divided by physical location, as would be detected in demographic studies. Nor could they be defined in terms of political, social or economical contrasts. Chasms between the two groups centered more on differences in philosophical *outlook* and *focus*.

In simplest terms, the numerically smaller of the two showed, in certain ways, a much more radical embrace of Sid's insights.

The characteristic most noticeable about this group was their observably *reflective* demeanor or style. As members in society from all walks of life, they were otherwise indistinguishable from the rest of the population. They went to work; they shopped; they maintained themselves, their families and homes. But, they did those things in a sort of *heightened* thoughtful, contemplative state. When they were engaged in talks about *ideals*, yet another odd aspect of their "new being" showed.

Views this group held of their *significance* in the world were shocking to the majority. They were each, according to them, the result of processes no more or less meaningful than an event like plant pollination. It was with a certain irreverent humor that they stated their opinions, when asked to speak on such matters. The world around them, they said, was very *natural*. And every creature *born* in it is *natural* and no different, qualitatively, than any other creature. To expound, they often added the following, or something similar:

"You see that bird? From an *all natural* point of view, it and I *have the same value*. We are each natural products of the earth."

It was just that sort of talk that earned this group, found in societies all about the world, the name that stuck to them. It was contrived from a mixture of sounds in the letters, JSS, taken from Sid's Seine's full name. Some *one* or some *group* initiated the term that emerged: "*J'SeSians*." The spelling was derived to reflect the pronunciation generally used. Other derivatives of Sid's name could have been chosen: *Sid-ians, Sein-ians*, and the like. But, somehow, it was the sound of "Jay-See-Shians" or "Juh-See-Shians" that achieved consensus with the public.

Attempts at a rough estimate of their numbers resulted in projections of between three and nine percent of populations. Somewhat surprisingly, that guesstimate turned out to be fairly accurate. Later it would be given the more accurate six percent, with a small margin of differentiation per society.

In addition to their thoughtful manner, and talk of things "all natural," and their existential humility, the *J'SeSians* evolved another peculiarity. It was in their view of procreation. Down to the single one of them, each reported revulsion at the idea of his or her own reproduction, or *continued* reproduction. Those without children vowed never to have them. Those *with* children loved and honored their offspring with the same fervor as any good parent. But, in the course of preparing them for success in the world, they would try to instill a special value. It was for them to view procreation in the same way as their parents.

At first, the *Order of Neo-Euthenics Strategists* found the evolution of *J'SeSians* endearing. As the Order learned more about their views, however, a certain apprehension began to set in. Members began to look at implications of the *J'SeSians'* outlook, for their (the *J'SeSians'*) own future. But, they realized it would take passing of much more time to know, really, how to evaluate and interpret what might result.

When sufficient time had passed to gather definitive sociological data, a heartening determination could be made. Conditions over the world were changing for the better. Everything from a decrease in impoverished populations to more responsible governments was in evidence. Improvement was slow but steady, and real. But farther scrutiny of conditions and circumstances revealed that positive change resulted mainly from the actions of a relative few. And in every case, that few was composed of *J'SeSians*.

The revelations compelled the Order to plan a series of meetings. These occurred even as Sid continued his travels about the world, inspiring throngs of people with his messages. The moods of those in convention ranged from *concerned* to profoundly *anxious*. Genealogical statisticians among Order members had made some startling estimates, which they presented. Given the *J'SeSian* ill-regard for reproducing, they could well be *no more*—within a century.

From Sid's discourses, the *J'SeSians* had all reached the same conclusion. No truly enlightened human being could be satisfied to perpetuate existence on earth. Life here, they determined, was suitable only under two conditions undesirable to them. One was as an animal of lesser intellect. The other was as an animal with higher intellect but with a propensity for existing in a state largely distracted from truth. The latter, in short, involved a life steeped in delusion.

What, then, would happen to the positive changes in societies being realized all over the world? Did it mean that the *Euthenics successes* so laboriously worked for, and obtained, were to be lost? Such loss certainly did not relate to finances. The "fortune" spent by the Order on the Euthenics Project was returning, in good measure.

But what of the sacrifice that came with more than half a century of planning, and three years of painstaking execution? Was success enduring only over the space of a mere four to five generations worth the monumental effort? Positing possible answers to such questions brought a measure of disquiet and even anguish to the euthenics ideologists.

Order members advanced one theory after another. Desperately they tried to identify the condition that would signify continued flourishing of the J'SeSian outlook. Order members in attendance of the consortium volleyed back and forth on their issue.

Member A: "It's not as if the J'SeSians are a bloodline which, with cessation of offspring, will terminate like a royal family."

Member B: "Nevertheless, without posterity, what is there to stop their group from, essentially, becoming extinct?"

Member C: "Well, think about it: Sid's *messages* will surely survive not only *his* inevitable passing but also that of the current population of J'SeSians, old and young. According to this scenario, other J'SeSians will emerge inspired by *recorded versions* of his teachings. The desired product—that is, altered and expanded thinking—will continue.

Member D: "There's a rather sobering possibility that we need to consider. As time passes and the current J'SeSians die away without progeny, a phenomenon *common with religious faiths* will likely occur. In all faiths are the purists, the pragmatic practitioners, and the pretenders. In our experiment, it has been the purists—those who most strongly embrace Sid's message—who have brought the desired changes to the world's societies.

"This is my prediction: Non-purist J'SeSians will find a way to water down Sid's message. As I said, the radical J'SeSians are the leaders, the flag bearers, of positive change in their societies. Later, when they are all gone, due to non procreation, the remaining population will find a way to pick apart James Sid Seine's enlightenment."

The latter was a disappointing forecast. In summary, that which Order members envisioned was this: In the absence of J'SeSian purists, "softer" adherents to Sid's philosophy would make compromises. The more radical tenets would be deemphasized, maybe even bleached *neutral* with added interpretations.

Regarding the milder parts of Sid's insights, non *J'SeSians* would extol them, make claims of embracing them. These, they would hold up as the *essential* elements of his teachings. In this way that group would appear to be *true J'SeSians*, in spirit. The door would be open for pretenders to claim the title of neo *J'SeSian* pragmatists and purists. Claiming the status of a *true J'SeSian* would be made as simple as following a few cursory and superficial directives.

For several months, the ONES discussed the matter and possible solutions, sometimes heatedly. Accepting that the fruits of all their work would, in all likelihood, not be preserved was not easy for them. In their minds they saw those "fruits" slowly losing ripeness on the vine, until each fell, void of further benefit.

The *Order of Neo-Euthenics Strategists* had sought to cause the emergence in societies of individuals whom they regarded as socially enlightened. These latter, they thought, would lead the way to *universal acceptance* of doctrines proclaimed by the "manmade prophet." But a factor totally unforeseen also developed. Individuals truly enlightened by tenets Sid preached, resolved to *discontinue their own procreation.*

Sadly, the *Order of Neo-Euthenics Strategists* all reached the same conclusion. Mankind, due to some innate flaw, cannot tolerate "vision" that is wholly *undistracted.* According to the Order's definition of the term, *unabridged human enlightenment,* creates too bright a "light" for the "mind's eye" to receive comfortably

In final pages of massive documentation the Order kept on their "Manmade Prophet" or "Created Faith" project, they entered the following:

"At the project's final stage, we find that the embrace, by mankind, of unabridged truth is a sword with two edges. The one gleams with man's enlightenment and achievement of vast improvements in societies. The other, in a blinding glint, reveals him willfully opting for his own extinction."